"The Holly Barker police procedurals are fun to read. . . . Mr. Woods just keeps getting better with each book he writes." —*Midwest Book Review*

HOTHOUSE ORCHID

After Special Agent Holly Barker lets an international terrorist slip through her fingers for a second time, the CIA thinks she might want a long vacation. So Holly returns to her hometown of Orchid Beach, Florida, where she was police chief for many years. But a very unpleasant surprise awaits her. Many years earlier, while she was in the army, Holly and another female officer brought charges against their commander for sexual harassment. Holly managed to fight him off, but the other woman, a young lieutenant, didn't. The officer in question was acquitted of all charges, and left the army—for a job as Orchid Beach's new police chief. Now Holly must decide whether to return to the CIA—or seek her revenge.

Praise for the
Holly Barker Novels

Iron Orchid

"A page-turner. . . . Readers will root for Barker." —The Associated Press

"A compelling and entertaining cat-and-mouse caper." —*Midwest Book Review*

continued . . .

Blood Orchid

"Woods's popular heroine, police chief Holly Barker, returns for her third adventure . . . a suspenseful, exciting mystery that is sure to please Woods's many fans."   —*Booklist*

"The prolific, bestselling novelist revisits savvy, sexy [Holly Barker] . . . fast-paced . . . strong action scenes."
—*Publishers Weekly*

Orchid Blues

"Mr. Woods delivers smart characters and dialogue with a nice swing to it. . . . Holly and Ham are engaging . . . with a lot of gumption and tough-talking banter between them."   —*The New York Times*

"Starts with a bang. . . . His action scenes are clean and sharp."   —*Publishers Weekly*

Praise for the
Stone Barrington Novels

Hot Mahogany

"[A] fun ride from Stuart Woods."—*Bangor Daily News*

"Series fans will find all their expectations nicely fulfilled."
—*Publishers Weekly*

Shoot Him If He Runs

"Fast-paced . . . with a whole lot of style."
—*Bangor Daily News*

"Woods certainly knows how to keep the pages turning."
—*Booklist*

Fresh Disasters

"Fast-paced, hilarious, and tragic."
—*Albuquerque Journal*

"Good fun."   —*Publishers Weekly*

BOOKS BY STUART WOODS

FICTION

Mounting Fears[‡]

Hot Mahogany[†]

Santa Fe Dead[§]

Beverly Hills Dead

Shoot Him If He Runs[†]

Fresh Disasters[†]

Short Straw[§]

Dark Harbor[†]

Iron Orchid[*]

Two Dollar Bill[†]

The Prince of Beverly Hills

Reckless Abandon[†]

Capital Crimes[‡]

Dirty Work[†]

Blood Orchid[*]

The Short Forever[†]

Orchid Blues[*]

Cold Paradise[†]

L.A. Dead[†]

The Run[‡]

Worst Fears Realized[†]

Orchid Beach[*]

Swimming to Catalina[†]

Dead in the Water[†]

Dirt[†]

Choke

Imperfect Strangers

Heat

Dead Eyes

L.A. Times

Santa Fe Rules[§]

New York Dead[†]

Palindrome

Grass Roots[‡]

White Cargo

Under the Lake

Deep Lie[‡]

Run Before the Wind[‡]

Chiefs[‡]

TRAVEL

A Romantic's Guide to the Country Inns of
Britain and Ireland (1979)

MEMOIR

Blue Water, Green Skipper (1977)

[*]A Holly Barker Book   [†]A Stone Barrington Book

[‡]A Will Lee Book   [§]An Ed Eagle Book

HOTHOUSE ORCHID

STUART WOODS

A SIGNET BOOK

SIGNET
Published by New American Library, a division of
Penguin Group (USA) Inc., 375 Hudson Street,
New York, New York 10014, USA
Penguin Group (Canada), 90 Eglinton Avenue East, Suite 700, Toronto,
Ontario M4P 2Y3, Canada (a division of Pearson Penguin Canada Inc.)
Penguin Books Ltd., 80 Strand, London WC2R 0RL, England
Penguin Ireland, 25 St. Stephen's Green, Dublin 2,
Ireland (a division of Penguin Books Ltd.)
Penguin Group (Australia), 250 Camberwell Road, Camberwell, Victoria 3124,
Australia (a division of Pearson Australia Group Pty. Ltd.)
Penguin Books India Pvt. Ltd., 11 Community Centre, Panchsheel Park,
New Delhi - 110 017, India
Penguin Group (NZ), 67 Apollo Drive, Rosedale, North Shore 0632,
New Zealand (a division of Pearson New Zealand Ltd.)
Penguin Books (South Africa) (Pty.) Ltd., 24 Sturdee Avenue,
Rosebank, Johannesburg 2196, South Africa

Penguin Books Ltd., Registered Offices:
80 Strand, London WC2R 0RL, England

Published by Signet, an imprint of New American Library, a division of Penguin
Group (USA) Inc. Previously published in a Putnam hardcover edition.

First Signet Printing, May 2010
10 9 8 7 6 5 4 3 2 1

Ⓟ REGISTERED TRADEMARK—MARCA REGISTRADA

Printed in the United States of America

This book is for Suzanne Alley.

I

Holly Barker arrived at CIA headquarters, in Langley, Virginia, at her usual seven thirty a.m., parked the car in her reserved spot and took the elevator to her floor. She set her briefcase on the desk, hung her coat on the back of the door and sat down, ready to do the work she always did before her boss, Deputy Director for Operations, or DDO, Lance Cabot, arrived. To her surprise, the door between their adjoining offices opened, and he stood there, looking at her in his wry way.

"Good morning," he said, "and no cracks about how early I'm in."

Holly smiled. "Good morning," she replied.

"Come in." He stood aside and let her pass into his office, which was much larger and more luxuriously furnished than hers. Rumor was that Lance had furnished the office out of his own pocket, but Holly knew him better than that. He was much more likely to have found a way for the Agency to pay the tab. He waved her to a seat.

"Coffee?" he asked, picking up a pot from the paneled cupboard that contained a small kitchenette and a fully stocked bar.

"Yes, thank you."

Lance poured them both a cup and sat down at his desk. "Have I ever told you how good you are at your job?" he asked.

Holly blinked. "Not in so many words."

"We've both been working on this floor for three years," he said, "and, quite frankly, I think you could do my job as well as I do."

Holly blinked in astonishment. Lance had always been miserly with praise, apparently believing that a "well done" sufficed.

"Except for the politics," Lance said.

He was right about that, she knew. "Well . . ."

"You're hopeless at the politics."

"I'm working on that," she said.

"Yes, but you're still hopeless."

"Not without hope of improvement," she said, contradicting him.

Lance smiled a little. "Well, you can hope."

"Lance," she said, "I hope this is all a prelude to a big promotion, a larger office, a huge increase in salary and a Company Cadillac." This was said less than half in jest.

"As I said, Holly, you can hope." Lance pushed

back from his desk, crossed his legs and sipped his coffee. "Actually, you have to leave us."

Holly clamped her teeth together to keep her jaw from dropping. "I don't know how to respond to that," she managed to say.

Lance's eyebrows went up. "Oh, it's only for a time, say a month."

Holly stared at him, uncomprehending.

"I'm not firing you," he clarified.

"Good, then I won't have to kill you," she replied. "Now what the hell are you talking about?"

"I'm not doing the talking; other people are."

"Talking? Not about you and me, surely."

"Well, maybe that, too. What they're talking about is Teddy Fay."

Teddy Fay was a name never mentioned at Langley, a great embarrassment to everyone in the building, except to those who secretly rooted for him. Teddy was the former deputy chief of Technical Services, the division that supplied operational officers with everything they needed to accomplish their missions: a weapon, a wardrobe, an identity or a cyanide capsule. Whatever, Tech Services obliged. But Teddy Fay, after retiring, had gone off the reservation, had started killing right-wing political figures, Middle Eastern diplomats—anyone who Teddy felt did not have the best interests of his country at heart—and no combination of the Agency's and the FBI's resources had been able to stop him or even find him. Holly was the only CIA employee who had ever even seen him since his retirement and then only when he was disguised.

"Am I getting blamed for Teddy Fay?" she asked.

"Not exactly," Lance replied. "It's just felt that you've had a number of opportunities to kill him and you haven't done so."

"Lance, I've seen the man only once when I knew who he was, and, on that occasion, I managed to put a bullet in him."

"Yes, but not in the head or the heart," Lance pointed out. "And given that, during your schooling at the Farm, you ran up the highest scores with a handgun of any trainee ever; some wonder why you didn't do just a little better. In fact, I myself have wondered."

Holly had wondered about that, too. "I won't dignify that with a response," she said, by way of saying nothing. She almost said that she was not an assassin but thought better of it.

"Be that as it may, you are just a little too hot around here at the moment, so take some leave. The director has had a word with the higher-ups, complaining about the unused leave time that some officers have allowed to pile up, and you're high on the list. You've got nine weeks coming, and it's time you took some time."

"Lance, I've got an awful lot on my plate right now."

"You need a change of diet," he said. "And, you might recall, we've made a few modifications in that house of yours in Florida."

Holly had nearly forgotten about that, and she had not visited the house since. "That wasn't my idea."

"Go there. E-mail or call, if you can't stand being out of touch, but go."

Holly sighed. "Well, I guess I could clean up my desk in a few days," she said.

"You've got two hours to write me a memo on what's pending, so I can reassign the work, then you're out of here." He paused for a reaction and got none. "Are you hearing me?"

"I'm doing that job for the director," she said. She had grown fairly close to Katharine Rule Lee, the director of Central Intelligence, and she wanted to further that relationship.

"This request comes from the director; I'm only passing it on. Give me the file; I'll handle it."

Holly threw up her hands.

"Why are you still sitting there?" Lance asked.

"All right, all right," Holly said, then slouched out of the big office and to her desk. Her work was neatly filed, and she made a stack of folders as she wrote her memo. She was done in exactly two hours. She knocked on Lance's door.

"Come in."

She walked into the room to find the director sitting where she, herself, had sat earlier that morning.

"Good morning, Holly," Kate Lee said.

"Good morning, Director," Holly replied. She set the bundle of file folders on Lance's conference table, then handed him the memo and watched while he read it through.

"I thought I'd stop in and reassure you before you leave," the director said. "It's not that we're trying to get rid of you; it's just that we're . . . well, trying to get rid of you for a little while. We needn't go into why."

"I understand," Holly said. "At least I think I do."

"This will pass," the director said. "After all, Lance has assured me that Teddy Fay is still dead."

Holly nodded as if she agreed.

"Oh, by the way, Lance probably hasn't told you this, if I know him, but we're bumping you up to executive grade, and, in addition to the salary increase and a few perks, you now have a new title: Assistant Deputy Director of Operations—ADDO—effective immediately."

"Thank you, Director," Holly said with real appreciation, "and no, Lance didn't tell me." She shot him a glance.

Lance tossed her memo on his desk. "Oh, get out of here," he said. "Let us know your whereabouts." He tossed her an envelope. "You'll need this."

The director stood up and offered her hand. "Congratulations, Holly. Now go and buy yourself a very nice present."

Holly flew.

2

Holly packed her Cayenne Turbo as lightly as she could and spoke to Daisy, her Doberman pinscher. "All right, Daisy, you can get in now." Daisy, who had been sitting by the car, waiting for instructions, leapt lightly into the front passenger seat of the SUV.

Daisy had been beautifully trained by an old army buddy of her father's who had met an untimely end. Holly had bought her from the man's daughter, and she and Daisy had bonded at once.

Holly got onto I-95 south, set the speed control at eighty and switched on the radar detector. The device was illegal in Virginia, but what the hell, it was cleverly concealed, and it looked for cops both ahead and behind while jamming their lasers long enough for her to slow down.

*   *   *

They spent the first night in a motel near Charleston and got moving early the next morning. She called her father, Hamilton Barker, from there and told him she was on the way. By late afternoon she was at the bridge over the Intracoastal Waterway; then she turned onto the side road that led to her father's house, on a little island, where he lived with his longtime girlfriend and recent wife, Virginia.

She pulled into the yard and let Daisy out of the car. Daisy ran through the open door and came back with Ham and Ginny, and hugs and kisses were exchanged, not least by Daisy.

"You want a drink?" Ham asked.

"No, I want to get to the house and settle in," Holly said. "I just wanted to say hello on the way. How about dinner tomorrow night?"

"Sure," Ginny said. "Come here, and I'll cook."

"You're on," Holly replied.

"I went to take a look at your place a few weeks ago," Ham said, "but I was met by some grim-faced guy packing a handgun and told to go away. I figured he was one of yours."

"Yeah, he was," Holly said. "The Agency did some work on the house."

Ham made a grunting noise. "I never knew they were building contractors," he said.

"You'd be surprised at some of the things the Agency does," Holly replied. "Come on, Daisy, let's go home." Daisy jumped back into the car. "See you tomorrow night," Holly said, and drove away.

She crossed the bridge and turned south on A-1A, the road that ran the length of the state's barrier islands. She drove through the little community of Orchid Beach and a couple of miles south turned onto her driveway. She was immediately brought up short by a heavy wrought-iron gate hanging on reinforced concrete posts. "What the hell?" she muttered.

She opened her briefcase and took out the envelope Lance Cabot had given her. There were some papers, some keys and a remote control. She pressed the remote's button, and the gate swung open, closing behind her automatically as she drove through.

Holly stopped at the front door and got out of the car with Daisy, who was obviously glad to be home. She fumbled with the new keys, noticing that they had none of the usual teeth, just what seemed to be a row of magnets. The door, of painted steel, was new. She got a key into the lock, and it took two complete turns to open the door. She checked the door's edge, and when she turned the key again, not one but three six-inch steel bolts emerged that would slide into the steel doorframe. Impressive. She heard the security system beeping and found a new keypad next to the door. The papers in the envelope Lance had given her revealed her new entry code, and she used it to disarm the system. She noted in the instructions that any breach of security would be sent electronically, not to a local security company but directly to Langley.

She unloaded her things while Daisy ran around sniffing at everything in the house. Holly walked into the living room and looked around. Everything seemed exactly the same, even the old magazines on the coffee table. Then she noticed that her view of the beach and ocean through the picture windows and sliding doors had a slightly greenish cast. She inspected them and found that the glass in the windows and doors was now an inch and a half thick. Good for hurricanes, she reckoned.

She slid open a heavy door and smelled the ocean air. Daisy raced outside and around the dunes, inspecting everything. Holly took her bags upstairs, unpacked them and came back down. Near the bottom of the stairs she saw a new interior door that had not been there before, with a keypad next to it. Checking the paperwork for a code, she opened the door and found a neat little office with an ordinary desktop PC alongside an Agency computer and printer, secure fax machine and plenty of cupboards and shelves. She opened one cupboard to find weapons racks containing a

12-gauge Remington riot gun and two handguns: a custom model 1911 .45 and a SigArms P239, a compact 9-mm with holsters. In another cupboard she found set into the wall a safe with a capacity of about 2 cubic feet. She memorized the combination, left the room, closed the door and heard the locks operate. Home Sweet Home, she thought.

Holly fixed dinner for herself and Daisy and fell asleep in bed with the new, flat-screen TV on. She was awakened early the next morning by a ringing telephone and groped for it. "Hello," she croaked.

"Good morning," Lance said. "I knew you'd be up early."

Holly sat up in bed and noticed that the TV was still on. Then she noticed that Lance's face had appeared on the screen.

"I didn't know you slept naked," Lance said.

"Beast," she said, pulling the covers up to her chin. "What do you want?"

"Just checking to be sure you made it in all right. Do you like our improvements to your place?"

"Very impressive," she said.

"We also did some strengthening of the structure and slated the roof with double fasteners. You have hurricanes down there, you know."

"I seem to remember."

"Go back to sleep," he said. "All is well here." The phone went dead, and the TV returned to CNN.

She was almost asleep when the phone rang again. She yanked the covers over her breasts, grabbed the phone and looked at the TV. This time, it was just CNN. "Hello?"

"Holly? It's Hurd Wallace."

Holly had retired from the army with the rank of major after twenty years and as the commander of a military police company. An old army buddy of Ham's, Chet Marley, had been chief of police in Orchid Beach, and he had offered her a job as his deputy chief, which she had jumped at. Hurd Wallace had been the man she had displaced when she was hired.

Chet Marley had been murdered, and Holly had become chief, with Hurd as her deputy. After a rocky beginning they had established a good, even warm working relationship, and by the time she had left to join the CIA, they had become friends. Hurd was now chief of police in Orchid Beach.

"Hey, Hurd," she said.

"Too early for you?"

"Nah, I'm wide awake," she lied. "What's up?"

"Just wanted to welcome you back; Ham told me you were coming. Can I buy you some lunch today? There's something I'd like to talk to you about."

"Sure."

"Ocean Grill at one o'clock?"

"Sure. See you there." She hung up, and by that time she was wide awake. She struggled out of bed and into a shower.

3

Holly walked into the Ocean Grill in nearby Vero Beach, a barnlike, old-fashioned Florida seafood restaurant, and found Hurd Wallace waiting for her. Hurd was still tall and thin, but his black hair was half gray now. They hugged.

"Long time," she said.

"Too long."

They were shown to a table and given menus.

"What brings you back to Orchid Beach?" Hurd asked.

"Something really weird," Holly replied. "A vacation."

Hurd laughed. "You haven't changed; you always worked too hard."

"Well, there's always too much work and never enough time to do it," she said.

"Are you enjoying your work?"

"I really am."

"I guess you have a bigger ocean to cast your net."

"Bigger than you can imagine. I wish I could tell you about it."

Hurd held up a hand. "I didn't mean to fish; I know you folks never talk about anything."

"Thanks for understanding."

They ordered iced tea and lunch, and soon Holly was enjoying tiny bay scallops in a lot of butter. "So, how's police work these days?"

"Much the same, but we do more drug work now."

"Yeah, I still get the local paper, and I read about that."

"Most of the officers you knew are still with us—a few new ones."

"I'll stop by and say hello."

"I'm retiring," Hurd said without preamble. "Today's my last day."

Holly was shocked. "I thought you'd never do that," she said.

"I've been offered a job with the state police as head of a new investigative unit. The money and the pension are better, and I don't have to move to Tallahassee. I can work out of the department's offices here in Vero."

"Well, congratulations, Hurd. Who's replacing you? Anybody I know?"

"That's what I wanted to talk to you about,"

Hurd said. "I expect you recall the circumstances under which you left the army."

"Of course." Holly and another female officer had brought charges against their commanding officer for sexual harassment, attempted rape and rape. Holly had managed to fight him off, but the other woman, a young lieutenant, had not. When the man was acquitted by a board of his fellow officers, Holly realized that she had no place to go in the army, so she retired. The chief at Orchid Beach, Chet Marley, an old army buddy of Ham's, had offered her the job as his deputy. When he had been killed, Holly had replaced him. "Why do you bring that up?" she asked.

Hurd unbuttoned his shirt pocket and took out a sheet of paper. "I Googled you," he said. He unfolded it and handed it to her. It was a newspaper account of the trial and her testimony. "I wish I had done it sooner."

Holly scanned it. "It's accurate," she said.

"The city council has hired Colonel James Bruno as the new chief," Hurd said.

Holly felt as though someone had struck her. Bruno had been her commanding officer.

Hurd saw the shock on her face. "It was a fait accompli before I found out who Bruno was; there was nothing I could do."

Holly recovered her voice. "How did this happen?"

"Ironically, the council's experience with you had been such a good one that they decided to look for another MP officer. Bruno looked good on paper, so they interviewed him. Apparently, your name didn't come up at the time."

"Does the council know now who he is?"

"I wrote a memo to the chairman, so that it would be on the record."

"Is it still Charlie Peterson?"

Hurd shook his head. "Charlie died last month: heart attack, at his desk. I'm surprised you didn't see it in the paper."

"I guess I'm behind a few issues," she said. "Who is his replacement?"

Hurd sighed. "Irma Taggert."

During and after Holly's first meeting with the Orchid Beach city council and during Holly's entire tenure as chief, Irma Taggert had been a constant thorn in her side. "That horrible pain in the ass?"

"One and the same," Hurd said. "She had seniority on the council, and the town's bylaws made her chairman until the next election, which isn't until this fall."

"Hurd, Irma would have voted to hire James Bruno, even if she had known who he was—maybe because he was who he was."

"I can't argue with that," Hurd said.

"Let me tell you what's going to happen," Holly

said. "Jim Bruno will use spit and polish mixed with charm to get the people on the force to like him. The man does have charm, I'll give him that. Then, when he feels secure, he'll start in on the female officers, and he'll find a way to get rid of anybody who doesn't come across. This is going to be bad."

"I wish there was something I could do," Hurd said.

"You can take the women aside and let them know who they're dealing with. They need to be warned."

"That I can do," Hurd said.

"Does he know I'm in town?"

"No. I don't think anyone but me knows, except Ham and Ginny, of course."

"When does Bruno start the job?"

"He's already in the office."

"Does he know I was chief before you?"

"I don't know, but he certainly will soon. Your name is bound to come up in the normal course of things. Maybe I'll tell him myself, just to see the look on his face."

"I'd be interested to know how he takes the news," Holly said. "Oh, and don't mention it to Ham; he might go down to the station and shoot Bruno."

"It'll be in tomorrow's paper," Hurd said.

"I'm having dinner with them tonight; I'll break

it to him and then sit on him if I have to. Ham was at the trial, you know."

"I didn't know."

"He retired a couple of weeks after I did, and I think it was so he wouldn't have to serve on the same base with Bruno. Or maybe even in the same army."

"I wouldn't want Ham mad at me," Hurd said.

"You're right about that," Holly said.

4

Holly dressed for dinner in starched designer jeans, a blue chambray work shirt and skinny lizard cowgirl boots. Ham had always liked it when she dressed like a boy. She checked herself in the mirror. Since she had lost the weight and colored her hair a lovely auburn, she had liked her looks a lot better. She was a good five-ten in the boots, and Ham liked that, too. She wanted him happy tonight.

Holly and Daisy arrived at Ham and Ginny's only ten minutes late, and she could smell the meat roasting on the back-porch grill. Ginny greeted her with a hug at the front door and let Daisy put her paws on her shoulders and give her a big kiss. Ginny poured them both a Knob Creek on the rocks and another for Ham; then they went out on the back porch to watch his beef-burning skills on display, searing the biggest, thickest porterhouse steak Holly had ever seen.

"Did you shoot that yourself?" Holly asked.

"I roped it down at the prime butcher's shop," Ham replied. "You wouldn't believe what it cost."

"Yes, I would."

"I charged it to your credit card," Ham said. Holly had given him a very special kind of credit card, one that tapped into a secret bank account she kept in the Cayman Islands.

"Figures."

"So, what's happening in your life, baby girl?" he asked.

"Well, I've got some good news and some bad news," she said, sighing.

"I always like the bad news first."

Holly took a deep breath. "Hurd Wallace is retiring as chief, and the new chief is Colonel James Bruno."

Ham dropped the tongs he had been holding and bumped his head on the hot grill when he picked them up. "How the fuck did that pig happen here?" he demanded.

"Try and relax, Ham; it's not a conspiracy." She told him what Hurd had told her at lunch. "Promise me you're not going to go down there and shoot him."

"Don't you think I have *any* self-control?" he asked.

"Yeah, sure."

"I'll wait until after dinner to go down there and shoot him."

"That's what I thought. I hope I didn't ruin your supper, but you wanted the bad news first."

"Tell me the good news; maybe it'll help me get over it."

"I got promoted."

"To what?"

"Assistant Deputy Director of Operations—ADDO."

"What was it you were before?"

"Assistant *to* the deputy director of operations."

"There's a difference?"

"Of course there is. Assistant *to* made me sound like a glorified secretary, though, of course, I was a lot more than that. Assistant deputy director means, I think, that I'll have some authority of my own."

"Authority to what? Assassinate people? Because if that's the case, James Bruno ought to be your first hit."

"No, no, Ham. It just means that when I give an order I don't have to preface it with, 'Lance Cabot asked me to tell you to . . .'"

"Does it mean that if Lance dies you get his job? Because if it does, I'll shoot him for you."

"No, it doesn't, Ham, and I want you to get your mind off shooting people. You'll screw up your digestion, and that chunk of cow you're flaming is going to take a lot of digestion."

"I guess Lance's job is a lot of politics," Ham said.

"You're right, and Lance says I'm shitty at the politics. Not as shitty as he thinks I am, but I could do better, and I'm going to surprise him by doing it."

"Pretty soon you're going to have Kate Lee's job," Ham said.

"Not while Will Lee is president," Holly said. An act of Congress had allowed the president to appoint his wife, who was a career CIA officer, as director. Holly looked at Ham closely. "How's your blood pressure?"

"Returning to normal," Ham said, taking a swig of the Knob Creek. "Well, almost normal. I hope Bruno likes to fish, because if he does, I'll catch him on the water and drown him."

"Careful, the BP is going up again. Drink more bourbon."

Ham did.

"You doing any flying?" Ginny asked, by way of changing the subject. Ginny ran her own flying school at the Vero Beach airport.

"No time," Holly said. "I miss it, too."

"Why don't you come out to the airport tomorrow, and I'll give you a biennial flight review and an instrument competency check."

"Good idea," Holly said. "Let me call you in the morning and set it up."

"You want your steak rare?" Ham asked.

"No, I want it medium rare, and that means when I stick it with a fork, I don't want it to moo."

They dined on the huge steak, which Ham had sawed into human-sized chunks, baked potatoes and a Caesar salad along with a big, fat California cabernet. Daisy dealt with the bone.

Ham, who had been quiet, finally said something. "Tell me, what was the most fun you've ever had at your job?"

"You just want me to tell you some secret stuff, don't you?"

"If you really want to. I just want to know if you're having any fun."

"Well, a few months ago I got to pose as an assistant director of the FBI and serve a phony court order on the editor of the *National Inquisitor*."

"You're shittin' me!"

"I shit you not."

"God, I hate that rag," he said. "I hope you gave the guy a really hard time."

"Oh, I did, and I savored every moment of it."

"I thought the Agency wasn't supposed to mess around in domestic stuff," Ham said with false naïveté.

"Oh, I was never there," Holly said. "The minute I left his office I ceased to exist, and so did what I did there. Or rather, what I didn't do."

"Just don't get caught not doing it," Ham said.

"I'll do my best."

"How was the Farm?" The Farm was Fort Peary, the Agency's training facility for new officers.

"Hard but fun. You'd have been proud of my shooting."

"I heard," Ham said. "The best ever scores by a trainee."

"You *heard*? You're not supposed to hear; we're talking about the CIA."

"I heard. I got a call from your instructor. He was properly awed, and, of course, he gave me all the credit."

"He said he knew you, but . . ."

"I kicked his ass in the national championships one year."

They ate and drank on, enjoying each other. Holly hadn't had such a good time since she had joined the Agency.

5

They ate and drank and talked until nearly midnight; then, after a cup of strong coffee, Holly stood up and said, "If I'm going to sleep in my own bed tonight, I'd better get going."

Ginny came out of the bedroom. "Daisy's dead to the world on our bed; you want me to wake her up?"

"Let her sleep," Ham said. "We haven't seen her for a long time. I'll bring her home tomorrow."

"Okay," Holly said. "Great grilling, Ham."

He handed her something wrapped in aluminum foil. "Take some home; we've got enough for a week."

Holly kissed them both, looked in on Daisy, who was having a dream, running on her side and making muffled woofing noises, then got into the Cayenne and started home. As she stopped before turning onto the bridge over the Indian River she noticed a car parked on the shoulder to her left: dark color, nothing fancy, like an unmarked patrol car. Its headlights came on, bathing her in bright light, and as she started to cross the bridge, it pulled onto the road behind her.

She had the odd feeling that she was being followed, and she couldn't get the idea out of her mind, so she did something unexpected: after the bridge, she turned right onto Indian River Trail, a dirt track that ran about five miles down Orchid Island, parallel to A-1A. It was wild and beautiful in the daytime but completely dark at night, and there was no moon. A deer ran into her headlights, and she slammed on her brakes. It scampered away. She checked her rearview mirror: no headlights behind her. She relaxed and continued down the trail, comfortable at thirty miles per hour.

She had driven a couple of miles when suddenly very bright headlights came on a few yards behind her. Holly's first reaction was to accelerate, but instead she just continued steadily down the trail. Then, as she approached a wide spot in the road, a flashing blue light came on behind her. In her rearview mirror she could see a uniformed figure illuminated in the blue flashes. She pulled over to the right and stopped to see if he just wanted to get past her or if this was a traffic stop. She wasn't particularly worried. How much trouble could she get into going thirty, and, anyway, she had the Orchid Beach chief's badge and ID the department had given her when she left.

The car pulled up even with her rear bumper, and she heard the door slam. She looked over her shoulder and was blinded by an extremely bright flashlight. Probably a Surefire, she thought, with the lithium batteries. She switched off the car, rolled down the window and began fishing for her driver's license in her handbag.

"Good evening," a male voice said.

She turned left and was met by the blinding light. "Good evening," she said.

"May I see your driver's license, registration and proof of insurance?" he asked politely.

"Of course," she said, and then something struck her in the head, hard. Only the seat belt kept her from falling into the floorboards. She blinked, trying to see and think again; then she felt a sharp stab in the left side of her neck, and she lost consciousness.

"Ma'am?" a male voice was saying. "Ma'am?"

"She's coming to," a female voice said. Both voices were young. She realized she was bathed in light from a car parked behind her. She tried to get up.

"Don't move around, please," the male voice said. "An ambulance is on the way."

Her head hurt, and she realized that something

was pressing on it. She felt and discovered a female hand, holding something against her head. "What?" she managed to say.

"I said, an ambulance is on the way," he replied.

Holly felt oddly uncomfortable; there was a blanket over her, and she seemed to have sand in her jeans. She reached down and discovered that she wasn't wearing any jeans, only her shirt. From a distance she heard the siren of an ambulance. It would be all right, she thought, and then she passed out again.

A stab of pain in her head brought her around. She tried to sit up, but someone held her shoulders.

"Just lie still," a male voice said. "I'm almost done."

She tried to lie still, but he was hurting her.

"There," he said.

"I know this is a cliché," she managed to say, "but where am I?"

"Emergency room, Indian River Hospital," he said. "How are you feeling?"

"Oh, just great," she replied. "What were you doing up there? Brain surgery?"

"Next best thing," he replied. "Giving you eight stitches in your scalp. Don't worry, I took as little hair as possible."

"What happened to me?" she asked. "Was I in an accident?"

"What do you remember?"

"I remember driving away from my father's house," she said. "What happened then?"

"There's a police officer down the hall talking with the couple who found you," he said. "We'll know more soon."

"What happened to my neck?" she asked, rubbing it.

He took her hand away and inspected it. "There's a tiny wound, like a needle prick," he said.

"Where's my bag?" she asked.

Somebody set it on her belly. "Here it is," a nurse said, cranking her bed until she was sitting up a little. "Your jeans and underwear are here, too; you weren't wearing them when the couple found you, and you had no shoes on."

Holly found her cell phone and pressed a speed-dial button.

"This better be good," Ham's voice said. "You woke me up."

"Ham," she said, "my car is on the Indian River Trail, a couple of miles south of the bridge. Will you bring it to the hospital? I don't have the keys, so they must still be in the car."

"Are you all right?"

"Somebody hit me over the head. Just come to the ER."

"Twenty minutes," Ham said, then hung up.

Holly closed the phone and looked up. A stocky

young man in a police uniform was standing there.

"Holly? You all right?" he asked.

"Jimmy!" she said, glad to see him. Jimmy Weathers had been a rookie in her department.

"A couple found you out on Indian River Trail, lying in the road. You got any idea how you got that way?"

"None at all," she said. "I had dinner at Ham's, and the last thing I remember was driving away from his house."

"The kids who found you said there was a car parked behind yours with a flashing blue light. Almost as soon as they saw it, it drove away, and they nearly ran over you."

"I'm sorry, Jimmy," she said, "but that means nothing to me. I mean, I remember some people taking care of me, but I must have passed out. Ham's going to be here in a few minutes. Will you stay until he comes? Somebody besides me needs to tell him I'm all right."

"I'll help with that," the doctor said, and she looked at him for the first time. He was fiftyish, athletic looking, with thick salt-and-pepper hair. "You're going to stay with us overnight; you may have a concussion."

"Whatever you say," Holly replied, suddenly exhausted.

6

Holly woke up in a hospital room, and Ham was sitting beside her bed. Ginny came into the room holding two paper cups of coffee.

"Hey, Ham," Holly said sleepily. "Hey, Ginny."

Ham pressed the call button beside her bed. "How you feeling, baby?"

"Headache," Holly said, groping for the bed control that would sit her up.

A nurse came into the room. "Will you tell Dr. Harmon she's awake?" Ham asked. "He wanted to know."

"I'll call him," the nurse said, then left.

"What happened?" Ham asked.

"I wish I knew," Holly said.

"You have any idea who did this?"

"No, none at all."

Ham held up her lizard boots. "These were in your car," he said. "I thought you might need them when you walk out of here. There are socks inside."

The doctor walked into the room. "You're alive!" he said, in mock amazement. "Do you remember me?"

"The ham-handed stitcher-upper," Holly said. "How could I forget?"

"We X-rayed you after you drifted off; you'll be glad to know you don't have a fractured skull, just a mild concussion. We've sent a blood sample out to see if there was anything odd in your bloodstream."

"Just bourbon and red wine," Holly said, "but not enough to be illegal."

"That's not our department; I was just concerned with the apparent needle mark on your neck and your propensity for becoming unconscious."

"Okay," she said. "What's your name?"

"Josh Harmon," he said, offering her his hand. "At your service."

Holly shook his hand. "I hope I didn't cause you to overstay your shift."

"Nah, you're my last call, then I'm out of here."

"When am I out of here?" she asked.

"Let's get you some breakfast and decaf. If, after that, you're not suffering the aftereffects of some drug, we'll give you the boot."

"Please do; I'm feeling pretty good, except for the headache."

"I'll prescribe a painkiller."

"Aspirin will do."

"I'd like you to take it easy for a couple of days," he said. "No running, no exercise. Just lie around the house and watch TV."

"I can do that," Holly said. "Where's Daisy?" she asked Ham.

"In the car."

A nurse came in with a breakfast tray and set it before her.

Holly sipped the coffee. "This is awful," she said.

"We make it that way especially, because we don't want you to like it here too much," Dr. Harmon explained.

"It's working," Holly said, wolfing down some eggs. She finished her breakfast in record time.

"Before I go, I just want to do a little exam," Dr. Harmon said. He held a finger before her eyes. "Follow this," he said, moving it slowly back and forth. He finished the neurological exam. "Why are you taking up a bed?" he asked. "Get out of here."

"Yes, sir," Holly said, throwing off the covers and exposing more of herself than she had intended.

"I'd better get out of here while I can," Harmon said. "I'll call you later today and see how you're doing."

"You have my number?"

"Your dad was kind enough." He gave her a little wave and was gone.

Ginny put her clothes on the bed. "I'll bet that call isn't going to be entirely medically oriented," she said.

"I'll go shoot him," Ham said.

Later in the day, Holly woke from a nap and tried to remember what she had been dreaming. Something about being stopped by a cop. Her headache was gone, but her hair looked awful. They had apparently washed the blood out at the hospital, but they hadn't exactly styled it when they were done. She got into a shower, then dried her hair properly. She put some antibiotic cream on her scalp wound and covered it with her hair. It looked perfectly normal.

She was hungry, so she dressed and went downstairs for a sandwich. She had just finished it when the phone rang.

"Hello?"

"Hi, it's Josh Harmon, your friendly ham-handed stitcher-upper. How are you feeling?"

"Pretty good, actually," she replied, "and I want to thank you for not taking any more hair than you did."

"A nurse would have taken a big chunk, but I knew that would annoy you, so I did it myself. How's the headache?"

"Gone. I mean, I can feel the wound, and it hurts a little, but not the whole head, like before."

"Aspirin is a miracle drug," he said. "By the way, just so I can have a medical excuse for this call, your rape kit was negative—no bruising or tearing, no semen or seminal fluid. I didn't want to mention it in front of your father."

"Thanks, I appreciate that."

"Are you a free woman?"

Holly laughed. "I am."

"No doubt about that, is there? I wouldn't want to ask a lady to dinner who was otherwise committed."

"No doubt," she laughed. "When?"

"Tomorrow night?"

"You talked me into it. I'll make you dinner. Say seven o'clock?"

"That works for me."

She gave him the address. "There's a rather formidable gate, but press the buzzer on your left, and I'll let you in."

"I'll bring the wine—red or white?"

"Both. See you tomorrow evening."

"See ya."

He hung up, and so did she. She put her dish in

the dishwasher and looked around. The place was pretty neat, but she tidied it up a bit anyway.

She opened the sliding glass door to the beach with some effort and went for a little walk with Daisy, thinking about her dream. When she got back into the house, the doorbell was ringing. She opened it to find Jimmy Weathers there.

"Hey, Holly. Your gate was open."

"Hi, Jimmy. Come on in." He did. "Thanks for being there last night."

"My pleasure, Chief," he said. "That's my neck of the woods when I'm working. I just wanted to see if you're okay."

She showed him to a seat. "Jimmy, I think I was stopped by a police car last night."

"On Indian River Trail?"

"I guess. I don't remember anything else, just a flashing blue light and a bright flashlight."

"Well, that's really interesting, Holly."

"How so?"

"That would make the third incident like this in about six weeks."

"Women stopped by a police car?"

"And raped by a police officer," he said. "The doctor said you weren't raped."

"I know."

"I think you got lucky."

"Do you have any leads at all?"

Jimmy shook his head. "Not a one. I don't think

it was a police officer, though; I was able to account for all our guys at the time of the rapes. Maybe somebody from another jurisdiction, but more like somebody posing as a cop to get women to stop their cars. Both of the women reported a single blue flashing light behind them. Have you been able to remember anything else?"

Holly shook her head. "Just the blue light and the flashlight."

"Maybe some more will come back to you. Will you let me know?"

"Sure, I will."

Jimmy stood up. "I'd better go," he said. "We've got a staff meeting to meet the new chief."

"You don't want to miss that," Holly said, walking him to the door.

Jimmy stopped at the door. "I hear you've had some dealings with him in the past."

"You heard right," Holly said. "Keep an eye on the female officers; he's a predator."

"I'll do that," he said, and walked out to his car.

Holly watched him drive away, then got out the security system instructions and used the keypad to close the gate. She spent the rest of the afternoon reading the instructions for operating everything new in the house.

7

Holly slept a lot for the rest of the day, and the following morning she went to her favorite grocery and got the makings for dinner. She went home and prepared osso buco, which she had first had at Elaine's with Stone Barrington. She left it to cook for four hours, then set the table and laid out the pans and ingredients for the rest of dinner. By noon, she was done. Holly liked to be prepared.

She had a sandwich for lunch, and shortly afterward Hurd Wallace called. "Jimmy Weathers took me aside at the station yesterday and told me what happened to you," he said. "Are you all right?"

"Sure, Hurd. I'm feeling very well. I've got a cut on my head that has to heal but nothing else. Thanks for asking."

"I knew about the two earlier cases, of course, but we've been unable to come up with anything, not even a description from the victims. I had to leave that in the hands of Jimmy and Jim Bruno."

"Has he started work?"

"Yes. I introduced him to the department yesterday, and he gave them the sort of pep talk you said he would."

"I've heard some version of it many times," she said.

"I briefed him on our open cases, including the two rapes, but he didn't seem much interested."

"He's interested in other people doing his job for him—God knows, I did his work for two years. He likes golf and tennis more than work. The good news is, he won't get in the way much."

"I'm going to keep in touch with half a dozen officers and get their readings as time passes."

"Good. Have you started your new job yet?"

"I'm sitting at my desk now," Hurd said. "I've got some unpacking and settling in to do, and then my people are going to start looking into these rapes. Problem is, we need a request from Bruno to get involved."

"Call him and ask him; he'd love to have you involved. But if you clear the case, he'll manage to take the credit."

"I'll keep that in mind," Hurd said. He gave her his new office and cell numbers. "Call me if you remember anything about the other night. Or if you need anything."

"Thanks, Hurd, I'll do that." She said good-bye and hung up.

Shortly after seven, the phone rang, and Holly picked it up. "Hello?"

"It's Josh Harmon; I'm at your very formidable gate."

"Hang on," she said. She tapped the code into the phone and hung up.

Shortly, Josh appeared at the front door, holding two bottles of wine. Daisy took an immediate but polite interest in him.

"You have a formidable dog as well as a gate," he said, handing her the wines. He turned his attention to Daisy. After a little introductory affection, she brought him a tennis ball.

"That means you're friends now," Holly said.

"I can't believe he's a watchdog, too."

"She. And she's a very well-trained watchdog. But, if you behave yourself, I won't have to give her the kill command."

"That's a relief," Josh said.

"Drink?"

"Scotch?"

"You ever drink bourbon?"

"Only under duress."

She poured him a Knob Creek. "You have to drink one of these; after that, you can have anything you like."

"Oh, all right," he said, taking a sip. "Not bad."

"Faint praise," she said.

"Give me time. What smells good?"

"Osso buco—it's been in the oven all afternoon. I'll make risotto before dinner." She poured herself a drink. "Let's sit outside for a while."

Josh walked to the sliding door to the beach and opened it with difficulty. "Wow," he said, "that's one heavy door." He looked closely at the glass. "Now, *that* is what I'd call major hurricane protection. It must be an inch thick."

"An inch and a half," Holly said.

"May I ask why?"

"Courtesy of my employer. They like for their people to be well protected."

They sat down in deck chairs. "And who might your employer be? I've no idea what you do."

"Hardly anybody does," Holly said.

"Does that mean I'm not supposed to ask?"

"Probably."

"All right. I'll respect your privacy and keep my nose out of your employment."

They sat and watched the evening light on the sea for about a minute.

"All right," he said. "What do you do, and who do you do it for?"

Holly had to make a decision; usually she told people she was an official at the Department of Agriculture, which pretty much prevented any further conversation, but she liked him, and it wasn't strictly against the rules to tell someone where she worked. "I work at the CIA," she said. "I'm an assistant deputy director of Operations."

He looked at her sideways. "You're not kidding, are you?"

"I kid you not."

"What does an assistant . . . whatever that title is . . . do?"

"At the top is the director of Central Intelligence," she said. "Under her are the two principal deputy directors: one for Intelligence, one for Operations. The Directorate of Intelligence deals with analysis—many, many analysts working on information from all over the world. The Directorate of Operations runs spies all over the world."

"Are you supposed to be telling me this stuff? Because, if you're not . . . Oh the hell with it, keep talking."

"I haven't told you anything that the brochure for the Agency won't tell you."

"So, you're a spy?"

"I'm trained to be, but essentially I'm an administrator."

"That's not what your title says. It says you're the assistant head spy."

"One of a few assistant deputy directors. I'm not sure I'm supposed to tell you how many."

"I'm not sure I want to know. You did say you were trained to be a spy?"

"There's a place, Fort Peary, in Virginia, commonly called the Farm, where prospective officers are sent for a considerable period of time and punished in all sorts of ways, not to mention trained in all sorts of ways."

"May one ask about the punishment and the training?"

"One is punished with long runs over difficult terrain and physical training of all kinds, especially self-defense."

"Killing with a single blow? Like that?"

"Like that."

"And the other training?"

"One may not know about that." She took his empty glass. "Can I get you a Scotch?"

"I think I'll have another bourbon."

"It's the patriotic thing to do," she said.

8

Holly started the risotto, then handed Josh the wooden spoon. "Now you work," she said. "Just keep pouring in the stock, a little at a time, and constantly stir until the rice absorbs it all, then add more stock, et cetera, et cetera, until it's all gone."

"And what are you going to do?"

"I'm going to set the table, then watch you, to see if you have any stamina at all. I guess risotto must be the most physically demanding of all cooking chores."

"I have stamina," he said.

"Don't tell me; show me." She set the table and got out her good Baccarat wineglasses, then returned to the kitchen. "How are you doing?"

"I'm doing just great," he said, "but I'm getting a blister between my thumb and forefinger."

"Chef's hazard; switch hands."

He did so. "This better be delicious when it's done," he said.

"It will be delicious after I add the final ingredients," she said, going to the refrigerator to fetch them.

"You used to be chief of police in Orchid Beach, didn't you?"

"That's right."

"Were you always a cop?"

"I was a military cop from the age of eighteen for twenty years, and don't start doing the arithmetic for my age."

"Oh, I think I can figure that out without arithmetic," he said, continuing to add stock and stir.

"You'd better not," she said. "Remember, I can kill with a single blow, and Daisy is trained to attack genitals."

Josh winced. "I'm fifty," he said. "Let's forget your age."

"What a good idea," she said. "All right, I have to add the final ingredients, now," she said.

"And what are they?"

"Crème fraîche and grated Parmesan cheese— Parmigiano-Reggiano, the real thing."

"I thought Parmesan cheese came from Wisconsin."

"Wash your mouth out with soap, then taste this." She held up a pinch of the grated cheese for him to taste.

"Mmmm, tangy!"

"Exactly. Now will you set the iron skillet on the dining table, on the trivet, please, not on the nice wood."

He did as he was told, then came back. "Anything else?"

"There's a corkscrew over there," she said, pointing to a drawer. "You can open the red wine." She got a potholder and carried the copper risotto pot to the table and set it down. "I think we're ready," she said.

He held her chair for her. "I'm certainly ready; I never got around to eating lunch today." He sat down, poured a little wine and tasted it. "I think we'll drink it," he said, pouring them both a glass.

"Okay," she said. "Your turn. Full bio, please."

"Okay. Born Delano, Georgia, fifty years ago, to a small-town general practitioner and his nurse. Educated local schools, then at the University of Georgia, Emory Medical School in Atlanta. Interned at Georgia Baptist Hospital, then did a residency in surgery at Emory Hospital. Practiced general surgery for fifteen years, then did a two-week stretch in the trauma center at Piedmont Hospital, subbing for a friend. Loved the ER, got a job there, and I've been doing emergency medicine ever since."

"Why do you like it?"

"Variety, intensity, a constant challenge to diagnose and treat quickly, and you don't have time to form a bond with your patients, so when they die it isn't the kind of personal loss it is if you've been treating them for weeks or months."

"My, but you're a sensitive soul."

"Watching people die while trying to prevent them from doing so is not fun, but it's less painful if you're not acquainted with them."

"Okay, I buy that. Who's your least favorite patient to treat?"

"A rape victim," he replied without hesitation. "That's why I was so glad you weren't raped."

"On behalf of rape victims, I thank you."

"You were raped before?"

"No, but someone has tried twice. Daisy dealt with the would-be rapist the first time, and I got lucky the second, when that young couple arrived in time to scare the guy off."

"Ex-cop that you are, are you going to try to catch the guy?"

"So far, I'm just keeping in touch with the investigation through old acquaintances," she said. "I wouldn't mind the opportunity to stick a nine-millimeter in his ear, though."

"Would you pull the trigger?"

"Probably not, but my father would."

"Ham? That's his name?"

"Yep."

"He looked like retired military."

"An old first sergeant, tough as boot leather, but squishy soft if you work your way inside far enough."

"His wife seemed nice."

"Yes. Ginny taught me to fly."

"That's something I've thought I'd like to try," he said.

"I'll introduce you. She's a first-rate instructor and has her own flying school at the Vero Beach airport."

"I'll look forward to it."

"How'd you come to be working in Orchid Beach?" she asked.

"Heard about it on the grapevine, liked the idea of a warm winter. With my skills, it's easy to work wherever you want to. There's lots of demand for good ER physicians. I've been here eight months, and I like it."

"Where do you live?"

"I'm renting a house in Vero at the Orchid Island development. I have an option to buy."

"Good golf there."

"Yes, you play?"

"Yes, but I haven't had time for a few years. I'd like to play while I'm here."

"I'll arrange it. How long will you be in town?"

"My boss told me not to come back for a month."

They finished dinner, and Holly served them ice cream; then they took coffee in the living room. The door to the beach was still open, and they could hear the waves lapping at the beach.

"Nice house," he said.

"I inherited it," she replied, settling next to him on the sofa.

"From whom?"

"My late fiancé. He was a local lawyer. He went into a local bank the day before our wedding to get some cash for our honeymoon and wound up in the middle of a bank robbery. He got in the way of a shotgun."

"I'm sorry for your loss."

"So am I, but enough time has passed that it hurts less than it used to."

"Were you ever married?"

"No. How about you?"

"Once, twenty years ago, to a nurse. Lasted three years."

They sat quietly, sipping their coffee, listening to the sea.

9

Holly felt his naked body slide down hers, until his head was in her lap, facedown. His tongue did wonderful things, and then she climaxed.

She woke alone, with Daisy sitting beside the bed staring at her. Josh had given her a prim good-night kiss the night before and had left her randier than he knew. It was the first wet dream she had ever had.

The phone rang, startling her. She grabbed at the sheet to cover herself, in case Lance was on the line, then she picked it up. "Hello?"

"Holly?" A woman's voice.

"Yes."

"It's Annie Ryan."

Annie was a female officer on the Orchid Beach force, one Holly remembered fondly. "Hello, Annie, how are you?"

"I'm not sure," Annie replied. "Would you mind if I stop by this morning and talk with you?"

"Not at all," Holly replied. "Any time after, say, ten?"

"Ten fifteen?"

"See you then." Holly explained about the gate and hung up. She showered, dressed, fed Daisy and let her out, then made herself some breakfast. She was still on coffee when the phone rang, and Holly saw the gate button light come on. She buzzed Annie in and found another coffee mug.

Annie Ryan was a petite redhead, maybe five-two, who looked very good in her tailored uniform. Holly poured her a cup of coffee and sat her down on a counter stool.

"I see you made sergeant," Holly said, gesturing at the stripes.

"Yes, last year. I'm a supervisor on the day shift now."

"I'll bet you're a good one, too," Holly said. "What did you want to see me about?"

"It's this Colonel James Bruno," she said.

"Ah, yes."

"Jimmy Weathers told me about your experience with him in the army."

"Good. I wanted all the female officers to know about him."

"Well, I guess we do, now," Annie said. "It's

just that we're not quite sure how to handle him. I mean, the guy is our chief, after all."

"My advice is, be pleasant but not friendly; keep him at arm's length, and don't ever get into a car with him alone. Always have a witness."

"Does he have a thing about cars?"

"Apart from having a shot at me," Holly said, "which I was able to fight off, he raped a young woman lieutenant, and he did it in a car."

Annie was quiet for a moment. "If we do like you say, will that be enough to keep him off us?"

"I think it will, if you never give him an inch, if you never let him cross the line without calling him on it. I realize you're walking a fine line here, but you have to give him the respect of his rank while seeing that he returns that respect. Believe me, he will take any display of friendship or warmth the wrong way."

"How did this guy manage to spend thirty years in the military while getting away with that?"

"My guess is that his problem was sublimated for a long time. He had a nice wife, and after she died of breast cancer he started to get too friendly with female soldiers. He played on the sympathy he got from his wife's death, used that to get friendly with women, then abused them."

"Okay, I'll have a talk with the other women."

"You can protect each other," Holly said.

"I guess that's what we'll do," Annie said. The

radio on her belt squawked, and she answered the call. "I'd better get going," she said. "One of my shift has arrested two men on a drug charge after a traffic stop, and I need to cover that."

"You go ahead," Holly said, "and feel free to call me if you need to talk."

Annie got back into her patrol car and headed back up the driveway.

Holly was glad to have talked to her. She wished she had had somebody to talk to when she was dealing with Bruno.

She cleaned up the kitchen, polishing the copper risotto pan she'd used the night before, then realized that, in spite of her shopping trip for dinner, she had little else to eat in the house. She made a list and drove into Orchid Beach to the market.

Holly had been in the store for a minute when she heard a woman's voice behind her.

"Major Barker?"

She turned and saw a young woman with short, blond hair, wearing the Florida State Patrol uniform with sergeant's stripes. "Yes?"

"You don't recognize me, do you?"

Suddenly, the penny dropped. She was the lieutenant James Bruno had raped—Lauren Cade. "Lauren!" Holly said. "I'm sorry. The uniform and the haircut threw me off, and nobody has called me major for a long time." They shook hands.

"I'd heard you were chief in Orchid Beach after

you retired," Lauren said, "but I thought you had left town."

"That's true," Holly replied. "I'm working in Virginia now; I'm just back for a little while on vacation. I still have a house here."

"I left the army a year after you did," Lauren said. "I came to Florida for the weather, had a couple of nothing jobs to pay the rent, then I applied to the State Patrol and was accepted. I made sergeant a few months ago."

"Congratulations," Holly said.

"I just came in here to get a sandwich for lunch."

"Why don't we have lunch together, if you have the time?" Holly said.

"Thanks. I'd like that."

They went to a deli a couple of doors down from the market, found a table and ordered sandwiches.

"Is Orchid Beach a regular part of your patrol duty?" Holly asked.

"Yes, I'm through here every day."

"Lauren, have you heard the latest about Jim Bruno?"

Her face hardened. "Do I want to?"

"I think you'd better hear this; he's the new chief in Orchid, my old job."

Her face fell. "No, I hadn't heard that."

"I thought it best to tell you before you ran into him."

"Thanks. I appreciate it. I'm sorry to hear he's in the state, let alone on my beat."

"I'd hate to see you have to transfer somewhere else just to avoid him," Holly said.

"Not likely," Lauren replied. "I just bought a house; I'm dug in here. I've applied to a new investigative unit that's going to be based in Vero Beach. Haven't heard anything yet."

"The one that Hurd Wallace is running?"

"Yes, that's the one. Do you know him?"

"He was my deputy chief when I was in Orchid. I'd be happy to put in a word for you, if you like."

"Oh, yes, that would be great!" Lauren said. "What's Captain Wallace like?"

"Good guy; no worries there. He came to see me to tell me about Bruno, said he would have done what he could to block his appointment if he'd known earlier who he was."

They changed the subject and chatted through lunch, then Holly said good-bye and went back to the market to complete her shopping. When she was back in her car, she called Hurd Wallace and recommended Lauren Cade highly. He said he'd interview her.

10

Holly awoke early the next morning, fed Daisy and herself, then took them both for a walk on the beach. Daisy ran freely among the dunes, as she always did, looking for just the right spot, then she returned to Holly with a stick of driftwood in her mouth, demanding that Holly throw it. Holly obliged, and Daisy dutifully retrieved the stick and returned it to Holly, wanting more. They made progress up the beach as Daisy retrieved. Then Holly threw it once more, and Daisy stopped after a few feet and sat down on the sand.

"What's the matter?" Holly asked, catching up with her. "You tired already? You haven't even worn me out yet."

Daisy made an urgent rumbling noise in her throat, then got up and began to walk up the beach, this time very slowly. Holly watched her, mystified. In their time together she had never seen Daisy behave this way. She followed the dog at her pace, and after another hundred yards Holly saw something in the surf ahead.

Daisy trotted ahead a few yards, sniffed at what seemed to be a lump on the sand, then sat down beside it and barked. Holly began to jog toward her. She was ten feet away when she recognized the lump. It was a body, female, naked, with long blond hair, lying facedown in the sand. One ankle had a length of rope tied around it. Holly stopped, called Daisy back, then reached for her cell phone.

The sun was well up now, and a small knot of people was gathered inside a taped-off area on the beach. Holly sat on a dune with Daisy, watching them, thinking. She heard a car door slam behind her, and she turned to see James Bruno trudging through the dunes toward the taped-off area. He joined the group inspecting the body, chatted with them for a few minutes, then turned back toward his car. Then he spotted Holly.

He walked slowly toward her, as if to ascertain her identity, then he stopped a few steps away. Daisy was already on her feet in a guarding stance.

"Good morning, Holly," Bruno said.

"Is it?"

"Will your dog attack?"

"I haven't decided yet."

Bruno thought about that and decided to stay where he was. "I understand you found the body."

"My dog did. I never got closer than ten feet to the woman."

"Do you know her?"

"She was facedown in the sand."

He nodded. "If you've formed any opinions, I'd appreciate hearing them."

Holly stared toward where the body was being loaded into the coroner's wagon. "White female, mid- to late twenties, five-five or -six, a hundred and thirty pounds. No deterioration, just some puffiness associated with being in the water, so she was probably put into the sea last night from a small boat with an outboard engine and with a weight tied to her ankle. Her killer was clumsy, and his outboard cut the rope. She came ashore with the tide, and when it went out, it left her there."

"That's very good," Bruno said.

Holly didn't reply, just stared out to sea.

"Cause of death?"

"Unless there were wounds on the front of the torso, strangulation. There was a faint mark on the back of her neck. You'd be wise to order a tox screen from the state lab. Hurd Wallace could hurry it up for you, if you call him."

"Why a tox screen?"

"You've probably heard that a serial rapist has been operating locally over the last six weeks."

"Yes, but he hasn't killed anybody."

"Maybe he's graduated to bigger, more satisfying acts," she replied. "Maybe rape isn't doing it for him anymore; maybe he's decided to become a serial killer."

He was quiet for a moment. "I understand you've had some communication with some of my female officers. I don't appreciate that."

"You think I care what you don't appreciate? What did you expect me to do? Get you dates?" She looked at him and saw him go red.

"Good morning," he said finally; then he started across the dunes toward his car.

Holly thought of siccing Daisy on him, just for the fun of it, but she didn't. She got up, dusted off the sand and went back to the house. She found Hurd Wallace's number and phoned him.

"Captain Wallace."

"Morning, Hurd. It's Holly."

"Good morning, Holly."

"I thought you ought to know, about an hour and a half ago Daisy and I discovered the body of a woman washed up on the beach, not far from my house."

"Who's investigating?"

"Orchid Beach. Jim Bruno turned up an hour late and asked for my impressions."

"Which were?"

She repeated the assessment she had given Bruno. "I also think that if you search the garbage cans at the nearest marinas you might find her clothing and handbag."

"Did you tell Bruno that?"

"No, I thought it would be more fun for someone else to discover what he had overlooked."

"Is this the first time you've seen him since . . ."

"Yes. He's lucky I wasn't armed."

"I understand. By the way, I had a talk with Lauren Cade late yesterday afternoon. I'm going to offer her a job. It's good that she's already on the state patrol; it will just take a transfer, not all the rigmarole that would be involved if I were hiring her off the street. I'm grateful for your recommendation."

"You're welcome, Hurd."

"Thanks for the tip about the murder. I'll get somebody on it." He said good-bye and hung up.

Holly tried to remember if she had told Hurd that James Bruno had raped Lauren Cade. Probably not; it wasn't relevant.

II

Holly had just hung up after talking with Hurd Wallace when her phone rang. "Hello?"

"Good morning, it's Josh," he said.

"Good morning."

"I'm coming back for more; would you like to go out to dinner tonight?"

"Yes, I would," she replied without hesitation.

"Where would you like to go?"

"You choose; I'm easy."

"I hope so," he said, laughing. "I'll come and get you at seven."

"That's good," she said.

"See you then." He hung up.

He appeared at her door on time, and she let him in.

"Would you like a drink before we go?" she asked.

"I'm hungry; let's have a drink at the restaurant."

"Okay by me." She patted Daisy on the head. "Guard the place with your life, and you can sleep on the bed while we're gone."

Daisy turned and trotted upstairs. Holly secured the house and left with Josh, who was driving a newish Mercedes convertible, top down.

"Nice car," she said, when they had cleared the gates. "How do you afford it on a public hospital salary?"

"The money isn't all that bad, really," Josh said, "especially if you don't have to buy a wife a car, too. It isn't as good as my general-surgery practice, but then I don't have to support an office and a staff. How does the CIA pay?"

"It's civil service pay, but I've been operating at a fairly high grade, and now that I've been promoted to the executive level, I'll do even better. To tell the truth, I was afraid to ask how much better. I'll find out when I get back to work. Where are we dining?"

"At the Ocean Grill in Vero Beach," he replied. "Do you know it?"

"One of my favorites," she said, "and I'm in the mood for seafood."

They were halfway through their first drink when he changed the subject.

"I got your tox screen back," he said.

"I thought that could take weeks," Holly said.

"Not if you have a friend in the lab and not if you ask for a specific test."

"And?"

"It was a benzodiazepine, trade name Rohypnol."

"I know about that," she said. "It's a date-rape drug. But doesn't it take fifteen or twenty minutes to take effect?"

"If you're ingesting it in a drink, yes. But the perpetrator probably dissolved it in alcohol and injected it, so it would work much faster. I'm very pleased with myself for taking your blood as soon as you were admitted. The body metabolizes the drug quickly, and if we had waited, we might have gotten a negative result on the test. As it was, only a very small amount was detected."

"Rohypnol is illegal, right?"

"Right. It would have to be obtained through a street dealer, like crack or pot, but it is available."

"Or," Holly said, "in a drug bust."

"Pardon?"

"If the perp is a cop he might well have found the drug in a search of a suspect or a car. He could learn how to use it effectively from the Internet."

"I guess you can learn almost anything from the Internet these days," Josh replied.

"How much Rohypnol would it take to kill someone?" she asked.

"I'd have to look that up on the Internet," he

replied, "but I suppose it would depend on how it was administered: a lot, if ingested—it has the same effect as alcohol, only more powerful. It would take less if injected—even less, if it were injected into a vein or an artery."

"Now there's a thought," Holly said.

"Come again?"

"This morning Daisy and I discovered the body of a young woman washed up on the beach not far from my house. I have a gut feeling she's a victim of the same perp who's doing the raping. Suppose he's injecting Rohypnol and he accidentally finds the jugular vein or the carotid artery?"

"I get your point," Josh said. "That could result in death instead of just unconsciousness."

"Probably surprised the perp," Holly said. "He was aiming for a neck muscle, but he hit the vein or artery instead, and she dies. He had to get rid of the body in a hurry, so he takes it out in a small boat, ties a weight to an ankle and throws her overboard. Only his outboard severs the rope, and she ends up a floater. Did I mention that she had a rope tied to a leg and that the rope had been severed?"

"No, but that makes sense. I suppose you must have a very rattled perp."

"Maybe," Holly said. "Or maybe he ended up enjoying the experience."

"The experience of killing someone?"

"Maybe. Or maybe the experience of sex with a dead body."

Josh gave a little shiver. "Creepy."

"When you think about it, it's not a very big step from sex with an unconscious body. Either way, she's not going to fight back, and maybe he feels safer with his victim dead."

"This is all outside my experience," Josh said. "I mean, if somebody walks into my ER who appears to be psychotic, I just patch him up, then call for a psych consult and hand him off. Chances are, I never see him again."

"Lucky you," Holly said. "Eventually, the cops have to deal with him, and, like our serial rapist, they don't even know who he is."

"From what you said before about his finding the Rohypnol in a search, I take it you're considering the possibility that your perpetrator is a cop?"

"He had a flashing light on his dashboard, and in the dark, a driver seeing the light wouldn't see much of the car in her rearview mirror. The cop who's investigating the crimes—you met him, Jimmy Weathers—brought up that possibility right away. He said he had already eliminated the men on the Orchid force as suspects, so he's thinking of somebody in a neighboring jurisdiction."

"I guess that makes sense." Josh cocked his head and looked at her. "You enjoy this process, don't you?"

Holly laughed. "It's the cop in me, I suppose. Until a few years ago, I had never done anything but be a cop. My new work is very, very interesting, but it doesn't involve much in the way of criminal investigation, and I guess I miss that."

"My guess is, you're not going to stop thinking about this until you've caught the guy," Josh said.

"Until *somebody* catches the guy," she replied, "and I guess it would be satisfying if it were me."

12

Lauren Cade got out of Hurd Wallace's car at the Indian River Marina and followed him across the parking lot.

"Here we go," Hurd said, pointing at two Dumpsters. "You take the one on the right; I'll take the left."

They both donned lightweight plastic jumpsuits and latex gloves.

Lauren opened the lid of the Dumpster and peered inside. It was nearly full, and to judge from the smell, it hadn't been emptied for a few days. She took a deep breath, grabbed the edge of the Dumpster and vaulted inside, landing on her feet, but immediately losing her footing and falling backward into the steel side. She struggled to her feet, glad of the plastic jumpsuit, then looked over at Hurd, who was having the same problem.

"We might get lucky and find some loose clothing," Hurd said, "but they could be in a bag, so let's toss everything out and work from the tarmac."

Lauren began picking up plastic garbage bags and tossing them out of the Dumpster. During the process, she found one loose towel but no clothing. When the Dumpster was empty, she crawled out and stood on the tarmac, surveying her work. Most of it was small, kitchen-sized bags, which is what she would have expected from boats. "Are we just going to dump everything out of the bags?" she asked.

"Yes," Hurd said. "I've already called for a garbage pickup from the county, so they'll do the cleanup."

"I've got one loose item," Lauren said, holding up the towel.

"Bag it, and set it aside."

She did so, then took a knife from her pocket and began opening bags, shaking the contents onto the bare tarmac and poking carefully through them before going on to the next bag.

"Look for anything like a wallet or purse, too," Hurd said.

Lauren looked at every single item in every bag: tin cans, paper plates, condoms, tampons—everything. An hour later she stepped out of the refuse and onto clean tarmac, just as a garbage truck drove up and two sanitation workers got out.

"What a mess!" one of them said. "You had to open every bag?"

"Every one," Hurd replied.

"We're gonna have to bag all this again," the man said.

"Well, you can put it back in the Dumpsters, then use your equipment to dump everything into the truck."

"I guess that makes more sense. Get some pitch-forks and brooms, Eddie," the man said.

Lauren picked up her bagged towel and took one last look in her Dumpster. "Hang on!" she shouted. She vaulted back into the bin and peered into a corner. "Car keys," she yelled, and tossed them to Hurd.

She climbed out of the Dumpster and went to take a closer look at them.

"Hertz," Hurd said. "Ford Focus." He read out the license plate number. Then they both started walking around the parking lot: not a single Ford Focus.

Lauren walked back to the parking lot entrance and looked up and down the road. "Hurd?" she called. "What color is the Focus?"

"Blue," he called back.

"I've got one," she said and began trotting down the road. She came up on the car and walked carefully around it, looking inside.

Hurd drove up in their car. "Anything?"

Lauren struggled out of the dirty jumpsuit and pulled on a fresh pair of latex gloves. "Rental folder," she said, opening the car door and reaching for the folder, which had been tucked into a cup holder. She opened it and read the contract. "Patricia Terwilliger," she said, "Atlanta address. Rented the car at Melbourne Airport three days ago. Here's her Georgia driver's license number," she said, walking toward the car.

Hurd was already tapping computer keys. In seconds, the driver's license was displayed on the screen. "Looks like our girl," he said.

"You saw her?" Lauren asked.

"At the morgue."

"Can I have the keys, please?" Lauren asked.

Hurd handed them to her.

She walked around to the rear of the car, inserted the key and opened the trunk. "I've got a wheelie carry-on and a purse here," she said. She lifted the carry-on out of the trunk and set it on the ground, then reached for the handbag and stopped. "Hurd, when you saw her corpse, was it missing anything?"

"No," he replied.

"Then you'd better get out an APB for a female body missing the right hand."

Holly, naked and sweating, was lying in her bed with Josh next to her. "What time do you have to be at work?" she asked.

"Noon," he panted.

"Good," she said.

The phone rang. "Hello?"

"Holly, it's Hurd."

"Hey, Hurd."

"Your idea about checking marina Dumpsters paid off, right out of the box."

"You found her clothes?"

"First her car keys, then her car—a rental out of Melbourne three days ago. The contract was inside with her license number, and we pulled up her license: Patricia Terwilliger from Atlanta. Then we opened the trunk and found her carry-on, her purse and another woman's right hand."

"Oh, shit," Holly said.

"I'm going back to the office to work this. I just thought you'd like to know."

"Thanks, Hurd," she said. "I appreciate the call. Maybe you'll get a print or two off the car."

"Lauren's with me. She's staying with the car until Forensics gets here."

"Keep me posted?"

"You bet I will."

"Will you call Jimmy Weathers? He's the lead on the case, and I know he'd appreciate it."

"Sure. I'll do it right now. I'm going to keep Jim Bruno out of the loop for as long as I can."

"Good. Oh, Hurd, I had a call from the doctor who treated me the other night. He got the tox screen back. The perp used Rohypnol on me."

"I'll let the morgue know."

"He says it metabolizes quickly, but the girl could have died from it very quickly if the perp hit a vein or artery, so you might get lucky."

"I'll take all the luck I can get," Hurd said. "Bye-bye."

Holly hung up.

"What?" Josh said.

"They've ID'd the woman Daisy and I found on the beach. Sounds like a tourist." She didn't mention the hand.

"Will it help you catch the guy?"

"God, I hope so," Holly said. "He's not going to stop this now; he's having too good a time. It's all working for him."

"Anything I can do?"

"You can tell your ER to be on the lookout for any other women who come in—women like me, hurt or unconscious."

"I can do that," he said, sitting up and reaching for his clothes.

13

Holly parked a few yards behind the state van and walked up to the blue car.

Lauren Cade was looking into the backseat with a flashlight. She straightened up, then saw Holly. "Hey, there," she said.

"Hey, Lauren. I see you got your transfer pretty fast."

"I sure did, and I thank you again for the recommendation to Hurd. He's a good guy."

"Yes, he is. Found anything on or in the car yet?"

"There are some prints around the driver's window and some sand around the pedals. I guess Hurd must have told you about the stuff in the trunk."

"Yes. Can I see the hand?"

"You mind, Terry?" Lauren said to the guy from Forensics working the car.

"Go ahead. It's in the van, bagged."

Lauren went to the open van door, reached into a lab container, lifted out the zippered plastic bag holding the hand and held it up.

Holly took the bag by a corner and rotated it slowly. "This girl is thinner than the one we found," she said. "Longer fingers and the skin is freckled."

"I'll get that to Hurd," she said. "He's back at the office."

"Taller, too, I'd guess; it's a pretty long hand."

"Right."

"And look at this," Holly said, pointing at where the hand had been severed, a couple of inches above.

"Something cut it clean," Lauren said. "Maybe an ax?"

Holly rotated the bag a hundred and eighty degrees. "No. Same cut on the bottom. Something cut from both directions at once. Bolt cutter, maybe."

"The guy carries around bolt cutters?"

"It's the sort of thing you might find in a police car," Holly pointed out. "You found the hand in the trunk?"

"Yes. It was under the carry-on, next to the purse."

"Was there any blood?"

"A drop or two. Terry took a sample of the carpet."

"Good." Holly placed the bag with the hand back in the container. "Have you had a look around the marina yet?"

"No. Hurd left immediately after we found the hand, and I haven't had a chance yet."

Terry walked up and shucked off his gloves. "I'm done here," he said. "You can have the car towed now." He began to put his equipment back into the van.

Holly looked around to see a flatbed truck coming down the road. "Make sure the driver is gloved," she said.

Lauren went to speak with the man, and Holly walked around the rental car. She didn't see anything new.

Lauren came back. "You want to work the marina with me?" she asked.

"Sure," Holly replied. "Let's see if we can find the boat." They walked across the parking lot and down the dock, then down the hinged ramp to the pontoons. "Let's look for a small boat with one or more outboards. You take the south end; I'll start from the north, and we can work our way back here."

The women separated and began to examine the small boats moored there. Holly was nearly back to the ramp when Lauren called out.

"Come take a look at this," she yelled.

Holly trotted down the dock to where Lauren

stood, looking into a Boston Whaler, a flat-bottomed runabout of about eighteen feet, with a 75-hp Japanese outboard engine. She walked along the dock for the length of the boat, then back. "Looks pretty ordinary," she said. "What caught your eye?"

"The keys are in it," Lauren said, pointing to the ignition under the wheel.

"I missed that," Holly said. "Good going."

"If the owner habitually leaves the key in the ignition, then anybody could have taken it."

"You'd better get that Forensics guy back here," Holly said. "This boat is going to need a good going-over."

Lauren got on her cell phone just as a young man in shorts, a polo shirt and a baseball cap walked up.

"Can I help you ladies?" he asked politely.

Lauren held up her badge as she talked.

"What's your name?" Holly asked.

"Tim Pooley," he replied. "I'm the day manager here."

"Can you tell me who owns this boat?" Holly asked.

"It belongs to the marina," he said. "We use it for towing or whatever."

"Are the keys always in it?"

"Pretty much," Tim said. "I mean, the night guy may lock them up; I don't know."

"Is there somebody here all night?"

"No. He shuts the gate at midnight and goes home. There's a combination lock, so customers can get in if they've been out late."

"What are your working hours?"

"Eight to six."

"How many of the boats in the marina are based here?"

"Well, we've got eighty berths, and sixty-six are rented by the month or the season. We get a few transients just about every night; they're mostly alongside the outer, long pontoon. Once in a while, if we know a local is away for a few days—out to the Bahamas or something—we'll rent his berth by the night."

"How many live-aboards among the locals?" Holly asked.

"Maybe a couple of dozen."

"Are they grouped together?"

"No. They're just wherever."

"Can you give me a list of the names of the boats and owners? Addresses and phone numbers, too."

"Well, I guess the addresses are right here," Tim said. "Everybody's got a cell phone number these days. I'll go get the list." He ambled off toward the little house at the head of the dock.

Lauren snapped her cell phone shut. "He's on the way back," she said.

"Do you have some crime-scene tape?"

"No, Hurd took the car; he was going to send somebody back for me."

"When that guy shows up, you should tape off this boat until Terry is done."

"Sure."

"Tim, the day manager, is getting us a list of the live-aboards in the marina," Holly said.

Tim was ambling back toward them now. He approached and handed them several sheets of paper. "The first page is the live-aboards," he said. "The rest are just monthly or seasonal renters."

"We're going to need the night man's name and phone number, too," Holly said.

Tim scribbled the information on one of the sheets.

"Thanks for your help, Tim," Holly said.

"Let me know if there's anything else you need."

"There's a van coming in a few minutes. The driver works for the state, and he's going to take some fingerprints from the boat."

"I guess my fingerprints are all over it," Tim said.

"He'll take yours, too, so we'll know which ones they are."

"I'll be in the office," he said and walked back up the ramp.

Holly handed the sheets to Lauren. "Now the

police work starts," she said, "so I'm going to leave you and Hurd to it."

"Thanks for your help, Holly."

"Take care," Holly replied. She walked back up the ramp and to her car, thinking hard.

14

Holly drove out to Ham's place, and as she approached the turnoff to his little island, just short of the bridge, she abruptly pulled off the pavement and stopped. Something she had forgotten on the night she was attacked had just popped into her mind. "Stay, Daisy," she said.

She got out of the car and walked slowly toward the turnoff, a hundred yards ahead. When she had left Ham's that night, she had stopped for traffic before turning onto the bridge, and there had been a car parked, maybe ten yards before the turnoff—a plain Detroit model, one that might be an unmarked police car. She began walking more slowly, examining the ground. It hadn't rained since then; there might be something here.

There was. Less than a foot from the pavement, in the dirt, was a little scattering of cigarette butts: somebody had emptied his car's ashtray here. She went back to her own car, found an old evidence bag in the glove compartment, went back to the pile and, using a piece of nearby palm frond, raked the butts into the bag and zipped it shut.

She looked at them closely. Marlboros, all of them, smoked nearly down to the filter: probably a man, probably a chain smoker.

She looked around for other leavings and found none, so she went back to her car, put the evidence bag in the glove compartment and drove out to Ham's island.

Daisy jumped out the window before the car had stopped and ran through the open front door. Holly followed her and walked through the house to the back porch, where Ham was sitting in the swing with the *New York Times* and a glass of iced tea.

"You still reading that liberal rag?" Holly asked.

"Liberal it may be, a rag it may be, but it's still the best damned newspaper in the whole world," Ham said. "You want some tea? You know where it is."

"I want some lunch," Holly said. "Why else do you think I would drive all the way out here?"

"Ginny's gone to the store. She'll be back in a little while."

Holly went into the kitchen, got some ice and poured a glass of sweet tea from the jug in the fridge. Something in the oven smelled good. She gave Daisy a cookie from her own special jar, then walked back outside and joined Ham on the swing. "I remembered something," she said.

"Yeah? Seems like I'm remembering less and less these days."

"I mean from the night I had to go to the hospital."

Ham put down his paper and looked at her. "What do you remember?"

"When I left your house, there was a car parked by the side of the road, just before you turn onto the bridge."

"Was it like an unmarked police car? Maybe a Crown Vic or something?"

"Yes, it was."

"I saw it there," Ham said. "In the late evening, when we were coming back from the movies."

"Did you get a look at the driver?"

"No, I couldn't see inside. The car might have had dark-tinted windows."

"The driver emptied his ashtray there, I think," Holly said. "I collected the butts. Marlboros, sucked dry. Hurd might get some DNA from them."

"You think he might be the guy?"

"Maybe. He's still out there."

"Yeah, I heard about the one on the beach, up from your house."

"They found her car this morning. There was a severed hand in the trunk."

"He cut off her hand?"

"Not the body Daisy found; she still had both hands. This is a new one—taller, slimmer."

"Spooky," Ham drawled.

"Yeah."

"This guy has graduated from assault and rape to murder and now to dismemberment in hardly any time at all."

"You're the cop; tell me what it means."

"It means he's liking it more and more. No telling what he'll do to the next one."

"Was the hand cut off before or after the girl died?"

"I don't know, but the ME will. God, I hope it was after."

They heard a car pull up, and a moment later, Ginny's voice. "I could use some help with these groceries!" she called.

Ham and Holly got up, emptied her car and put everything in the kitchen.

"Tuna casserole in ten minutes," Ginny said.

They had a leisurely lunch with a bottle of white wine. Holly helped Ginny clear the dishes, then they sat on the back porch for a while and talked.

Holly's cell phone rang, and she answered it. "Hello?"

"Hey, it's Hurd. Thanks for helping Lauren this morning," he said.

"She's smart; she would have covered it without my help. Has the ME had a look at that hand yet?"

"Yep. You were right: she's taller and slimmer than the last one; older, too—probably late thirties."

"Did he offer an opinion on whether the hand was severed before or after death?"

"After, he says. He agrees with you about the bolt cutters, too."

"Hurd, I remembered something about the night this guy went after me." She told him about seeing the car parked near Ham's turnoff. "Ham saw it there once, too." She told him about the cigarette butts.

"You preserved them?"

"Yes, they're in my glove compartment."

"Where are you now?"

"At Ham's, but I'm going home in a minute."

"I'll stop by your place later this afternoon and pick up the evidence, if that's all right."

"Sure. If I don't answer the bell, I'm on the beach. You can get the bag from my glove compartment."

"See you later." He hung up.

"Is Hurd excited about your cigarette butts?" Ham asked.

"What's this about cigarette butts?" Ginny asked.

Holly got to her feet. "Ham will explain it to

you. I'm going to head home; drinking wine at lunch always makes me want a nap."

"We still going flying?" Ginny asked.

"How about tomorrow afternoon, say four o'clock?"

"I'm good then. See ya."

Holly kissed them both and drove toward home. Once, she looked into the glove compartment just to be sure the bag was still there.

15

As Holly approached her front gate she saw a car parked on the side of the road a few yards from the gate—a blue Chevrolet, she thought. As she pulled up to the gate, Jimmy Weathers stuck his head outside the window and waved. She beckoned him to follow.

They both got out of their cars at the front door, and Daisy ran to greet Jimmy. "Hey, Jimmy," Holly said.

"Hey, Holly, can I come in a minute?"

"Sure." Holly unlocked the front door, and they entered. "That your car?" she asked.

"No, it's an unmarked police car. Bruno promoted me to detective, so I'm working in a plain car and civvies now."

"Congratulations, Jimmy. You want something to drink?"

"Something soft would be good; I'm working."

Holly got a Diet Coke out of the fridge and handed it to him. "How's your investigation going?"

"Well, Hurd and Lauren have kind of started to get in my way. I just spent a couple of hours with Lauren at the marina."

"I guess that's partly my fault," Holly said. "I called Hurd when Daisy found the body on the beach. I don't think you're going to be able to do much about Hurd and his new unit, except develop your own leads, and even then you'll have to keep him updated on what you turn up."

"I talked to him a few minutes ago," Jimmy said. "He told me about the cigarette butts. Do you think you could give them to me?"

"Hurd's coming by to pick them up later," Holly said. "Anyway, you'd just have to send them to the state lab for testing, which is what Hurd will do, too."

"I guess I just wanted to impress Bruno with them," Jimmy said.

"Catch the perp," Holly said. "That'll impress him. Tell me, does Bruno smoke?"

"I don't think so."

"He was quitting when I knew him," Holly said. "I just wondered if he's started again."

"I've never seen him smoke. Is Bruno a suspect in your mind?"

"I don't have any reason to suspect him," Holly

replied, "but I don't have any reason not to, either."

"He has a boat at the Indian River Marina," Jimmy said.

"Oh?"

"But so do I."

"What kind of a boat do you have?"

"It's a twenty-two-foot sloop. I bought it cheap and did a lot of work on it. My girlfriend and I take it out on weekends. I got Bruno's berth for him; he bought a powerboat, a fisherman."

"Jimmy, you know the Boston Whaler that the marina uses as a workboat?"

"Yeah, it's always around."

"Have you ever noticed whether the keys are left in it?"

"No, I never took that much interest; it's just like a hundred other Whalers up and down the river. Lauren's talking to the night manager about it."

"Well, at least you don't have to duplicate your efforts," Holly said. "And they'll keep you posted on what they know, just as you should keep them posted."

"Holly, can I ask you something personal?"

"How personal?"

"It's about when Bruno tried to . . . you know."

"Tried to rape me? What do you want to know?"

"How'd you stop him?"

"I broke his nose," Holly said.

"How?"

"With a straight left. He wasn't expecting it. I'll give you a tip, Jimmy, if you don't already know it: men, even bullies like Bruno—maybe *especially* bullies like Bruno—don't like the sight of their own blood, especially when it's covering the whole front of a starched and pressed colonel's uniform."

"What did Bruno do after you hit him?"

"He backed off; in fact, he backed right out of the building. Bruno is not stupid," Holly said. "He got into his car, went down a stretch of country road and smashed it into a tree pretty good. Then he took off his seat belt, called nine-one-one, asked for an ambulance and went to the hospital to have his nose set and taped. That way, he had an excuse for looking like somebody who'd lost a street fight when he came back to the base."

"I guess that was pretty smart. How do you know he did that?"

"Because I saw his car later. At Bruno's trial, the prosecutor talked me out of testifying about breaking his nose, because he thought the humiliation might make his jury of other officers more sympathetic to him."

"It wouldn't make me sympathetic," Jimmy said.

"Yeah, but imagine if you were a brother officer, inclined to protect another officer, especially a full colonel."

"Were there any women on the jury?"

"One. She looked miserable when the verdict was read; I expect she was browbeaten into going along." Holly thought of mentioning Bruno's attack on Lauren, but she didn't know if Jimmy knew about that, and it was better for Lauren if he didn't.

The phone rang, and Holly pressed the gate button. "That will be Hurd," she said. She walked Jimmy outside.

"Hello, Holly, Jimmy," Hurd said. "Congratulations, Jimmy. I hear you made detective."

"Yeah," Jimmy replied. "Thanks, Hurd."

Holly got the bag of cigarette butts from her car and handed them to Hurd. "Here you go," she said.

Hurd accepted the bag. "We found the other body," he said. "The one with the right hand missing."

"Where?" Holly asked.

"A quarter of a mile down the road from where the rented Ford was found," Hurd replied. "A search dog found it for us. We found her handbag, too."

"Who was she?"

"A friend of the other woman's. They came down from Atlanta together on vacation. You were right about her: she was five-nine, a hundred and twenty pounds, forty-five years old."

"Any further evidence found with the body?"

Hurd shook his head. "She was taken down a well-worn footpath off the road, then dumped in a thick bunch of palmetto. We might not have found her without the dog."

"What does it tell us," Holly said, "that the murderer dumped one body down the road but took the other out to sea?"

"The question occurred to me," Hurd said, "and I don't have an answer."

"It doesn't make any sense," Jimmy said.

"Maybe after he had taken one body down to the boat, he thought it was too risky to take the other, so he drove it down the road," Holly suggested.

"And how did he control the two of them?" Hurd asked.

"What was the cause of death?" Holly asked.

"I just heard from the ME," Hurd said. "A twenty-two slug to the back of the head."

"Was the body naked, like the other one?"

"Yes, but there was no evidence of rape."

"He liked the other one better," Holly said, "and he managed them with the gun."

"Why did he take her hand?"

"As a souvenir," she replied. "He tossed it in the trunk, then apparently forgot about it."

Hurd winced. "How could anybody forget a thing like that?"

16

Holly waved good-bye to the two men and went back inside her house. She stood at the sliding glass doors, looking out at the ocean, thinking. Then she went to her newly constructed office, tapped in the code to unlock the door and sat down at the Agency computer.

She entered her passwords through three levels of security, and then she logged on to the National Criminal Database, which combined the FBI and a network of local law enforcement, and typed in "James Morris Bruno, Jr." The computer thought about it, then reported the messages, "No criminal convictions as an adult. No arrests as an adult."

Holly thought about that. *As an adult?* She hadn't seen that before. Bruno might have a juvenile record, but if so, it wouldn't be part of a national database; in fact, it probably would be sealed. Where did Bruno grow up? She racked her brain.

She had known all sorts of things about him when she had worked for him, but that had been years ago, and anyway she had worked at forgetting everything about him.

New Jersey, she finally remembered, but what city? She couldn't remember. She went to the state of New Jersey Web site and, after working her way through multiple levels, she found it: Juvenile Criminal Records. She typed in Bruno's name again, and the message came up: "Record sealed by the court."

So, he did have a juvenile record. She wrote down the URL, then minimized the Web site and returned to the Agency site. Giving her password again, she entered a subsite called Unlocksmith, which demanded her authority for entry. The system had already identified her by her password, but it wanted a higher authority. She knew Lance Cabot's entry code, even though she was not supposed to, and she entered that, followed by the URL of the juvenile case files.

After a few seconds, she was greeted with the message: "This site is available only to authorized personnel. Any attempt to enter without proper authority is punishable by up to one year in prison and a $10,000 fine." There would be a record that somebody had visited the site, but the New Jersey authorities would never be able to trace it back to the Agency, because Unlocksmith entries were self-obscuring. Any attempt to backtrack would be met with gobbledygook.

She typed in Bruno's name once more, and there was his record in all its glory: two assault-on-minor charges, one male, one female, and one conviction for statutory rape. She examined all three case files. The assault-on-minor charges consisted of one incident of schoolyard bullying that had put a younger boy in the hospital for two days and one incident of sexual assault on a twelve-year-old girl when Bruno had been fourteen—a harbinger of things to come.

The statutory rape charge had come when Bruno was sixteen and the girl thirteen. The initial charge was rape, but the girl had testified that her participation had been consensual, and, with the agreement of her parents, the charge had been reduced to one count of statutory rape and the sentence was one year in prison, suspended on condition of good behavior, record to be expunged after that, except it hadn't been expunged. All three incidents had occurred in Morristown, New Jersey.

Surely, these cases would have been of interest to an investigator or a prosecutor, but, since the file was sealed, they would be inadmissible in court. And Bruno had had a clean record since the age of sixteen. Or maybe he had just stopped getting caught.

She Googled New Jersey newspapers and went to the *Star-Ledger* Web site, where she searched various topics, from sexual assault on a minor to rape and rape-murders. She began calling up the news reports and reading them. Finally, she found what she had been looking for: the body of a fifteen-year-old Morristown girl had been found in a local river after she had been missing for eleven days. She had been raped and strangled. Holly found a dozen other articles on the case, the last one three years after the incident. The case had never been solved.

She dug through the local police department records but could find no mention of any suspects being questioned. All right, she thought, assume the worst: all this had happened thirty-five years earlier, before DNA testing; Bruno would never be connected with the crime, even if he had been guilty of it. She logged off the various sites, but before she could log off the Agency system, a message appeared on her screen:

CALL ME ON A SECURE LINE. CABOT.

She picked up the Agency phone and dialed Lance's direct line.

"Cabot," he said.

"It's Holly. You left me a message."

"What are you doing?" he asked.

"I beg your pardon?"

"You're visiting sealed court records, somewhere

in darkest New Jersey, using my authority. What are you doing?"

"Oh, that," she said.

"Yes, that."

"There's been a series of rapes and murders locally."

"Locally where?"

"In or around Orchid Beach."

"You are supposed to be down there, clearing your brain and resting up to reenter the fray, and you're messing with a serial rapist?"

"And murderer. He's killed two of them."

"The city and state still maintain police forces, do they not?"

"They do."

"Then why are you involved?"

"I was one of the victims."

Lance was silent for a moment. "You were raped?"

"No, but I was unconscious, and had passersby not come to my rescue, the worst could have happened."

"Are you all right, Holly?" Lance was almost solicitous.

"I'm all right, Lance—honestly I am. I spent one night in a local hospital, recovering from a dose of Rohypnol, administered by the perpetrator."

"Will you be able to identify him?"

"No. I hate to say this, but it all happened so fast."

"You're sure you're all right."

"I'm sure. I've had the proper medical care." Including two dates and one roll in the hay with Josh, she thought.

"All right, then, use my authority to do any searches you need to," Lance said. "Apart from being drugged and nearly raped and murdered, are you having a nice vacation?"

"Just lovely," she said. "Apart from that."

"I'm glad to hear it," he said. "Good-bye." Lance hung up.

Holly printed out the news reports and put them into a file folder; then she relocked the office and started thinking about dinner.

The phone rang. "Hello?"

"Hi, it's Josh. How about dinner?"

"You're on," she replied.

17

While Holly was working on her Agency computer, another user had logged on from the Bahamas, routing his connection through a number of other computers around the country. Teddy Fay knew the CIA computer system better than most of its employees, and he routed through the mainframe to connect with the Federal Aviation Administration's list of U.S.-registered aircraft at a level that allowed him to edit. He created a new entry, gave the airplane a registration number that had not been assigned to any other airplane and entered the name and bogus address in South Florida that he had chosen for himself. That done, Teddy packed up his laptop, got up from his makeshift desk in a corner of the ramshackle hangar he had rented for the past few weeks and put the case into the luggage compartment of his airplane, along with the possessions he considered necessary to maintain whatever identity and appearance he chose.

For some years now, Teddy had been retired from the CIA, where he had been a highly placed member of the Technical Services Department, the division of the Agency that supplies its agents with identities, passports, disguises, weapons, clothing and any other resource they require to roam the world, doing the bidding of their masters. Almost since the day of his retirement, Teddy had been a fugitive, having employed the skills he learned during his thirty-year career to deliver his own brand of justice to those who had disagreed with him, some of them highly placed in the government.

He had faked his death a couple of times, but he knew there were those at the Agency who still wanted him even more dead. His greatest protection lay in the fact that the denial of his existence was just as much in their interests as in his.

His Cessna airplane, a model 182 retractable, sported a new paint job that masked a number of replacement-skin panels where the aircraft had taken fire from one of the Agency's minions some weeks before. He shook a rolled-up sheet of plastic from a cardboard tube, peeled a layer of it away and applied it to the rear of the airplane, repeating the process on the other side. Then he peeled off another layer, leaving his brand-new registration number affixed to the airplane.

That done and the airplane packed, he swung open the doors of the battered hangar and, employing a tow bar, rolled the airplane out onto the weedy tarmac. Ten minutes later he was headed northwest at a very low altitude, nearly skimming the waves. Whenever he saw a boat in the distance he swung astern of it and kept far enough away so that no one aboard could note his tail number, then he resumed his old course, using the onboard GPS units.

He made landfall at the northern end of Amelia Island, Florida's northernmost barrier island. Shortly, he spotted the Fernandina Beach Airport a few miles away and climbed to pattern altitude. He announced his intention to land over the local radio frequency, entered the traffic pattern, set down and taxied over to the local fixed-base operator or FBO. He shut down the engine, went inside and ordered fuel.

"Where you in from?" the woman at the desk asked.

"I've been visiting my sister in north Georgia," he replied.

"Where you bound for?"

"Key West," he replied. "I'm based there." He paid for the fuel with a credit card from a Cayman Islands bank, where his comfortable wealth was on deposit, took off and headed south, under visual flight rules. Forty minutes later he called the Vero

Beach tower and received landing instructions. Once on the ground he arranged for a tie-down space, ordered fuel, then went into the SunJet Aviation terminal, carrying his briefcase, and found an attractive middle-aged woman waiting for him.

"Adele Mason?" he asked.

"Mr. Smithson?" she replied. They shook hands.

"Jack," he said.

"Jack, I have half a dozen properties to show you," Adele said. "My car is right outside."

Teddy followed her to the car.

"I thought we'd start with a couple of beach-front properties," she said. "They're more expensive than things on the mainland, though."

"That's all right," Teddy said. As she drove, he memorized the route from the airport to the beach.

Once on the barrier island, she drove south for a couple of miles, through a comfortable-looking, older neighborhood; then she turned down a driveway. They passed a 1950s ranch house.

"That's the main house," she said. "The owners live in Atlanta and don't get down all that often. The guesthouse is next." She continued past the main house, drove behind a hedge and stopped at a small cottage.

Teddy could see the ocean thirty yards away. He got out of the car and followed her to the front door. She unlocked it and led him inside.

The house reminded him of his childhood on Chesapeake Bay, on the eastern shore of Maryland. There was a living room with a small dining table, a kitchen with older appliances, two small bedrooms and a small room with a desk in it.

"How much?" he asked.

She told him.

"How long?"

"As long as you like."

"I'll take it."

She looked surprised. "Don't you want to look at anything else?"

"No. This is perfect. Did you bring a lease?"

She sat in a chair, put her briefcase on her lap and opened it. "I can fill in the blank form for you. You sign it, give me a check for one month's rent and a security deposit, and I'll mail it to the owners for their signatures."

"I'd like to move in right away," Teddy said.

"Let me call them and see if that's satisfactory. My office will run a credit check, as well." She handed him a form. "Please fill this out."

Teddy entered the information he had assembled for his new identity, including the social security number he had implanted in that agency's computers; then he walked around the house again while she made her calls. He came back, and she handed him the lease.

"Everything's fine," she said.

"I don't have a local bank account yet," Teddy said. "Will you take American dollars?"

She laughed. "Of course."

Teddy opened his briefcase and counted out some of the cash he had obtained on a recent trip from the Bahamas to the Caymans, then closed it again.

"Here's your lease," she said, handing it to him. "I'd better run."

"Could you drop me in town?" he asked.

"Of course."

She drove him back into Vero Beach and he pointed at a Toyota dealership. "Just over there will be fine," he said.

He got out of the car and stood at her open window. "Thank you so much for finding me just the right place."

"It was my pleasure."

"By way of thanks, I'd like to take you to dinner."

"I'd like that."

"Tomorrow night?"

"What time?"

"Seven o'clock?"

"I'll come and get you," she said, "since you don't know your way around yet."

"I'll look forward to it," he said as she drove away.

It took Teddy half an hour to find and assess a

four-year-old, low-mileage Camry and buy it, after which he returned to the airport, unloaded the airplane and began putting everything into the car. As he was doing so, a Beech Bonanza taxied onto the ramp and parked a couple of spaces down from his airplane. Two women got out.

Teddy's heart began to beat faster. He knew one of them; she had taken a shot at him once, but, of course, she wouldn't know him now, with his balding head covered with a clever gray hairpiece and his eyes hidden behind aviator glasses. They walked past him with hardly a glance and went into the little flying school beside the ramp.

Teddy got into his car, took a few deep breaths and let his pulse return to normal as he drove away. That woman, Holly Barker, worked for the Agency, for Lance Cabot; what the hell was she doing in this beach town that he had so carefully selected?

All the way to his new house, he made turns and checked his rearview mirror, and he didn't turn into his drive until he knew there was no one following him.

18

Holly sat in her living room with Hurd Wallace and Lauren Cade. She laid her file on Jim Bruno's juvenile record and the stories from the New Jersey newspaper on the coffee table and sipped a Diet Coke while they read it.

"Well," Hurd said finally, "this is all very interesting, but there's nothing here that ties him to the recent rapes and murders locally."

"Not in an evidentiary sense," Holly admitted, "but all this shows a past which gives him a predisposition to that sort of crime."

"None of this could ever be presented in court," Hurd said. "You haven't even tied him to the New Jersey murder when he was still a young man."

"Don't you think I know that, Hurd?" She tried not to sound irritated. "All I want to do here is place Bruno on your list of suspects. Oh, and you can add to this material that he keeps a boat at the marina that's tied to the death of two victims and the disposal of one body."

Lauren spoke up. "I have to agree with Hurd, Holly. Even that could be no more than a coincidence. Eighty or ninety other people, including Detective Jimmy Weathers, keep boats there, too."

"Maybe you should investigate all of them, Lauren, and when you're done I'd be willing to bet that not one of them would have the sort of background that Bruno has."

"You're convinced that Bruno is our perpetrator?" Hurd asked.

"Of course not, Hurd. I just think he's your best suspect right now."

"Our only suspect," Lauren said.

"All right," Hurd said, tucking the file into his briefcase, "James Bruno is a suspect. Is that what you want?"

Holly nodded. "Thank you, Hurd. And for God's sake, don't show his juvenile record to anybody. It was sealed by the court, and I don't want to have to explain how I got it."

"How *did* you get that record?" Lauren asked.

"Don't ask," Holly replied.

"Holly," Hurd said, "do you want to work on this full-time? Do you want me to get you a badge?"

"No!" Holly said. "Please, no! I'm on vacation here, and I don't want my head filled with this case. Of course, I would appreciate updates."

Hurd laughed. "You mean you want to be involved but not involved."

Holly laughed, too. "I mean I don't want to explain to anybody my past with Bruno or how I've looked into his past, especially in court. My boss would not like for me to be cross-examined by some hot defense attorney."

"All right," Hurd said, "we'll keep you out of the official record on the case."

"Thank you, Hurd. I appreciate your understanding."

Hurd got to his feet, and Lauren followed him out the front door. Holly waved them off, then turned back into the house. She had to shower and change before Josh came for her.

Josh arrived, and they took their drinks outside to Holly's deck and sat down in comfortable chairs to watch the light change on the ocean as the sun went down.

"I ran into the county ME at the hospital this afternoon," Josh said. "He told me something interesting about one of your crime victims, the one you found on the beach."

"Tell me," Holly said.

"He checked for needle marks on her neck, and he found how the Rohypnol had been administered. It wasn't by needle, it was by gun."

"I don't follow," Holly said.

"A vaccination gun," Josh explained. "Surely you had one of those used on you during your years in the army."

"Yes, you're right," she said, "but I remember those things as attached by hoses and electrical cords to things."

"There's a version that holds a vial of something and is powered by a fairly small battery, the way power tools are these days."

"Still, it wouldn't be something you could stick in your pocket, would it?"

"If you had a big enough pocket," Josh pointed out. "It would be easier to deal with than a hypodermic syringe. You'd just press it against the neck and pull the trigger."

"Where would a perpetrator obtain one?" Holly asked.

"Probably from the manufacturer or maybe even from a medical supply store—there's a big one in Vero Beach."

"Okay, I buy it."

"It makes the perpetrator more interesting, doesn't it?"

"I suppose," Holly said. "It also adds another way to find him. The police could visit that medical supply store in Vero and find out whom they've sold the things to. Anybody who wasn't a doctor or a hospital purchasing agent would stand out as a suspect."

"I think maybe I should have been a cop," Josh said. "I enjoy knowing about this stuff, even if I am a couple of steps removed from the process."

"Well," Holly said, "maybe you did miss your calling, but it wasn't as a cop."

"Really? What should I have been."

She laughed. "A porn star," she said.

Josh blushed. "First time I've been told that," he said.

"I don't believe it. When you're carrying around that sort of equipment, it gets noticed."

"Okay, it's been mentioned," he admitted, "but nobody ever suggested I should have been in porn films."

"You know what I think you need?" Holly asked.

"What?"

"Another audition." She took his hand and led him into the house and upstairs.

"We've got a dinner reservation in half an hour," he said.

"We'll manage," Holly said, unzipping his fly.

19

Teddy Fay awoke as the sun's rays struck his face. His right arm was numb. Adele Mason's head lay across it, and her leg was thrown over his. Gently, he extricated his arm and lifted her knee so that he could recover his leg. He slithered silently out of bed, walked to the window and looked out, opening and closing his hand, trying to get his circulation going. The sun had just broken the horizon. He closed the venetian blinds, walked into the bathroom and closed the door behind him.

He shaved, got into a shower, soaped up and then rinsed in cold water. He tiptoed into the bedroom, found some shorts in a drawer and put them on; then he went into the kitchen. He had managed a trip to a grocery the day before, and he put on some coffee and fried bacon in the microwave while he toasted a couple of English muffins and scrambled some eggs.

"Smells good in there," Adele called from the bathroom.

"Breakfast in five minutes," he called back; then he heard the shower running.

She came into the kitchen wearing only a towel and kissed him on a shoulder. "Jack, do you mind if I ask how old you are?"

"Sixty," he lied. "How about you?"

"Forty-nine," she replied.

"You look wonderful," he said, emptying the eggs onto two plates.

"You are wonderful," she said, "at least in bed."

"Thank you ma'am." He laughed.

"Oh, I forgot something," she said, hurrying from the room. She came back with the local newspaper. "I called the paper yesterday and got you a subscription; I always do that with a new client."

"Thank you," Teddy said and set the paper on the little table.

They washed down their breakfast with fresh orange juice and finished it with coffee.

Teddy sat back in his chair and picked up the paper. "My goodness," he said, "according to this you've got a serial rapist/murderer in this town."

"I'm afraid so," Adele said, "and I hope it's not going to be bad for business."

"Why? Doesn't everyone want to live in a town with murderous thugs?"

"Stop it. I'm serious."

"I know you are. I'm glad I arrived when I did, or I'd be a suspect, being the new guy in town."

"What sort of work do you do, Jack?" she asked.

"I'm retired."

"From what?"

"I've invented things all my life, the sort of gadgets you see in those infomercials on TV." This was not a lie; those little inventions had made him a comfortably wealthy man, and the continuing royalties went, eventually, into his Cayman bank account.

"Can you make a living doing that?"

"You can if you have a few great sellers and if you've negotiated a good royalty agreement."

"Why did you retire?"

"Oh, I just got tired of it, I guess. A few months from now, though, I'll get an idea for something, and I'll be back at work. I've retired before."

"Were you ever married?"

"Yes, but she died four years ago of ovarian cancer."

"I'm sorry."

"So am I, but I've had time to get over it."

"What brought you to Vero Beach?"

"I thought I'd like to live in a place with a warm winter, and I read something about Vero in a magazine or a newspaper, I forget which." He smiled at her. "So far, I like it just fine."

Adele looked at the kitchen clock. "Oh, I've got to run; I'm showing a house at eight thirty." She went back into the bedroom and came back ten minutes later, clothed and made-up.

Teddy walked her to the door and gave her a kiss. "Later in the week?"

She got out her calendar. "When's good for you?"

"Tomorrow night, here? I'll cook you dinner."

"You're on." She ran for her car.

Teddy went back to the table and finished reading the article about the crimes. It made him angry to think there was some animal hurting women out there. He'd like to get a shot at the guy, he thought.

He read slowly through the paper, getting a sense of the locality, when he saw a familiar face in an ad. It was one of the women he'd seen at the airport: "Ginny Barker, Certified Flight Instructor, Private and Commercial certificates," and a phone number. She must be related to Holly Barker, he thought.

He went to his computer and Googled Holly, finding news stories about cases she had solved when she had been chief of police in Orchid Beach, a neighbor of Vero. He learned that she had retired from the army after a career as an MP and that her father lived here, too. Ginny Barker was his wife. He wondered how Holly had made the transition to the Agency.

It was interesting to know more about a woman

he had once taken to the Metropolitan Opera, in
New York, when he had been disguised as an elderly Jewish gentleman, retired from the garment
industry. He wondered if she'd ever figured out
who he was. Probably so, for she had turned up on
the island of St. Marks, where he had also fooled
her for a while. Then she had taken that shot at
him.

He went into the Agency mainframe, to personnel, and read her file. She was getting good reviews
from her superiors, particularly Lance Cabot, and
had recently been promoted to assistant deputy
director. He was impressed.

He made a mental note to himself not to let his
disguise slip while he was in Vero Beach. He might
run into her at any time. It occurred to him that
his ease in fooling her before might be making him
cocky, and he didn't want to start underestimating
her now. He would like to know what she was
doing back in this area. She couldn't be looking for
him, because he had picked out this town only a
day or two before.

Now he knew that she was a pilot, or studying
to be one, taking lessons from her stepmother,
who was no older than she. Amazing what you
could pick up in the local paper, and it didn't hurt
to have access to the Agency mainframe.

Teddy stacked the dishes in the dishwasher and
cleaned up after himself. Then he took his briefcase

into the little spare room and began to make it his study. He went online and bought a safe from a local company that promised to deliver it the following day. In the meantime, he found some removal boards behind the sleeper couch and stashed his cash, weapons and other supplies there.

After a couple of hours of work around the place, he had made it livable and had also turned it into a base for himself, with provisions for a quick getaway if necessary. Some people, he reflected, might have been troubled by the stress of constantly watching their backs and planning escapes, but Teddy enjoyed it. He could change towns and his life anytime he chose, and he could invent and produce the IDs and backgrounds necessary to preserve himself. That was fun.

He put on some clothes and went for a drive. It was time he knew more about his new hometown.

20

Holly sat at Ham's dining table while Ginny filled out her logbook, entering the training exercises she had performed the day before.

"You know," Holly said, "I sometimes think about buying an airplane."

"It's a great time to do it," Ginny said, "what with the economy the way it is. Prices are depressed. Can you pay cash?"

"Probably," Holly said.

"Well, what do you want to do with an airplane?" Ginny asked. "Travel long distances or just fly around on Sunday afternoons?"

"I'd like to be able to fly down here whenever I feel like it," Holly said. "There's a nice airport at Manassas, Virginia, not far from my house."

"You want to make the trip nonstop?"

"Yes."

"Well, there's the Cessna 450—a turbocharged single—fast, with a good range."

"Is it pressurized?"

"No. For that you'd want a Piper Malibu Mirage, and that would cost you twice as much."

"I've got a friend who's got a Mirage," Holly said, "and I like it. He's had the engine upgraded to a turboprop."

"So, start with the Malibu, then do the conversion later if you need it. Right now I happen to know that the Piper factory in Vero has a couple of airplanes that buyers backed out on after the stock market crash. Let me look into it; I might be able to get you a deal."

"Sounds good," Holly said.

"You'd need to do the factory training course, which takes five days, but you have enough time to get that done before you go back to work." Ginny handed her the completed logbook. "There you go; you've had your biennial flight review, so you're good for another year, and your instrument competency check, too."

"I really like the idea of the Malibu," Holly said. "It's the sort of airplane that could go a long distance on a long weekend. Let's look at it."

Ginny got up. "I'll call a guy I know in sales at the Piper factory," she said. She got up and went into the little office she shared with Ham.

Holly got up and went out on the back porch, where Ham was reading the *Wall Street Journal.* "Making any money?" she asked.

"Nobody's making any money," Ham said. "My portfolio is way down."

"I'm glad I'm in Treasuries," Holly said. "I'm thinking about buying an airplane."

"Good idea. I'm sure Ginny can advise you on that."

"She already has; she's looking into it now."

"Heard anything about your roving rapist/ killer?" Ham asked.

"No. He was hot for a few days, now he's cooled off."

"Think he'll get hot again?"

"You can count on it," Holly said. "He was just getting started when he stopped. I'll bet he's already getting antsy again, looking forward to that thrill."

"You know, I've killed a bunch of people in my time—Vietnam gave me that dubious opportunity— and I didn't find one of those kills thrilling."

"That means you're a normal human being, Ham—well, *fairly* normal—and our guy isn't. He's all twisted up inside."

"You think it's Jim Bruno, don't you?"

"Right now, he's the only suspect, but I haven't decided he's the one. He needs to get tied to one of these cases directly, with some hard evidence."

"You ever miss being a cop?" Ham asked.

"Sometimes; it has the virtue of resolution: you solve a crime and send somebody to prison. The work I do now, the victories take longer, mostly. You get a short-term thrill now and then, when an operation goes just the way you hoped it would, but not very often."

"I know what you mean," Ham said. "In Vietnam, you had a good day or a bad day. You couldn't think a month ahead, because in a month you might be on the other guy's KIA list."

Ginny came out back to join them, a sheet of paper in her hand. She handed it to Holly. "They faxed me the specs on an airplane that's sitting out on the ramp at the airport," she said. "Take a look. It's loaded with the latest of just about everything. They took a big deposit on it, but the guy got hurt in the market, and he can't close the sale."

Holly read the list carefully, trying to imagine each piece of equipment on the airplane. "Wow," she breathed. "This is a dream machine. How much?"

"How about a hundred and fifty grand off list?" Ginny asked. "I talked to the seller, and he's highly motivated; he wants to get his deposit back, and he's willing to take a loss to do that. The factory wants the rest of their money, too, so they're chipping in something."

"Tell them yes," Holly said. She looked at her

watch. "I can get the money wired here today. Do you think we could buy it through your flying school? I don't want an expensive airplane registered in my name right now. It might raise questions with my employer."

"Sure, I guess so." Ginny went and got her checkbook, ripped one out and handed it to Holly. "You can wire the funds to this account."

Holly made a note of the information, then went inside and called her bank in the Caymans. She entered her account number and two passwords, then tapped in the amount and the receiving account number and routing code. A computerized voice repeated the information to her, she confirmed it, then she was asked to speak a code sentence. She did so, and the computer confirmed her identity and authorized the transaction. Holly returned to the porch. "The money's on its way."

"You want to go look at the airplane?" Ginny asked.

"Sure!"

They drove to the airport in two cars, so Holly wouldn't have to drive Ginny back, and she followed Ginny onto the field to a ramp outside the Piper factory where three airplanes were parked. A man was waiting next to a Malibu Mirage with the keys, and he opened it up for them.

Holly loved the smell of newness inside the

airplane—all-leather seats and wool carpeting. She sat in the pilot's seat, with Ginny next to her, and examined the big glass panels that displayed all the flight and instrument information.

"By the way," the Piper man said, "the training class starts Monday morning; by next Friday, you'll be qualified."

"I can't wait," Holly said. "How about insurance?"

"I'll put the airplane on my flight school policy," Ginny said, "and you can reimburse me."

"Great. When can we close?"

"How about tomorrow morning?" the man sitting behind them asked.

"That's good for me," Ginny said. "I'll stop by the bank on the way in tomorrow and get a cashier's check."

They got off the airplane and Holly walked around it. It was painted in a beautiful red and white color scheme. She wiped a finger across the paint and found grit. "It's dirty," she said. "How long has it been sitting on the ramp?"

"About seven weeks," the man said. "I'll have it washed today."

"Ginny, will you fly it before we close, make sure there are no maintenance squawks?"

"Sure, I will," Ginny said.

Holly was more excited than she had been since she had started training at the Agency's Farm.

"Ginny, can we fly her some over the weekend? Do you have the time?"

"Sure, we'll get a head start on your training."

Holly drove home, singing to herself. She hadn't been this excited since she began her training at the Agency.

21

Teddy Fay, now Jack Smithson, had a busy day. First, he went to the Department of Motor Vehicles and exchanged the Georgia driver's license he had created and planted in the Georgia database for a Florida license. Now he was perfectly legitimate. He had a fixed address and a government-issued picture ID.

He chose a bank near his house and opened a checking account and a savings account with a cashier's check from a Miami bank that his Cayman bank had arranged. He drove out to the western outskirts of Vero Beach, just past I-95, and found an outlet mall with a Ralph Lauren store. He owned few clothes, so he bought a lightweight suit, a blue blazer and a tweed jacket, plus trousers, underwear, shirts and ties, and a dozen Polo shirts in various colors. He thought of that as Florida camouflage. He found a Publix market near his rented

house and stocked up on groceries in some depth;
then he went home, put away the groceries and,
with a needle and thread, fixed the length on all his
new trousers, dress and khakis. He pressed everything and put the things in his drawers and closets,
then answered the doorbell.

He let the deliverymen in with his new safe and
showed them where to bolt it to the floor in the
closet in his study. As soon as they left he changed
the delivery combination to one of his own, then
removed his cash and equipment from the wall behind the sofa and stowed them, along with a number of weapons, in the large safe.

Holly attended the closing on the sale of her new
airplane with Ginny. After she was handed the keys,
the logbooks and a nylon briefcase containing all
the manuals and instruction books for the airplane
and its equipment, she and Ginny went for a test
flight.

"I flew it earlier today," Ginny said, "and all it
needed was to have the tires properly inflated."

"That's good news," Holly said. She ran through
the checklist and started the airplane, then called
the tower and got permission to taxi to a runway.
She did her run-up tests before requesting takeoff,
and she was cleared. She taxied to the centerline of
the runway, did her final checks and pushed the
throttle forward. The airplane accelerated down

the runway and lifted off with a tug of the yoke, and she was flying her very own airplane.

"This is exhilarating!" she cried.

Ginny laughed. "Turn right to two-forty, climb to eight thousand feet and we'll head out to a practice area." On reaching the practice area, Holly switched on the autopilot and let it fly the airplane, while she entered a flight plan and an instrument approach into the computer.

They did some slow flight and practiced turns and stalls, then flew a couple of low approaches before landing at Okeechobee Airport, where they refueled and had lunch in the airport's restaurant. After lunch, they practiced emergency landings and short-field landings, then flew back to Vero and flew another instrument approach to a full stop.

Holly shut down the engine and got out of the airplane. "That was really fun," she said. "I feel as though I could fly her home right now."

"You've still got a lot to learn about your airplane," Ginny said. "Now go home and start memorizing the Owner's Operation Handbook. You're going to need all that stuff, and you'll wow them when you show up for training."

Holly did exactly that, breaking only for dinner for herself and Daisy. She fell asleep that night with the operator's handbook open on her stomach.

*　　*　　*

Teddy greeted Adele Mason with a stiff Scotch.

"My, what's that wonderful aroma?" she asked.

"A lamb stew. It's been cooking for hours."

"I can't wait," she said, sipping her drink. "How have your first days gone?"

"I'm a Florida resident now," Teddy said. "Driver's license and all. I bought some new clothes, opened a bank account and made myself at home."

"The place looks wonderful with somebody living in it. The elderly couple who own the house have outlived their only daughter, and they don't have any grandchildren, so there was nobody to live in the guesthouse."

"I like living on the beach," Teddy said. "I like being able to hear the surf when I go to bed and wake up in the morning. Where do you live, Adele?"

"I rent a tiny condo farther up the island, half a mile from the beach. I was divorced six years ago, and I can't really afford to buy anything until I sell a lot more houses."

They had another drink. Then Teddy opened a bottle of California cabernet and served dinner. Adele raved about his cooking, and Teddy was suitably appreciative. He was enjoying himself as much as she was.

They took a brandy to bed and made enthusiastic love for the better part of an hour before falling asleep in each other's arms.

This time, Adele woke first, shortly after midnight. "I've got early showings this morning," she said.

"Why don't you get that done then come back and spend the weekend here with me?" Teddy asked.

"I'd love to," she said. "I could be back here around two o'clock tomorrow afternoon."

"Perfect," Teddy said. "We can go for a swim."

"I'd love that," she said, kissing him. "See you in the afternoon."

She left, and Teddy drifted off to sleep again.

Adele got dressed and drove back to the highway. She turned right and headed north on A-1A, the road that ran up the barrier islands.

Adele was very happy with the way her new relationship with Jack Smithson was going. She hadn't slept with a man for more than a year, and the last relationship had ended badly. She was looking forward to getting to know this very interesting man better, and she hoped they would last.

A few miles up A-1A she made a left, then a right onto Jungle Trail, a shortcut that would save her a mile or two. Anyway, she liked the dirt roadway and the trees and an occasional glimpse of a raccoon or a deer along the trail.

She had driven a mile or so when the car ran over something and began to pull to the left. She stopped the car and retrieved a small flashlight from the glove compartment, then got out of the car and walked around to the front.

Her right front tire was completely flat. Adele knew how to change a flat, but she hated doing it. Then she looked up and saw a car coming down the trail, behind hers. A flashing blue light on the dashboard came on, dimly illuminating a uniformed figure behind the wheel. Thank God, she thought, a man, and a cop into the bargain.

He got out of his car and turned a very bright flashlight on her. "Got a problem there, ma'am?" he asked, walking toward her.

"Yes, a flat tire."

"I'll give you a hand," he said, coming closer.

"Oh, thank you so much. I'm so lucky you came along."

He came closer, but the light blinded her. Then she felt a sting on the side of her neck.

"Just take it easy," he said. "You're going to get drowsy now."

"Oh, God, no," she whispered to herself as she sank to her knees.

22

Lauren Cade got out of her car and walked the forty yards to where the medical examiner's wagon and an unmarked police car were parked. Detective Jimmy Weathers stood, wearing latex gloves, looking at the front of a Tahoe SUV parked in the middle of the Jungle Trail.

"Morning, Jimmy," she said. "Thanks for the call."

"Morning, Lauren."

"What have you got?"

"Another woman, dead, probably raped. This time, she's been posed naked behind the wheel."

Lauren looked through the passenger window and saw the corpse, a middle-aged woman. Her handbag was lying on the floor next to her.

"Looks like she had a flat," Jimmy said. "Right front wheel, but there's no nail in the tire and, walking back down the trail, there's nothing there that would cause the flat. Slow leak, maybe."

"Spike strip?" Lauren asked. A spike strip was something that the police could throw in front of a car being pursued to blow out its tires.

"Good thought," Jimmy said. "Another cop thing to add to the rest."

"Have you been through her bag?"

"I just got here myself," Jimmy said.

"Mind if we do it together?"

"That's good."

Lauren donned her latex gloves, lifted the large leather bag from the car and emptied it on the hood.

"Lots of stuff," Jimmy said.

"She's a woman," Lauren replied, picking up a big diary with a card stapled to the front. "Adele Mason, Beachfront Realty, Vero Beach," she read.

"Yeah, they're across from the Holiday Inn," Jimmy said, picking up the woman's wallet. "Here's her driver's license. She lives not far from here, if the address is current."

Lauren opened the diary to where it had been marked with a rubber band and read the last entry of the day. "Dinner, Jack Smithson." She flipped open her cell phone, called information and asked for the number, then closed it. "No such listing," she said. She began going backward in the diary. "Here's another dinner with Jack, three nights ago. He's also down for two that afternoon at Sun-Jet. What's that? And the words 'Bingo, the Wald property!' are entered for that afternoon."

Jimmy went back to the rear of the car and came back with a plastic-covered book. "Looks like her listings," he said, then began flipping through the book. "Here we go: J. M. Wald, 2202 Ocean Close, Vero."

"She sold the Wald house, then. To Jack, maybe?"

"Let's go find out," Jimmy said.

Teddy Fay was surfing the Internet, looking for a local source of outdoor furniture, when there was a rap on the front door. Teddy started, alarmed that someone could approach the house without his noticing. Relax, he told himself. He took a deep breath or two, then got up and went to the front door.

An attractive blond young woman stood on the other side of the screen door, a bag slung over one shoulder, a badge in the other hand. "Good morning," she said. "I'm Lauren Cade, with the Florida State Police. Mr. Smithson, is it?"

Teddy's mind was working a mile a minute: something to do with the new license, maybe? "Good morning. Yes, I'm Jack Smithson."

"May I come in and speak to you for a moment, Mr. Smithson?"

"Of course," Teddy said, opening the door for her. As he turned, he found a young man standing behind him in the living room. He had come in the back door, and Teddy had heard nothing. He was slipping. Brazen it out, he thought. Be cooperative. "I'm sorry, you startled me," Teddy said.

"I'm Detective Weathers, Orchid Beach Police Department," the young man said.

"Won't you sit down?" Teddy asked, indicating the living room sofa.

They sat down, and Teddy took a chair on the other side of the coffee table.

"How can I help you?" he asked.

"Mr. Smithson," Lauren said, "are you acquainted with Ms. Adele Mason?"

"Yes, I am; she's the real estate agent who found this house for me."

"You bought this house?"

"Rented. The Walds, who own the property, don't have many guests, so they rent the guesthouse. They're not in Florida at the moment."

"I see," Lauren said. "And when did you rent it?"

"Three days ago. It was the first property she showed me, and I thought it was ideal."

"Where are you from, Mr. Smithson?"

"Here, now. I more recently lived in north Georgia, but I retired and moved down here."

"When was the last time you saw Ms. Mason?"

"Why, last night. She came for dinner here; I cooked for us."

"And what time did she leave?"

"Shortly after midnight, I believe."

"Mr. Smithson, would you submit to a DNA test?" She removed a plastic tube from her purse. "It's just a swab of the inside of your cheek."

"Wait just a minute," Teddy said. "DNA test? For what purpose?"

"For a comparison."

Teddy's face fell, and he wasn't acting. "Has something happened to Adele?"

"I'm afraid so," Lauren said. "She was murdered sometime last night and possibly raped. That's why we need a DNA sample, to eliminate you as a suspect."

"My God, she was here only last night. Is this to do with those murders I read about in the local paper?"

"It seems likely."

"Well," Teddy said, "we made love last night, so you might very well find my DNA on her . . . person."

"Thank you for that information, but what we need to learn is if someone else's DNA is present, and we'll need your sample for differentiation."

"Of course," Teddy said. "I mean, I watch those forensics shows all the time. I understand. Go ahead and take your swab."

Lauren uncapped the tube, removed the swab, ran it around the inside of his cheek and replaced it in the tube.

"When did you move in here?" Jimmy asked.

"Three days ago. I had found Adele's name on the Internet, and we had had a phone conversation about what I was looking for. She met me at the airport on Wednesday afternoon and drove me here."

"Which airport, sir?"

"Vero Beach. I fly a small airplane."

"Where is it parked at the airport?"

"At SunJet Aviation. I arranged in advance for tie-down space there."

"Is that your Toyota parked outside?"

"Yes, I bought it the same day from the local dealer."

The detective was writing in his notebook. "Name of the salesman?"

"Ah, Meadows. Leonard Meadows."

"What sort of work do you do, Mr. Smithson?" Lauren asked.

"I'm retired. I'm sort of an engineer. I invent small gadgets, the kind of thing you see on infomercials late at night."

They asked a few more questions, then thanked him and left.

Before they drove away, Jimmy called the airport and the Toyota dealer. "His story holds up," he said.

"He certainly looked shocked when we told him she was dead, and our perp's MO doesn't include having dinner with his victims before he kills them. I don't think Smithson is our guy."

"Neither do I," Jimmy said.

Teddy lay down on his bed and rested. He was disturbed that Adele seemed to be the latest victim of a local criminal. And he was deeply angry.

23

Holly had just finished lunch when the phone rang. "Hello?"

"Hi, it's Lauren Cade."

"Hi, Lauren. What's up?"

"We've got another victim, a real estate agent named Adele Mason, last night, Jungle Trail."

"Oh, shit. Well, I've been expecting another one."

"So have I."

"Was there anything at the scene that would tell us something different about the perp?"

"Not really. She was apparently dragged into the woods and raped there; the ME found sand on her body. Then she was posed, naked, behind the wheel of her car. One thing was different: her right front tire was flat. We think, maybe, a spike strip was used."

"That doesn't make any sense," Holly said.

"Why not?"

"You're saying he would lay a spike strip on Jungle Trail in advance of the crime? How would he know a woman alone would hit it?"

"Well . . ."

"I think it's more likely that he got lucky on the flat tire."

"Maybe you're right."

"I think you ought to close Jungle Trail to car traffic until this guy is apprehended. This is the second attack, if you include me."

"We've already done that. We thought we might have gotten lucky when we found a man's name in Mason's diary, a Jack Smithson. We talked to him, but he says that he arrived in Vero on Wednesday afternoon, and she met him at the airport and showed him a house, which he promptly rented. All that was in her diary."

"Doesn't sound right; all the other victims have apparently been strangers to our perp."

"That's what we figured. Smithson was cooperative, gave us a DNA swab."

"There was no semen from the other victims, though."

"Right."

"What time did the attack occur?"

"Sometime after midnight."

"Tell Jimmy Weathers he ought to have Orchid patrols stop any male who is driving what looks like an unmarked patrol car driving after dark."

"That could be a lot of cars."

"Well, at least take the tag numbers and run them."

"I'm sure they could do that."

"One thing you don't want to do, Lauren."

"What's that?"

"Don't drive around alone at night looking for this guy; you might find him under unfavorable circumstances."

"You have a point."

"If you want to be a decoy, make sure you have plenty of backup."

"All right. I just thought I'd let you know about the new attack."

"I appreciate that, Lauren. If I have any ideas, I'll call you. Bye-bye." She hung up, and the phone rang again almost immediately.

"Hello?"

"It's Josh."

"Hi, there."

"Dinner tonight?"

"We seem to be making a habit of that."

"I'll take you to the Yellow Dog Café, up near Melbourne."

"I like that place."

"Seven o'clock?"

"You're on."

Josh was on time, and they got into his car for the thirty-minute drive.

"I think I know where your rapist/murderer got the injection gun," he said.

"Where?"

"At our hospital. There was a routine inventory of medical equipment this afternoon, and an injection gun was missing."

"Wouldn't someone have noticed that before?"

"No. It's not the sort of equipment that's used every day; it's pretty much limited to flu-shot clinics and school vaccinations, that sort of thing. You wouldn't pull it out and load it for a single injection."

"That's interesting information. I'll pass it on. There was another murder last night, on the Jungle Trail."

"Jesus, where is this going to end?"

"Either they'll catch him, or he'll stop."

"Stop? Why would he do that?"

"It happens with serial criminals. Sometimes they get arrested and convicted on other charges. Years can go by. Sometimes they get nervous about getting caught and just back off for a while. Sometimes they hit a new locale, and hope new killings won't get paired up with old ones. There are more uncaught serial killers in this country than you'd imagine. Sometimes they move to another state, in midcareer; sometimes they go on for years, like Ted Bundy."

"That's a depressing thought."

"Yes, it is. Cops get depressed a lot."

"Do the police have any advantages against this guy?"

"Sure. There are more cops than murderers; they have good forensics tools. What usually happens is that the killer finally makes a mistake, and the cops pounce."

"Would a reward help?"

"Probably not in this case. Nobody who knows this guy knows he's doing this. He works alone; he's probably unmarried and living alone or with his elderly parents, usually a mother. He probably doesn't have a regular girlfriend, so he's not getting sex in a normal way. And he's smart and careful. He's been using condoms, so there's no sperm sample for DNA testing."

"I wish there were something I could do to help," Josh said.

"You've already helped by telling me about the missing vaccination gun. You might keep an eye out for a man who comes in with scratches on his face or arms. Sooner or later, some woman will fight back."

"He seems to render them unconscious almost immediately," Josh pointed out.

"Yes, but he's got to make a mistake sometime; every criminal does."

"Is somebody checking up on police officers?"

"Yes, the local detective in charge of the case has already canvassed his department and all the neighboring departments, and he's come up dry."

"Do you have a gun?" Josh asked.

"I'm carrying one right now," Holly replied.

"Dare I ask where?"

"Ankle holster."

"I'll keep that in mind."

"Excuse me a second." Holly called Lauren Cade and told her about the missing injection gun.

"That's very interesting," Lauren said.

"And it expands your field of possible suspects," Holly said. "It could be an orderly or a male nurse." She glanced at Josh. "Or even a doctor."

"Gee, thanks," Josh said.

24

Teddy Fay awoke, still worried about how the two police officers had approached his house without his knowledge. He couldn't have that.

He checked the Internet, then drove to a nearby electronics shop where he bought a driveway alert and half a dozen motion detectors, all operated by lithium batteries. Back at home, he installed the driveway alert just inside the entrance to the Walds' drive; then he planted the motion detectors around the guesthouse. Inside, he plugged in the control unit, ran a test and got a confirmation on all the sensors. The next time somebody turned into the driveway or approached the house on foot, he'd know about it.

He opened the safe and took out the briefcase that held the Czech sniper's rifle that he had stolen from the Agency before he retired. He assembled it and screwed on the silencer; then he opened a box of paper cups and took a stack of them out onto the beach. He looked up and down the strand for foot traffic and found no one near, so he pressed the cups upside down into the wet sand at the edge of the water, checked again for foot traffic, then walked back to the house.

He opened the kitchen window and the screen, then stood, cradling the rifle, and took careful aim at the first cup on the left. The bullet kicked up sand two inches to the right of the cup, so he made a minute adjustment to the telescopic sight and fired again. Bingo. In rapid succession he fired at the other cups and hit each one. He had not lost his touch.

He disassembled the rifle, cleaned it and returned it to its case; then he inspected his other weapons and relocked everything in the safe. He felt better now.

He picked up volume two of Winston Churchill's *The Second World War*, which he was rereading, settled into a comfortable chair and began to read, but he could not concentrate. His mind kept wandering to Adele Mason and her untimely death.

Teddy was accustomed to righting what he considered to be wrongs, and without any help from law enforcement. He would have liked very much to deal with Adele's murderer, he thought, but he was not by nature an investigator, and he had no access to what the police knew. This was a new kind of frustration for him, and he did not like being frustrated.

He put down the book and picked up the local newspaper instead. There was an article about the latest murder and a brief obituary. The funeral was the following day, and Teddy decided to be there.

A few miles up the beach, Holly Barker was restive, too. The silence of her newly fortified home made her feel that she was a flower in a hothouse, so she opened the sliding doors to the beach and sacrificed air-conditioning for the sound of the light surf lapping against her beach.

Bored, she unlocked her little office, logged on to the Agency computer and began to read cable traffic to Lance's office. It was a remarkably quiet day out in the stations around the world, and she found nothing worthy of her interest, so she logged off, locked the office and looked for a decent movie on television. A couple of hours with *The Maltese Falcon*, which she had seen at least a dozen times, made her feel better.

Teddy sat in his parked car across the street from the church and watched the people arrive. Seeing no familiar faces, he locked his car, went inside and took a seat in a rear pew.

The casket was open at the front of the church, and people wandered past it, viewing the corpse.

Teddy had always found this practice distasteful; if he had been fond of the deceased, he preferred his last memory of the person to be one in which the person was alive, not dead. Finally, the undertaker closed the casket, and the service began.

Teddy looked at the backs of the heads of the other mourners and wondered if one of them had murdered Adele Mason. It was said that killers sometimes attended the funerals of their victims. Then he looked to one side and saw the female detective, Lauren Cade, standing to one side near the front of the church, facing the pews, and on the other side of the church, the male detective, Weathers, and another man, doing the same. Apparently, great minds thought alike.

Teddy took in the man standing next to Weathers. He was fiftyish, a little over six feet tall, a hundred and eighty pounds and unusually fit-looking for a man his age. Another cop, probably, maybe Weathers's boss. Weathers whispered something to him, and the man leaned toward him to listen but kept his eyes on the pews.

The mourners were asked to stand for a hymn, and Teddy took the opportunity to leave the church, tucking a funeral program into his pocket. He stood outside on the steps for a moment, and, as he did, Detective Weathers came outside, too.

"Good morning, Mr. Smithson," he said. "I'm Jimmy Weathers; we spoke . . ."

"Yes, I remember," Teddy said, and the other man joined them.

"This is my chief, James Bruno," Weathers said.

Teddy shook the man's hand and found that he had too strong a grip. He didn't like gym rats who tried to prove their manhood by crushing others' hands. "How do you do?" he said.

"What's the matter, Mr. Smithson?" Bruno said. "Weren't you enjoying the service?"

"Was I supposed to?" Teddy replied.

"Well, no, but . . ."

"Do you think Ms. Mason's murderer is inside?" Teddy asked.

"You never know," Bruno replied.

"No, I guess you don't. I'm new in town, so I don't know anybody—except Adele, of course—so I'm not into guessing who it might be. I hope you get the bastard."

"So do we," Weathers said.

"Good day to you," Teddy said, then walked down the steps of the church, crossed the street and got into his car. When he drove away, Weathers and Bruno were still standing there, watching him.

Teddy took the funeral program from his pocket and looked at the back page. Burial was to be at a local cemetery, and there was a map. He began to follow it.

He found the cemetery with no problems. He

parked the Toyota and walked toward the hearse, where the coffin was being unloaded, and people were starting to gather. He stood perhaps fifty yards away and watched the brief service. He saw Lauren Cade and the two local cops standing apart, viewing the gathering as he was.

Finally, the coffin was lowered into the grave, and the group started to walk back to their cars. Teddy watched until Lauren Cade and the two cops moved, too, then he walked back to his car and drove away.

25

Teddy stopped at the Vero Beach Book Center and went inside. He needed a book more absorbing than a second reading of Winston Churchill to take his mind off Adele Mason, now lying in the sandy Florida soil.

He was impressed. It was a very large bookstore, with everything he could have asked for in reading matter. He bought a *New York Times* and, after half an hour's browsing, a new biography of Andrew Jackson. A review of the book had stirred his interest, and he didn't know a lot about Jackson's period of American history. When he walked up to the counter to pay for his purchases, he was surprised to find Lauren Cade ahead of him in line.

She bought a novel, and when she turned was equally surprised to see him. "Hello, Mr. Smithson," she said.

"Good morning, Ms. Cade." He laid his purchases on the counter, along with some cash.

"I saw you at the funeral," she said, "and again at the burial. Why did you stand so far back?"

"For the same reason you did," Teddy replied.

"And what would that be?"

"To see if I could spot the killer in the crowd."

She smiled. "Well, you never know. It was worth the effort, I think."

Teddy took his purchases and walked with her to the parking lot. "Did you spot him?"

"No," she said. "Did you?"

"I'm afraid my instincts misled me," Teddy said.

"How so?"

"I saw a man who struck me as a possible suspect, but he turned out to be a police officer—the chief, in fact."

Lauren looked at him sharply. "Why do you say that?"

"I can't explain it; I just didn't like the look of him, and when Detective Weathers introduced him to me outside the church, I liked him even less."

"That's very interesting," she said.

"You suspect him, too?"

"I shouldn't talk about it," she replied.

"I'm sorry. I didn't mean to pry. I suppose you consider me a suspect as well."

"Off the record, I don't," she said. "Everything

you told us turned out to be true when we checked. Much of it was confirmed by Ms. Mason's diary."

"Are there any suspects besides this Bruno character?"

"No," she said, "and I can't concentrate too much on him, because I have personal issues with him that might cloud my judgment."

Teddy didn't ask what they were. "Ms. Cade, as long as I'm not a suspect, is there any reason why you and I couldn't have dinner this evening?" He looked at his watch. "It's past six, and I don't mind dining a little early."

"Neither do I," she said. "There's a very good restaurant called Carmel's just over there," she said, pointing across the parking lot.

They had no trouble getting a table so early, and soon they had drinks and were perusing the menu. Teddy wondered how old she was: midthirties, he guessed. He also wondered how she felt about older men.

"Mr. Smithson . . ." she began.

"Please, call me Jack."

"And I'm Lauren. How old are you?"

He smiled. "I'm sixty."

"I had thought a bit younger," she said.

"I think of myself as younger. And you?"

"I'm thirty-eight," she said. "And I think of myself as older."

"That's odd," Teddy observed.

"I suppose it is," she agreed.

"Have you had a hard life?"

"Not particularly," she said. "I've had some rough moments."

"So have we all, some rougher than those of others. How did you come to be a state police officer?"

"I came from a family who had little, and I joined the army as a means of getting a college education. I majored in criminology, and I applied for Officer Candidacy School with an eye toward the military police. I served for fourteen years, then left and applied to the Florida State Police."

"Were you disappointed in the army as a career?"

"On the contrary, I liked it and thought I would do the full thirty years."

"What happened?"

"Let's just say I was disappointed in some of the officers I served with."

Teddy felt he shouldn't question her too closely about that. If she wanted to talk about it she would. "My life was more mundane," he said. "I did an apprenticeship as a machinist after high school, and then started inventing gadgets, mostly kitchen stuff. Somewhat to my surprise I was able to make a good living at it. I married, and she died four years ago of ovarian cancer. No kids."

"I didn't marry," Lauren said. "The only men I

met were army officers, and they always seemed to be either just timeservers or too ambitious to be promoted."

They talked on over their dinners and shared a bottle of wine. When they were done, he walked her back to her car.

"Am I too old for you?" he asked.

"I don't think so," she replied.

"Then may we have dinner again?"

"I'd like that."

"Perhaps tomorrow night?"

"That's good for me. I should warn you that sometimes I get called to work on short notice."

"I'm flexible. May I cook for you at my house?"

"That would be lovely."

"Seven o'clock?"

"I know where to find you," she said, getting into her car. She handed him a card. "That's how you can reach me, should something come up."

He wrote down his own number and gave it to her. "Nothing will come up," he said. "I'll see to it."

"Until tomorrow evening, then," she said, starting her car.

He closed her door and walked back to his own car. This had been an unexpected but very pleasant surprise, he thought. And he was curious about her past relationship with James Bruno.

He went home and fired up his computer. He

didn't need to go into the Agency mainframe; there was enough on Bruno through Google. He read about the man's trial for rape and even found a photograph of Lauren, who looked much younger at the time.

And another surprise: Holly Barker was in the photo, too.

26

Ham Barker sat in his Boston Whaler, a rod in his hand, casting into the shallows of the Indian River. As he reeled in his line, a roar came from the river behind him, and his boat rose alarmingly on the wave from a wake.

Ham turned and watched the sportfisherman as it passed him at about twelve knots, not on the plane but with its stern low, pushing out a small tsunami behind it. He saw the name on the stern, *Party Girl,* and made a mental note to remember it, in case he ever met its owner ashore. Then he caught sight of the man at the helm: one James Bruno. Ham recognized him from his court-martial. A young woman in a bikini sat in the stern, sunning herself.

Ham laid his rod in the boat, pulled in his anchor, started the engine and turned upriver, following *Party Girl.* He crossed half its wake, then settled dead astern, where the wake was smooth. Ham felt a flush of anger just at the sight of Bruno. It was a good thing he wasn't armed, he thought, or he might have put a couple of rounds into the retired colonel.

He followed the boat upriver and watched as it put in at a marina where Ham knew fuel could be bought at a discount, then he slowed and stood off a dozen yards while Bruno tossed his lines to a dock man, then hopped off his boat and walked up the ramp to the marina office to order fuel.

Ham put his boat into gear and motored slowly alongside *Party Girl*. "Excuse me, miss," he said to the young woman, who was applying suntan lotion to her body.

She looked up from her work. "Yes?"

"May I ask, how long have you known James Bruno?"

She blinked. "Not long. Why?"

"Are you aware that he has a history of raping women?"

"Don't be ridiculous!" she said. "He's a perfectly nice man."

"That's what the women he raped thought, until he raped them."

"But he's the chief of police."

"Ironic, isn't it? Don't take my word for it; Google him and read about his court-martial when he was in the army. I tell you this only for your protection." Ham looked up and saw Bruno walking back down the ramp toward his boat. Ham put the engine in gear and slowly motored out of the marina.

He looked back and saw an angry discussion taking place on the sportfisherman; then he watched as the woman grabbed a duffel, stuffed some things into it, hopped off the boat and practically ran up the ramp. Ham smiled broadly.

Bruno stood in the stern of his boat, shaking his fist. "You son of a bitch!" he yelled. "Come back here!"

"You're lucky I don't," Ham said to himself; then he put the throttle forward and began running downriver again, laughing aloud. At least he had ruined Bruno's afternoon, and maybe he had spared the girl an awful experience. He felt very pleased with himself.

Bruno came through the back door of the Orchid Beach police station and stalked down the hall toward his office, still white with rage. As he reached the door he looked across the squad room and saw Lauren Cade leaving Jimmy Weathers's cubicle. She glanced at him, then turned her head and walked out the front door of the building.

Bruno walked down to Weathers's cubicle and leaned against the doorjamb.

"Hey, Chief," Weathers said.

"What was that little bitch doing here?" Bruno demanded.

"She's working on the rape case, too—you know, with Hurd Wallace's new unit?"

"You're the detective in charge of the case," Bruno said. "Why do you need her?"

"Well, nominally, it's our case, but Hurd's outfit has authority from the governor to participate in any case they like. I don't mind, really, since they can get things like lab work done faster than we can. They have priority."

"I don't like that," Bruno said. "Resign us from the case and let them do the fucking work."

"Excuse me, Chief, but I don't think that's a very good idea."

"And why not?"

"Well, I've put a lot of time into this case, and I think the more hands we have on it the better we'll do."

"And when you break it, you want to share the credit with Hurd Wallace and that bimbo?"

"She's not a bimbo, Chief; she's a good police officer and very smart."

"Yeah, I know how smart she is; she worked for me in the army."

"I didn't know that, Chief."

"She was a disloyal officer."

"Disloyal? How?"

"She was lazy, undisciplined and tried to take

credit for the work of others. She'll try to take credit for your work, too."

"Chief, I don't really think she's like that," Jimmy said. "That hasn't been my experience with her."

"Well, I have a lot more experience with her than you do."

"You really want me to resign us from this case? These things are happening on our turf, and if we don't take responsibility for our jurisdiction the local paper will be all over us, and, believe me, the city council members read the local paper."

Bruno thought about that. "Do whatever the fuck you want to, then." He spun around and strode back to his office, slamming the door behind him.

The detective in the next cubicle stood up and looked over the partition at Jimmy Weathers. "What's the matter with him, Jimmy?"

"I don't know," Jimmy said, "but I'm going to find out."

He flipped open his address book and dialed Holly Barker's number.

"Hello?"

"Holly, it's Jimmy Weathers. I got a little situation here."

"What's up, Jimmy?"

"Well, the chief just saw Lauren Cade here talking to me, and he pitched a fit."

"I'm not surprised," Holly said.

"Well, I was. Can you tell me what's going on?"

"There's a history between them, Jimmy, and I guess you should know about it."

"What kind of history?"

"Bruno . . . Look, just Google him and read about his court-martial. That'll tell you everything you need to know."

"All right, I'll do that."

"But, Jimmy, don't mention what you find out to Lauren; just be aware of it."

"Whatever you say, Holly, and thanks." He said good-bye and hung up; then he turned to his computer and typed in Bruno's name.

He read the news stories with wide eyes.

27

Teddy Fay went busily about preparing for Lauren Cade's dinner visit. He put the duck into the preheated oven and laid out the ingredients for their first course, then cleaned up the mess he had made during his preparations and adjusted the light in the kitchen to a more welcoming level.

He set the table in the living room for two and put new candles into their holders, then opened the bottle of cabernet he had selected and left it on the table to breathe.

Teddy enjoyed not just cooking but all the preparations that went into having a woman over for dinner. When she arrived, he wanted to look well prepared and have everything go smoothly.

An electronic chime sounded from his study; a car had turned into the driveway, the first time that had happened since he had installed the warning system. He was happy to know it worked. He took off his apron and hung it next to the stove, then went to the door to greet her. She was just getting out of her car with a bottle of wine in her hand.

"Good evening, Lauren," he said as he opened the screen door for her and pecked her on the cheek. "Come in."

"I thought this might be useful," she said, handing him the wine.

It was a very nice French burgundy. "Thank you so much," he said. "I hope you don't mind if we don't drink it this evening; I've already opened a bottle. Can I get you a drink?"

"Scotch, if you have it," she said.

"I've got Johnnie Walker Black or a single malt, Laphroaig."

"Johnnie Walker would be lovely."

He seated her on the couch and poured them both a Scotch.

"Something smells good," she said.

"I hope you enjoy duck."

"I do."

They chatted idly for a few minutes, and he poured them a second drink.

"Why don't you come into the kitchen while I prepare our first course?" he said, and she followed him. He put her on a stool at the kitchen counter, then proceeded to dust the sweetbreads with flour, drop them into a pan with hot clarified butter and sauté them. When they were ready, five minutes later, he transferred them to a small platter and led her to the table. He lit the candles, then poured a little wine into his glass, tasted it, and then poured them both a full glass.

She tasted the wine. "Oh, this is better than what I brought," she said.

"You chose well, and it would have been just as good with our dinner as mine."

Teddy sat down and watched for her reaction as she tasted the first course.

"Delicious!" she said. "But I don't know what it is."

"Sweetbreads," he said, stopping himself from telling her that they were the thymus gland from the neck of the calf.

"I've never had them, but I like this."

"I'm glad."

They ate the first course slowly, sipping their wine. When they finished, Teddy glanced at his watch: perfect timing. He cleared away their dishes, put them into the dishwasher and then removed the roasting duck from the oven, crisp and juicy. He cut the duck expertly into pieces and arranged them on two plates, leaving room for the small potatoes and haricots verts he had already prepared; then he served them.

"It looks wonderful," she said.

"I hope you think so when you've tasted it."

She signaled her approval with her first bite.

"No one has ever cooked me a dinner as good as this," she said. "Certainly not a man."

"Cooking is one of my pleasures," Teddy replied.

"What are your other pleasures?" she asked.

"Shooting, building technical things and . . ." He stopped.

"What?"

"I was about to go too far," he said.

"You were going to say sex, weren't you?"

Teddy laughed. "You don't know me well enough for that, yet."

"I like shooting, too," she said, "and . . ." She stopped, and they both laughed.

She reached over and touched his hair. "This isn't original equipment," she said.

Teddy laughed. "I'm vain, and I look better with hair, even if it isn't original equipment."

"It looks good on you," she said, "but my guess is you'd look just as good without it."

"You have a liking for bare scalp, do you?"

"On some men it looks good."

"I'll keep that in mind," Teddy said, "but I'll keep my hair on, at least in public." Especially while he was in the same town as Holly Barker, he reflected.

He took their dishes away and brought them both ice cream; then he put a coffeepot and cups on the living room coffee table.

She took a seat on the sofa, near the center, and he sat close to her. They were both warm with the Scotch and the wine, and it didn't take long before they were kissing.

"It's been a long time for me," she said.

He knew from his research that she meant since Bruno had raped her.

"I won't rush you," he said.

She kissed him again. "I think I'd like to be rushed."

Teddy picked up the tempo.

When he awoke the following morning she was in the shower, and she came back to the bedroom toweling herself, but naked. He liked it that she wasn't modest about what was a very beautiful body.

She lay down next to him for a moment. "I'd really like to make love to you again," she said, "but I have an early staff meeting that I can't be late for."

"I understand," he replied. "Is this about the rapist/murderer you're looking for?"

"Yes. We're having everybody sit down together at the same table: the local cops, the medical examiner, the forensics people. Maybe we can get a little synergy going."

"I hope so," he said. "I'd like to see you clear this thing and get it off your mind."

"It's constantly on my mind," she said. "Sometimes I'd just like to go out and shoot Bruno. No trial, just execution."

"I read about his court-martial on the Internet," Teddy confessed, "so I know what he did to you. You won't have to have the burden of explaining."

"I'm glad you read about it. The newspaper accounts were accurate and pretty much told the whole story."

"There was another woman who was a witness against Bruno," Teddy said.

"Yes. Her name is Holly Barker. She managed to fight him off, and she was a good witness, but the deck was stacked against us." She got up and began dressing.

"I hope you get him," Teddy said.

"We will," she replied. "This time we're playing with a new deck." She kissed him, said good-bye and, telling him to stay in bed, left.

Teddy lay there, thinking about how he would like to end this whole thing for her.

28

Lauren arrived at work early and went to her cubicle to pick up a legal pad for use in the weekly staff meeting. She had been there for only a moment when Hurd Wallace came in and sat down in the chair next to her desk.

"Good morning," he said.

"Good morning, Hurd," she replied.

"I've got some difficult news: Jim Bruno is here, and he wants to attend our morning meeting."

"I don't know what to say," Lauren replied.

"I know this is awkward for you, Lauren."

"It's not that it's awkward for me," she said, "even though it is. It's that he's our only suspect, and we can't have a suspect attending a meeting at which we're going to discuss the crimes we suspect him of."

"That's a very good point," Hurd said. "How would you suggest I disinvite him?"

"Tell him we're not talking about the murders. Tell him we're discussing something from another jurisdiction that's confidential."

Hurd thought about that for a moment. "All right, that's what I'll do. But Jimmy Weathers is here, too, and he's the lead detective on the case. What do I do about him?"

"I'll call Jimmy later and bring him up-to-date."

Hurd stood up. "I'll go talk to both of them, then."

Hurd went back to his office and found James Bruno and Jimmy Weathers waiting for him.

"Morning, gentlemen," he said, shaking both their hands. "My secretary tells me you want to attend my staff meeting."

"That's right," Bruno said. "I think it's best if we know your thinking on these murders, so we can be of more use."

"I'm afraid the murders are not on our agenda for the meeting. I mean, they may come up, but for the most part we're dealing with investigations in other jurisdictions, and we have to hold those details in strict confidence, just as you hold the details of the crimes in your jurisdiction in confidence."

Bruno appeared to be trying not to seem annoyed. "I think it's important that we share knowledge on these murders," he said.

"That's exactly what we've been doing, Jim. At least, I thought that's what we're doing."

"Well, maybe you've been sharing with Jimmy, but not with me."

"Jimmy is your lead detective, Jim. Jimmy, do you feel left out of the case?"

"Well, no, Hurd. I can't say that I do."

"But *I'm* left out of the case," Bruno said.

"If that's true, Jim, it's because you haven't expressed much interest in it."

"I'm *very* interested in it," Bruno said.

"Then I'm sure Jimmy will be glad to brief you on all the details of the investigation," Hurd said.

"Jimmy has already briefed me," Bruno replied hotly.

"In that case, I don't know why you're here, Jim," Hurd said. "It's not as though we're keeping information from Jimmy. In fact, he's the one who's been keeping us abreast of his own investigation. We're not hiding anything from him."

"Why won't you let me attend the meeting?" Bruno demanded.

"Jim, I've already explained that we'll be dealing with other cases in our meeting, cases you have no reason to be privy to."

"I see," Bruno said, getting to his feet. "Let's go, Jimmy; we're apparently not wanted here."

"I don't think it's like that, Chief," Jimmy said.

"I said, let's go!" Bruno retorted.

"I'll certainly keep you posted if we get anything new, Jim," Hurd said.

Bruno walked out of the office without another word.

"I'm sorry about this," Jimmy said.

"Lauren will call you later," Hurd replied. "Keep that to yourself."

Jimmy looked puzzled. He shook hands and left.

Hurd watched to see that they were out of his office, then walked next door to the conference room, where Lauren, the medical examiner and the forensics guy were waiting. Everyone sat down.

"I'm sorry to be late," Hurd said, "but I had to ask Chief Bruno of Orchid Beach not to attend our meeting."

"Why?" the ME asked.

"Because he's our only suspect in the case," Hurd explained.

The ME looked shocked. "What evidence do we have against him?"

"He has a history of being accused of rape," Hurd explained. "We have no material evidence at this point, but I think it's best if we keep him out of the loop until we can exclude him as a suspect."

The ME shrugged. "If you say so, Hurd."

"This is confidential, of course."

"Of course."

Jimmy and Bruno were driving back to the Orchid station with Jimmy at the wheel.

"What was that about?" Bruno asked.

"Chief, I don't think it was about anything," Jimmy replied. "Hurd explained himself, and I think we have to accept his explanation."

"Why would he want to keep information from me?" Bruno asked.

"I don't think he does. Sergeant Cade has been in touch with me on a daily basis, and I've called her a lot, too. I think I'm fully briefed on the case."

"Well, I don't feel fully briefed," Bruno said.

Jimmy pulled into the station parking lot, and they got out of the car.

"I'll get the case file and go through it with you," Jimmy said.

Bruno slammed the car door. "Oh, fuck it!" he spat. "You handle the goddamned thing any way you like. I'm out of it." He stormed off and went into the station.

Jimmy went back to his desk, and he was reading the file again when his phone rang. "Detective Weathers."

"Jimmy, it's Lauren."

"Hi, Lauren."

"I'm sorry you were kept out of the meeting this morning, but we didn't want Bruno there."

"How come?" Jimmy asked.

"Because he's the only suspect in the case."

"Bruno?"

"Yes. He has a past history of rape."

Jimmy took a deep breath. "Lauren, I think you should know that I read the stuff on Bruno's court-martial, so I know about your involvement."

"It's just as well," she said. "I would have told you eventually. I hope you don't think I was keeping anything from you."

"Well, you kept the fact that Bruno is a suspect from me."

"We don't want him to know, and I think you can see how important it is that you don't tell him."

"That puts me in kind of an awkward position," Jimmy said.

"I know it does, but I can't do anything about that. For the integrity of the investigation you have to keep this from him."

"And what happens when he finds out and I get fired? Are you folks going to give me a job?"

"Don't worry. We'll see that it doesn't come to that. Either Bruno will find out when we get enough evidence to arrest him, or he won't find out at all."

"All right, Lauren, I'll play along, but please don't get my ass caught in a wringer."

"I won't, Jimmy. I've got to run now. Bye-bye." She hung up.

Jimmy hung up, too. "God in Heaven," he said aloud to himself.

29

Holly got out of her first day's training for the Malibu Mirage at dusk, and she was exhausted. She had spent half her day learning the airplane's systems and the rest in the simulator, which she had found trying. It didn't fly like the airplane, and, although she could look out its windows at the landscape, it was more of a schematic of a landscape, and it didn't help all that much. She decided she would rather fly the airplane itself.

She got into her car and was heading back toward the beach and home when, shortly after crossing the bridge, she saw two police cars, their lights flashing, with a silver sedan pulled over. She drove slowly past the cars and got a look at the driver, who appeared to be a sixtyish man, sitting in his car and talking with two police officers. She supposed that the Orchid force had started stopping every white male driving alone.

All she could think about now was a drink, some dinner and a hot bath.

Teddy had just crossed the bridge when the lights began flashing behind him. He considered whether he should make a run for it but decided against it. After all, he was a solid citizen with ID to back it up, so he pulled over, lowered his window and waited. To his surprise the police car pulled past him and blocked any escape, and another car pulled up behind him. A moment later there was a flashlight in his face.

"Good evening, sir," a young officer said. "May I see your license, registration and proof of insurance?" His hand was on his gun.

"Certainly," Teddy said, reaching for his wallet.

"Slowly, sir, please," the cop said.

Teddy slowly produced his wallet, removed the license and handed it over, then opened the center armrest for his registration and insurance information, while another cop watched him closely from the other side of the car.

"Mr. Smithson?" the cop read from the license. "What are you doing out tonight?"

"Driving home," Teddy replied.

"From where?"

"From the Publix market on US-1," Teddy said. "There isn't a big supermarket on the island."

"Would you step out of the car, please?"

Teddy got out.

"Place your hands on top of the car, please."

He did so and felt himself being searched. "What's this about?" he asked. "Why did you stop me?"

"Do you mind if I have a look inside your car, Mr. Smithson?"

"No, I don't mind, but I'd like to know why."

"Just a routine procedure, sir. Please have a seat on my front bumper, right behind your car."

Teddy walked back to the police car behind him and sat down. He watched as the two officers thoroughly searched his car and as one officer pressed the button inside the car that opened his trunk. The two officers moved around the four bags of groceries in the trunk and looked under the floor where the spare tire was stored.

"All right, Mr. Smithson," the cop said, handing him back his paperwork. "You may proceed on your way. I apologize for any inconvenience."

"Not at all," Teddy said, accepting his paperwork and returning to his car. The cop had not even mentioned that he had been driving at least ten miles per hour over the speed limit. He started the car, waited for the police car to move from in front of him, then pulled away from the curb and continued on his way.

This had to be about the search for the rapist/

murderer, he thought. He drove home, put away the groceries, took his laptop from the safe and switched it on. He logged on to the Agency computer through a handy computer in Birmingham, Alabama, and began compiling everything he could find on James Bruno, from his court-martial record, to his West Point transcript to his military personnel file.

Finally, he ran a complete background check on the man, discovering only some speeding tickets, the most recent four months ago. Except for those, the man was clean on the civilian side. Only the court-martial transcript told the story of his abuse of women.

Bruno, he concluded, was a type A personality, aggressive and bullying, though Teddy doubted that part of his personality would display itself when he was faced with someone his own size who had an equally aggressive attitude.

He pulled Bruno's recent Florida driver's license application from the state's DMV records, which gave him the man's current home address. He was going to have to start looking into Bruno's daily schedule and devote some thought to how to best deal with him.

Lauren Cade got home from work, poured herself a drink and called Jack Smithson.

"Hello?"

"Hi, it's Lauren."

"How was your day?"

"Long and tiring. I'm just having a drink and recovering."

"I was pulled over by the police on the way home from the grocery store this evening," he said.

"Oh? What crime did you commit, Jack?"

"White male alone in a car," Teddy replied. "I take it this is part of your investigation?"

"It's the Orchid Beach department's part of it," she said. "Our little unit doesn't have the resources to do that sort of thing. I take it they saw your innocent face and let you go."

"Something like that," Teddy said, chuckling. "You making any progress with your investigation?"

"Not really. Jim Bruno showed up at our office this morning to attend our staff meeting. Hurd had to tell him he couldn't but not why, which is because Bruno is a suspect. He got mad and left."

"That's awkward, isn't it, when a cop is a suspect?"

"Yes, it is. First time I've ever had a case where an investigating officer was a suspect, and I don't like it. I wouldn't like it, even if Bruno wasn't the guy."

"I've got a whole lot of new groceries here,"

Teddy said. "You want to come over and help me eat them?"

"I'd love to, but I'm just so tired. Tomorrow night?"

"That would be lovely. Seven o'clock?"

"I may have to come straight from work; mind if I have a shower there?"

"I'll be happy to assist you in that endeavor," Teddy said.

"Oooh, now you're making me wet."

"Hold that thought until tomorrow night," Teddy said.

"You'd better believe it," she replied. "Night-night now." She hung up.

The call made Teddy's evening.

30

Lance Cabot's secretary buzzed him. "There's a man from Computer Services named Ross Hilton who'd like to see you for a moment," she said.

"Why?" Lance asked. He was busy, and he didn't want to discuss his computer needs with some nerd.

"He says it's an Operations matter."

"Oh, all right, send him in," Lance said impatiently.

A kid who appeared to be about seventeen walked into his office. "Hey," he said.

"You're from Computer Services?" Lance asked.

"I'm twenty-five, and everybody in my department looks like me," the kid said.

"All right, ah . . ."

"Ross."

"Ross. Have a seat."

Ross had a seat. "I've come across some unusual activity on the mainframe," he said.

"What sort of activity?" Lance asked. He hoped he was going to understand this the first time.

"It looks like someone is logging on to our mainframe from a remote computer and using it."

"From where?" Lance asked.

"Once from the Bahamas, once from Birmingham, Alabama. I think the Birmingham computer was being used as a conduit from yet another location."

"And where is that location?"

"I haven't been able to figure that out yet, but the very idea of somebody using our mainframe is pretty scary, wouldn't you say?"

"Yes, I would say."

"I mean, anybody logging on from outside the building would have to go through at least three levels of security, with a different eighteen-digit password at each level."

"Then that person must be an employee, probably an operating agent."

"Inside the United States? I was told when I was recruited that the Agency is barred from conducting operations inside the U.S."

"That's perfectly true, Ross, but there are reasons other than conducting operations that might cause an agent inside the country to employ the mainframe. Research, for instance. If you can figure out where the user is located, then I'll know better if it's one of our people."

"So what do you want me to do about this?" Ross asked.

"You've already done the correct thing by bringing this to my attention."

"You want me to bring it to your attention if this happens again?"

"Yes, please do that. On second thought, bring it to the attention of one of my deputies, Holly Barker. She's on vacation now, but you can e-mail her through the system. She has an authorized terminal in her present location."

"Okay, I'll do that," Ross said. "Thanks very much." He got up to go.

"Thank you, Ross. Oh, to what use was this person putting the mainframe?"

"Sorry, I forgot to mention that. It was sort of a background check on a retired army colonel named James Bruno. The user dredged up the record of a court-martial and also went into the Florida Department of Motor Vehicles computer and extracted the guy's driver's license application."

Something sounded familiar to Lance about all this. "Who was court-martialed?"

"This Colonel Bruno."

"And what were the charges?"

"Rape and attempted rape."

"Ahhh," Lance said. "I think I know what this is about, Ross. I'll deal with this; don't bother any further with it."

"Whatever you say, Mr. Cabot. See ya." He gave a little wave and left the office.

Lance turned to his computer and sent an e-mail.

Holly returned from her second day's training, exhausted again. She had finally gotten a grip on the simulator and was flying it well, but she was still anxious to get into the real airplane. She went into the kitchen to get a beer and a small, green flashing light caught her eye. It was just outside the door of her Agency-provided office, and she hadn't noticed it before.

She tapped her entry code into the keypad and opened the door. A message was flashing on the monitor of the Agency computer: E-MAIL WAITING.

She logged on and went to her in-box. "Call me. Lance," the message read. She looked at her watch. He might still be in the office, so she dialed his direct number.

"Lance Cabot," he said.

"It's Holly. You rang, master?"

"Yes. I had one of those teenaged geeks up here from Computer Services this afternoon to tell me about someone from outside the Agency accessing the mainframe."

"What does that mean?"

"It means that someone has been using the mainframe to investigate the background of a retired army colonel named Bruno. That rang a bell."

"I'm surprised you remember," she said.

"I remember everything, Holly; never forget that."

"I'll try not to. What's the problem?"

"One of the things I remember was a conversation with you about your personal use of the mainframe."

"Yes, I remember that, too. When did this incident occur?"

"Today, apparently."

"I haven't been on the mainframe today."

"You aren't still digging things up about Bruno?"

"I think I already have everything I need to know about his past," she said. "Right now, he's a suspect in a series of rapes and murders in this town."

"Our geek says that someone accessed the mainframe from the Bahamas and then again from Birmingham, Alabama."

"I've never been to Birmingham, Alabama," she said.

"Actually, he says the user routed through a computer in Birmingham."

"Was he able to figure out where the original computer is? I mean, the one the user is actually using?"

"No, not yet. Who, besides you, would be interested in the background of Colonel James Bruno?"

"I haven't the foggiest. I mean, the local and state cops have an interest in him, but I've already given them the material on Bruno that I found, and anyway, they wouldn't have the codes necessary to access the mainframe."

"The user also accessed the Florida DMV computer and got Bruno's driver's license application."

"Well, this sounds like the cops, but if a Florida police agency can access the CIA mainframe, then I'd say we have a major computer security problem."

"It can't be the cops down there," Lance said. "That's just too preposterous. It's got to be one of our people doing this."

"I think I would agree with that. Certainly, it's a much less troubling idea for an Agency employee to be using the mainframe for his or her own purposes."

"Less troubling but annoying," Lance said. "If you think of anyone else in the Agency who would have an interest in Colonel Bruno, call me."

"Will do."

"Good night." Lance hung up.

Holly hung up, too, baffled.

31

Teddy Fay lay back and gazed into the face of Lauren Cade, which was contorted with passion. She moved rhythmically up and down on top of him, making little noises, and he moved with her. Then, they both climaxed together and ended up with her in his arms but still locked together.

"That was just wonderful," she said.

"It certainly was," he agreed.

"How do you do that?" she asked.

"It seems to me that you were doing the greater part of it."

"I suppose I was."

"And doing it extremely well, too."

She fell sideways and lay tight against him, her head on his shoulder and her leg over his, spilling his seed onto him. "Messy, isn't it?"

"Yes."

"I love it. I love your sweat, too."

"That's entirely involuntary; it doesn't require any talent."

"No, it's just part of you." She got up and went into the bathroom. He heard water running, and a moment later she came back with a hot facecloth and wiped down his body.

"The service is very good around here," Teddy said.

"I'm going to keep it that way," she replied. "What can I get you?"

"A cold beer, please."

"Oh, me, too." She trotted off toward the kitchen.

"There are cold glasses in the freezer," he called after her.

She returned with two perfectly poured glasses, and he sat up and rearranged the pillows for both of them.

"It's fun watching you walk around naked," Teddy said.

"Then I'll do that a lot."

They touched glasses and drank the cold lager.

Teddy experienced a rush of feelings for her. He wanted her to never leave his house again, but he could not express this desire. "What are your career plans?" he asked.

"I've got four years on the job," she said, "so I guess I'll put in at least twenty, for the pension—barring a better offer, of course."

"What would you consider a better offer?"

"A job with a federal agency, I guess—FBI, DEA, like that."

"Then you'd have to move," he pointed out.

"Probably. I suppose they employ agents in Florida, though. I'd like to stay here. Mind you, my new job is something meaningful; it's better than chasing down speeders on I-95."

"I suppose it is. You're a bright woman; you need something that requires intelligence."

"I do."

Teddy was trying to think about the future, but it was hard. What was he going to do? Ask her to marry him and run with him when the Agency stumbled across him somewhere? Could he confess to her the murders he'd done, necessary for the welfare of the country though they may have been. Could he ask her to share the risks in his life, to change her identity, to keep moving? He actually enjoyed the chase, but it seemed unlikely that she would. He tried to bring his mind back to the present.

"What about you?" she asked. "Are you going to settle down in Vero Beach?"

"Seems like a nice town," he said. "So far. Certainly the company is good."

"How'd you pick Vero anyway?"

"I read something about it somewhere. It's a nice size—not too big, not too small—and I don't mind a hot summer."

"I do," she said, "but there's nothing I can do about it."

That was something he could offer her, he thought: a better climate somewhere else. "Where would you like to live, if you could live anywhere?"

"Paris," she said unhesitatingly.

"That's a nice thought," Teddy said. "Do you have the language?"

"Two courses in high school. I can order dinner."

"That's about the extent of my French, too," he admitted.

"I think if I lived in Paris the language would come to me quickly enough."

Teddy changed the subject. "When you nail this Bruno character, what will your next job be?"

"The next big crime, I guess."

"Wherever it is?"

"Wherever in Florida."

So she might get yanked away from him. He didn't like that.

"Our charter from the government is to investigate 'major' crimes, but Hurd Wallace has a lot of discretion over what cases he works. Of course, the governor could call at any time and send him off to Miami or Jacksonville or someplace to solve some murder that had statewide or national implications."

"Are you having Bruno followed?"

"No, not yet, anyway. But I've told Jimmy Weathers—you met him—that Bruno is a suspect, so I expect he'll be paying a lot of attention to him until we break the case."

"Does he spend most of his time in the office?"

"Jimmy says he works odd hours. Sometimes he's at the station in the middle of the night. It's like he's always checking up on the people who work for him."

"I'm no cop," Teddy said, "but I should think that if he's your suspect, you'd follow him night and day, until he made an incriminating move."

"To do that, Hurd would have to request more manpower from the state police, and then it starts to get political. If he meets with resistance, he has to get the governor involved. I think Hurd is reluctant to do that, or we'd already be following Bruno."

"He'll make a mistake eventually," Teddy said.

"Let's hope so," Lauren replied.

Teddy was thinking he wouldn't wait for Bruno to make a mistake.

32

Jimmy Weathers worked until after midnight; then, as he was locking his desk, he saw a light go on down the hallway. Bruno was in his office.

He walked down the hall toward the rear door to the parking lot and stopped at Bruno's door. "Evening, Chief."

"Good evening, Jimmy," Bruno said.

"Did you just get here?"

"Yes," Bruno replied. "You, too?"

"No, I'm just leaving. You going to be late?"

"Probably an all-nighter," Bruno replied. "I'm working on personnel files, and, by the way, I'm giving you a good performance rating."

"Thank you, Chief. Good night, now."

"Good night," Bruno said.

Jimmy walked out to the parking lot, and, as he was about to get into his car, he noticed that Bruno's unmarked cruiser, parked next to him under a streetlamp, had the keys in it. If Bruno kept doing that, Jimmy mused, he was going to end up with a stolen police car.

The next morning Lauren Cade was fifteen minutes late for work, having spent longer in bed with Jack Smithson than she'd meant to. Hurd Wallace called to her as she passed his door.

"Lauren?"

"Yes, Hurd. Sorry I'm late."

"You're just in time. The Vero department called two minutes ago. They've had a call about a dead woman in a car, and they're en route now."

"Is it another one, do you think?"

"I think," Hurd said. "Do you know the fairgrounds west of town?"

"Yes."

"That's where they found her. You ready to go?"

"Sure."

"We'll take your car," he said, grabbing his jacket.

The fairgrounds were located on a grid of roads just west of Vero Beach, a place that Lauren passed when she was driving from her house to the Indian River Mall. There was a police car blocking the entrance, but Lauren identified herself and was allowed in.

She drove into the grounds, and it was immediately obvious where the crime scene was. Two Vero cars and a van were in the middle of the large, grassy field that served as a parking lot when there was an event at the grounds. She cut across the field toward them.

She stopped, and she and Hurd got out of their car and identified themselves to the detective in charge.

"I'm Ed Rankin," the detective said. "I've heard about you folks. You going to take this one away from us?"

"We don't want to do that," Hurd replied. "We just want to help."

"Well, I hope you don't help like the FBI helps," Rankin replied. The Bureau had a reputation among cops for letting them do the work, then taking the credit.

"Nothing like that," Hurd said. "This is probably one more in a series we've had. You know about that."

"Sure, I do, and I think you're right," Rankin said.

The medical examiner's truck pulled up next to them, and the ME got out. "What we got here?" he asked.

"Let's look together," Hurd said, leading the way around the victim's car.

The driver's door was open, and a naked woman was on her knees in the driver's seat, her head toward the passenger door. There was blood on her buttocks and thighs and on the back of her head.

Lauren winced when she saw the position, and she was immediately struck by the difference between what she and Jack had been doing an hour ago and what this woman had experienced.

The ME conducted his on-site examination, then stood back.

"Tell me what you think," Hurd said.

"I think she was forced to strip and kneel on the driver's seat, then was raped vaginally and anally from behind, then shot once in the back of the head, probably with a twenty-two pistol, eight to ten hours ago."

"I concur," Hurd said, looking at Lauren.

"So do I," she said.

"Can I take the body?" the ME asked.

Hurd turned to Rankin. "Ed?"

"Sure. We can look at the interior of the car better with her gone."

The ME and his assistant removed the body from the car, loaded it on a gurney and put it into his truck. Shortly, they were gone.

"We got a handbag," Rankin said, holding it up by a strap. It was on the seat under the body. He walked to the front of the car and emptied the bag onto the hood. "We got a wallet," he said, opening it, "and a driver's license." Rankin took the license from the wallet and peered at it. "Oh, shit," he said.

"What?" Lauren asked.

"I know her. Jeanine Clark. She sells tickets at

the mall movie theater. My oldest boy went to high school with her. The family lived a couple of blocks from us."

"How late would she work at the movie theater?" Hurd asked.

"I think they have shows as late as midnight," Rankin replied. "I'll check out there and see what time she left last night; that'll probably give us a time of death, and I'll bet it agrees with the ME's estimate."

Lauren stepped away from the car and made a phone call.

"Detective Weathers," Jimmy said.

"It's Lauren. We've got another one."

"Where?"

"In the Vero jurisdiction, out at the fairgrounds."

"He's moving around, then."

"Yes. I want to know where Bruno was last night. Can you find out without alerting him that he's a suspect?"

"I already know," Jimmy said. "I left here a little after midnight, and he had just arrived, said he was going to be working all night on personnel files. He's gone, now—probably at home asleep."

"That's interesting," Lauren said. "Was anybody else in the station last night?"

"Just the switchboard operator; everybody else would have been on patrol until the shift change, at eight a.m."

"Would the operator have seen Bruno there?"

"Probably not. She's in her own space, with the door closed. She has to stay by the switchboard in case of a nine-one-one call, and she has her own john back there."

"What does Bruno drive?"

"An unmarked Crown Vic cruiser, dark blue. I noticed when I left last night that the keys were in it. I suppose you could make a case that somebody took the car and returned it later, but that's kind of far-fetched, isn't it?"

"Yes, it is."

"You need me out there?"

"No, I'll ask the DIC, Ed Rankin, to fax you a copy of his report. The ME just left; you can get his report later today, probably. I'll talk to you later, Jimmy." Lauren closed her phone and noticed that Hurd Wallace was standing a few yards away, looking down. She walked over to him. "Got something?"

"Maybe we got lucky," Hurd said, pointing down. "There was some rain last evening, and there's a bare spot in the grass right here. Look at that tire print."

Lauren looked down. "Nice and clear," she said, "and it looks like there's a cut in the tire." She moved along a few feet. "Here it is again, from when the tire turned. It's a right tire."

"Let's get a cast of that track," Hurd said.

33

Teddy was working in the kitchen when the chime went off, signaling a car entering the driveway. That would be Lauren, he guessed, but he still went to the door and looked outside to be sure. She was spending more and more time at his house; some of her clothes were in his closet and chest of drawers. He liked that.

Lauren came in the door and gave him a wet kiss. "Whatever that is smells good," she said.

"It's only meat loaf."

"My favorite!"

"Then you came to the right place."

"I know I did."

"How was your day?"

"Another murder," she said. "Out at the fairgrounds, west of town. A young woman who worked as a ticket seller at the Indian River Mall cineplex."

"Any new clues?"

"We may have gotten a break," she said. "We know that Bruno said he was working all night at the police station, and there was nobody there who could give him an alibi. We also found a tire track with a cut in the tread."

"Is that tire on Bruno's car?"

"We don't know," she said. "Hurd and I drove past his house, and his car was parked in the driveway, so we had a look at the tires. We couldn't see a cut, but it could have been on the ground, and we couldn't move the car without a warrant. Of course, we don't have enough evidence to get a warrant."

"And while you're waiting for enough evidence, he could kill a few more women."

"Please don't say that," she said. "That's my worst nightmare."

Teddy fixed them a drink and handed her one. She took a stool at the kitchen counter. "I'm getting tired of looking at corpses," Lauren said. "This one was posed in the driver's seat, kneeling."

"I think I get that picture," Teddy said. "No more details, please."

"I don't want details myself," she replied, "but details are my job."

"Details were always what made my work fun," Teddy said; then he realized he was talking about his career at the CIA and stopped talking.

"Go on."

"I was just going to say that when you're inventing gadgets, everything is in the details." He held up a plastic frame with a blade in it. "Like this potato slicer," he said. "It would have cost too much to make the blade adjustable, so I had to cook a lot of potatoes to get the slicing thickness just right."

"A crime scene is nothing but details," Lauren said. "I just can't imagine how murders got solved fifty years ago before gunshot residue and knife blade matching and DNA came along."

"Isn't that when the cops just beat confessions out of the suspect?"

"Wash your mouth out with soap," she said. "Well, maybe, but we don't do that."

"But the Supreme Court says you can lie about evidence to the suspect, in order to get a confession."

"That's not twisting science," she said, "it's using human nature against him. If the guy is already feeling guilty and he thinks you've got him, likely as not he'll spill the beans with a video camera running."

"I heartily approve of that technique," Teddy said. "I don't know how any murderer can think he'll get away with it these days, what with all the science involved, all the ways he can get caught."

"Somebody like Bruno," Lauren said, "who has

police training, has an advantage. He knows what we'll look for, and he works at not leaving any evidence. He uses condoms, so that he won't leave his DNA; he wears latex gloves . . ."

"I get the picture," Teddy said. "But I'll bet that if he has a cut tire, he doesn't know it."

"We didn't get tire tracks at any of the other scenes," Lauren said, "just this one."

"Maybe he cut his tire since the last murder, ran over something sharp."

"Maybe." She took out the phone. "Excuse me a minute. I just thought of something." She selected a number from her phone's address book.

"Hello?"

"Jimmy, it's Lauren Cade."

"Hey, Lauren."

"There's something you could do that would be a big help," she said.

"Sure, anything I can do."

"Can you check the right tires on Bruno's cruiser for cuts?"

"What are you looking for?"

"A cut across the tread. I checked his car at his house today but couldn't see anything; it might have been parked with the cut on the ground."

"I get you," he said. "Sure, I'll check the car every chance I get. You're sure it's on the right side?"

"I think so. You can check all four."

"Will do."

"Thanks, Jimmy." She hung up.

"That was Detective Weathers?" Teddy asked.

"Yes. He's going to check Bruno's tires for me."

"And if you find a cut, you can get a warrant?"

"Maybe. Then, if we can match the cut in the tread to the cast we took, we'll have some material evidence."

"I'll be the first to congratulate you," Teddy said, slicing and serving the meat loaf before adding mashed potatoes and beans to the plates. Then he put them on the table, and they sat down to eat.

"I fantasize about searching Bruno's house and finding the panties," she said.

"What panties?"

"Oh, I guess I didn't tell you," Lauren said. "He keeps his victim's panties—at least, we've never found any at the crime scenes."

34

Lauren Cade was at her desk the following morning when her phone rang. "Detective Cade," she said.

"Lauren, it's Jimmy Weathers."

"Hey, Jimmy."

"I checked Bruno's tires this morning, and there's a cut on the right front one. It's deep, wedge-shaped and crosses about three-quarters of the tread."

"Jimmy, I love you," Lauren nearly shouted. "Tell me you didn't manipulate the car in any way."

"I didn't touch it. The wheels were sharply turned to the left, and the cut was visible to any passerby. You shouldn't have any trouble with the warrant."

"Thank you, Jimmy! I've got to go see Hurd now." She hung up and hurried down the hall to Hurd Wallace's office, smiling.

"What?" Hurd said when he saw her face.

"Jimmy Weathers found a cut on the right front tire of Bruno's car. He described it, and it sounds identical to the one we've got the cast of."

"That's great news," Hurd said, picking up the phone and buzzing his secretary, Shirley Medved. "Shirley, call Judge Landry and get me an immediate appointment. Tell him it's for a search warrant in an important case." He hung up. "Here's how we handle this," he said to Lauren. "We tow the car to a garage of our choice, and we go over the whole thing with a fine-tooth comb. The DA is going to want more than the tire cut to ask for an indictment."

"Maybe we'll find the panties in the car," Lauren said.

"DNA from the panties would guarantee a conviction," Hurd said, "though I'm not going to get my hopes up about that. Bruno is too smart to keep something like that in his car; if he has them, he'll have thought of a better hiding place."

The phone rang, and Hurd picked it up. "Yes? Thank you, Shirley." He hung up. "We can't see the judge until four o'clock this afternoon. He's in court nonstop until then."

"Oh, God," Lauren said. "I'll be on pins and needles until then."

Lauren sat in her car outside the courthouse and waited impatiently for Hurd's return. She felt an excitement she had never felt before; her stomach churned, and her knees were weak. She looked up to see Hurd coming down the courthouse steps.

Hurd got into the car and held up a warrant. "Got it," he said and gave her a rare smile. He got out his cell phone and punched in a number. "Fred? It's Hurd Wallace; I need an immediate tow, a flatbedder. Right, meet me at the Orchid Beach police station parking lot as soon as you can get there. We'll be going back to your garage." He hung up. "Let's go."

Lauren drove quickly to the police station, resisting the temptation to use her lights and siren. She pulled into the parking lot. Bruno's cruiser was in his labeled parking space. "There it is," she said. "And here comes the tow truck."

"You want to serve the warrant?" Hurd asked.

"No, I'm too nervous; you do it, please."

Hurd got out of the car and walked into the police station through the back door. He was gone for no more than a minute; then he returned. Jim Bruno came out the back door and stood at the top of the steps, watching.

"Fred, there's the car," Hurd said. "The keys are in it."

"You want to drive it, then?" Fred asked.

"No, I don't want to take any chances."

Hurd and Lauren watched Fred go through the

motions with practiced ease. In five minutes, he had the car on his flatbed.

Lauren and Hurd got back into the car and followed the tow truck. Hurd got on the phone and reached the unit criminalist and gave him directions to the garage.

"How did Bruno react?" Lauren asked.

"With astonishment," Hurd replied. "I mean, he really looked amazed. He demanded to know the reason for the warrant, and I refused to tell him. I told him the car was material to an investigation that's under way."

"Now I wish I had served it," Lauren said.

"It's better that I did it," Hurd replied. "We don't want him to try and make a case for harassment because of your past dealings with him."

"I suppose you're right," Lauren said.

The tow truck pulled into the garage. Fred unloaded it and drove it into an empty bay, then raised the hoist.

"Lift it so that the tires are at eye level," Hurd said to him.

The hoist stopped, and Hurd and Lauren walked to the right front tire. Hurd spun the wheel slowly. "I don't see a cut," he said.

"I thought Jimmy said it was the right front," Lauren replied. "You check the right rear, and I'll check the other side." She inspected both tires and found no cuts. Then she walked back to where

Hurd was standing. "No cuts on the other side. I don't understand."

"Lower the car, Fred," Hurd said to the garage owner, who was standing by watching. He lowered the car. "Pop the trunk, Lauren. Let's look at the spare."

Lauren put on latex gloves, opened the driver's door and pressed the trunk lid release, then went to the rear of the car. Hurd was unscrewing the wing nut that held the spare in place. In a moment, he had the tire out, and they inspected the tread.

"I don't get it," Hurd said. "There's no tire cut anywhere."

Lauren walked back to the right front tire and knelt to look at it again. "Look at this," she said.

Hurd walked over and squatted. "What?"

Lauren flicked a little piece of rubber that extended from the tire like a pin. "It's a new tire," she said. "These little appendages fall off after a while."

"Shit," Hurd said. "That means he bought a new tire after Jimmy saw the cut this morning."

"But why would he have done that?"

"I don't know," Hurd said.

Lauren got out her phone and called Jimmy Weathers's cell phone.

"Hello."

"Jimmy, it's Lauren. We got the warrant, and we're inspecting the tires now. There's no cut on any one of them, and there's a brand-new tire on the right front."

"Damn," Jimmy said. "He must have seen the cut. It was deep enough to bother you; I wouldn't have wanted to drive on it. One good bump, and you'd have a blowout."

"I guess you're right," Lauren said.

"I'm sorry, Lauren. I don't know what else to say."

"Not your fault, Jimmy," she said. "Bye-bye." She turned to Hurd. "Where does the Orchid department buy its tires?" she asked.

"Up US-1 a couple of miles. Let's go." Hurd headed for the car, and Lauren followed.

The crime lab van pulled up behind the garage.

"The car's on the hoist," Hurd said. "This is about the rape/murders; check everything, and be careful to properly preserve any evidence. We'll be back."

Lauren got into the car, and they drove away.

35

Holly was driving back from the airport after her day's training when an unmarked police car suddenly passed her, moving fast. Lauren Cade was looking at her in the rearview mirror, waving, with Hurd Wallace sitting next to her. Holly's curiosity was piqued: another murder? She accelerated and fell in behind the car.

They pulled off the road at Vero Discount Tires, and Holly followed. What were they doing? Getting a flat fixed? If so, what was the hurry? She got out of the car. "Hey, Lauren, Hurd."

"Hey, Holly."

"What's up?"

"We've got a lead in the rape/murders," Lauren said.

"At a tire place?"

"We found a tire print with a deep cut in it at the crime scene yesterday," Hurd said, "and we got a report from Jimmy Weathers that Jim Bruno's cruiser had such a tire cut, but Bruno replaced the tire earlier today. Join us?"

Holly went with them into the tire store.

"Afternoon," a clerk behind the counter said. "What can I do you for, folks?"

Hurd flashed his badge. "Did Police Chief Bruno buy a replacement tire here today?"

"Sure did. Right before lunch."

"Can we see his old tire?"

"Sure, if we can find it. Follow me."

They followed the man through the back door into a shop, then out behind the building.

"The chief's old tire will be in this pile over here . . ." The man stopped; there was no pile of tires. "I'm sorry," he said. "Looks like we had a pickup this afternoon. The pile was here this morning." He called to one of the men in the shop. "Hey, Mike, did we get a pickup today?"

"'Bout an hour ago," Mike yelled back.

The man turned back to Hurd and his group. "We get a pickup from an outfit in Melbourne about once a week. They specialize in disposing of old tires, batteries, that sort of stuff."

"Can you give me the name and address of the company?" Hurd asked.

"Sure. I've got it inside." He went back into the front room, rummaged through a desk drawer and came up with a business card. "Here you go," he said, handing Hurd the card. Environmental Disposal Corporation. They're out beyond the Melbourne airport."

"Thank you," Hurd said. "Holly, you want to come with us?"

"I can't Hurd; I've got to cook dinner for a friend, and I haven't even been to the store yet. Good luck." Holly watched them drive away.

They found the EDC sign between the airport and the interstate, and Lauren turned onto a road leading toward a group of steel buildings. She parked the car in front of a building with a sign that said OFFICES, and she and Hurd went inside.

Hurd showed his badge. "May I speak with the manager, please?"

"I'll tell him you're here," the woman said. "Please have a seat."

They did, and ten minutes passed before a man in a shirt and tie appeared.

"I'm Charles Meeton," he said. "What can I do for you?"

"We need to find a tire that you picked up in Vero Beach today," Hurd said.

"Sir, we've got *lots* of tires here," Meeton said.

"This one would be on a truck that picked up tires at Vero Discount Tires an hour and a half, two hours ago," Hurd said.

A noise came from outside that practically drowned him out. "What's that?" Hurd asked.

"Just some of our equipment," Meeton said. "Alice, can I see the dispatcher's log?"

Alice handed him a clipboard.

"Let's see," Meeton said, "that would be Al Parker's truck. What number is Al Parker's truck, Alice?"

Alice consulted another clipboard. "Fifteen," she said.

Meeton handed her back his clipboard. "Come on, folks, let's take a look outside." He led the way out the way they had come in.

Outside, the noise was deafening. "There's Al's truck," Meeton shouted over the din, pointing. A hundred yards away, a dump truck was depositing its load in what appeared to be a steel-sided container about fifteen feet across. The three of them began to walk toward it.

Hurd fell in alongside Meeton. "What's making the noise?" he shouted.

Meeton shouted something back.

"What?"

"The shredder," Meeton yelled. "You see, we shred the tires, and then . . ."

But Hurd was already running toward the truck, waving his arms. "Stop!" he was yelling at the driver. "Stop!"

Lauren caught up with him as he was yelling at the driver. The man got into the truck and worked a lever, and the back of the dump truck went down. Lauren hopped onto the running board and looked into the truck bed: empty.

Hurd was yelling at Meeton again to shut off the shredder. Meeton walked from behind the dump truck, waved at the shredder operator and drew a finger across his throat. The man pulled a lever, and the noise stopped.

Hurd turned to Meeton. "We've got to get into the hopper," he said.

Meeton led the way up a rickety flight of stairs next to the hopper, and Hurd and Lauren followed. Lauren looked into the huge hopper and saw a dozen or so tires lying on a conveyor belt, ready to be fed into the shredder.

"There's a ladder over here," Meeton said. He flung a leg over the edge and found the top rung of a steel ladder bolted to the inside of the hopper. Hurd and Lauren followed him down.

"Your chances of finding a specific tire are slim and none," Meeton said, pointing to the remaining tires. "But you're welcome to look."

Lauren spoke up. "Bruno's tire would have gone onto the top of the pile," she said, "which means it would have been at the bottom of the truck bed. We've got a shot."

She and Hurd began picking up tires and looking at them. "Bruno's was a Michelin," Lauren
said. "I remember that."

Hurd was looking at the names on the tires and
pushing them aside. "Lots of Goodyears," he said.

Lauren looked, too. "Here's a Michelin," she
said. Hurd joined her as they rolled the tire so as
to see the whole tread. "Not this one," she said.

They continued to look through the remaining
tires but found nothing.

"Well," Hurd said, "it's gone." As they climbed
back to the top of the ladder, he pointed to the
rear of the shredder. There seemed to be no piece
of a tire larger than what would fit into his hand.

They stopped back on the stairs and Lauren
looked at the shredded rubber. "I guess we could
go through all that," she said.

"What's the point?" Hurd replied. "Even if we
found exactly the right piece, we couldn't prove it
came from Bruno's car."

"I guess you're right," she said. They were both
filthy from handling the old tires. "Is there some
place we can wash up?" she asked Meeton.

Lauren and Hurd were glum on the ride home.

36

Teddy Fay sat at his computer, looking at a digital map of Vero Beach. He found James Bruno's street. It was a few blocks from the local airport. Teddy printed out the map, then got into his car and followed it to Bruno's neighborhood.

He turned off Indian River Boulevard, drove past a large church and found himself in a neighborhood of ranch houses that appeared to have been built in the 1950s. They were well-kept, their lawns mown and their flower beds tended, but Teddy suspected that when demand for land grew in Vero, this would become a neighborhood of teardowns, with single houses bought up, razed and their lots combined to accommodate larger, more ostentatious houses.

Teddy found Bruno's house. There was no car in the carport, but Lauren had said that Bruno worked odd hours, so Teddy had no way of knowing when to expect Bruno to be at home. He drove past the house, then turned right at the corner and right again, to put him behind Bruno's property.

He found himself looking across a concrete drainage channel that had only a small stream of water flowing through it. After a tropical storm or a hurricane, Teddy reckoned, this would be a raging torrent.

On the other side of the hedge was a tall, ill-kempt hedge with a number of gaps in it that was the rear border of Bruno's property. Through the gaps, Teddy could see a weedy backyard and the back of the house, whose trim needed painting. This had all the earmarks of a rental, since the other houses on the street were so well kept, but it looked good to Teddy. It would have old hardware and easy locks.

It was late afternoon, and people were arriving home from work, a lot of them probably from the Piper aircraft factory only a few blocks away. A light airplane flew overhead, then made a turn toward the airport. There were lots of students studying at the flight safety school, which trained hundreds of new pilots every year.

Teddy drove away from the neighborhood and stopped at a large home-building supply store, where he bought a few things, then stowed the paper bag in the trunk of his car. Then he headed toward the Publix market on US-1 to pick up a few things for dinner.

Holly was coming out of the market, carrying two bags of groceries, when her cell phone vibrated. She set the bags down on the sidewalk and took the phone from its holster. "Hello?"

"It's Josh. Don't cook; I'm bringing dinner."

"Now you tell me? I'm just coming out of the market with a bunch of stuff."

"We'll save it for another time. Have you got red wine at home?"

"Yep."

"Then I'll see you at seven. Bye-bye."

Holly returned the phone to its holster and bent to pick up her bags. As she did a gray-haired man got out of a silver Toyota and came toward her across the street, heading for the market.

As he passed, he gave her a little smile, and she smiled back, as people in Vero and Orchid Beach usually did in their small-town neighborly way. Holly continued to her car.

Teddy had recognized her immediately but had not altered his course to the market. It was as good a time as any to see if she would recognize him. He passed her with a smile, and she smiled back. Inside the store, he stood behind a stack of canned goods and watched her through the window. She opened the rear door of her car—a Porsche Cayenne Turbo, he noted—put her groceries inside, got into the car and drove away without a second glance at the market.

That went well, he thought, and he wondered how a woman on an Agency salary could afford a car that cost around a hundred thousand dollars. Maybe he would look into that.

Holly drove home, let Daisy out onto the beach and put her groceries away. She showered and changed, then went downstairs to watch the news before Josh came.

Teddy put his groceries away and started a roast chicken. Then he went to his computer and found a meandering route through several cities, until he found an idle machine in San Diego, California. From there he logged on to the Agency mainframe, then navigated to personnel, where he opened Holly Barker's file.

He read through the file slowly, from Lance Cabot's initial letter of recommendation for her hiring, through her training at the Farm, where she had done exceptionally well in every category and had run up the highest pistol score in the history of the Agency. He made a note not to put himself in a position, as he once had, where she might have an opportunity to shoot at him. He felt lucky to have gotten away with the leg wound.

There had been a break in her training at the Farm, when she had been transferred to special duty in New York, under Cabot. He was clearly her rabbi at the Agency, and she had chosen him well, if, indeed, she had done the choosing. This was the period when Teddy had met her at the Metropolitan Opera, when he was disguised as an elderly Jewish gentleman, retired from the garment trade. A short time later, she had come uncomfortably close to him again, but he had managed to escape from the city.

He noted that she had recently been promoted to assistant deputy director, again under the aegis of Lance Cabot, and that she had, accordingly, received a substantial raise. Still, her Agency income didn't seem to support the purchase of an expensive German SUV with a 500-hp turbocharged engine.

He went to her original application and read, in fairly telegraphic form, of her progress through her army career and her hiring as chief of police in Orchid Beach. Then he came to her financial disclosure form.

"Ahhhh," he said aloud to himself. The woman had a substantial estate, amounting to nearly three million dollars, nearly all of it inherited from her fiancé, who had been killed as an innocent bystander in a bank robbery the day before her wedding. Teddy felt sorry that she had experienced such pain, but her personal wealth accounted for the ownership of the Cayenne as well as for her Orchid Beach house.

Teddy logged off the mainframe and closed his computer. What an interesting woman she was, he thought. It was a pity that he couldn't know her better. Still, from what he had just read, he knew more about her than most people did.

He went back into the kitchen, checked on the roasting chicken, and began preparing the rest of their dinner.

He couldn't do what he wanted to tonight, because Lauren would be there. Jim Bruno would have to wait a little.

37

Lance Cabot was at his desk in the early morning when there was a rap at his door. His secretary was not in yet, and no one was screening his visitors. "Come in," he said.

The door opened slightly and the disheveled head of the computer geek who had visited him before appeared. "Got a second?"

"What is it?" Lance asked, not a little annoyed. He couldn't remember the kid's name, but he thought he had solved his problem.

"Our visitor returned to the mainframe early last evening," he said, "this time via a chain of computers around the country ending in San Diego."

"And?"

"And he got into Holly Barker's personnel records."

This stopped Lance in his tracks. "Are you sure about this?" he asked, giving himself time to think.

"Absolutely. I still haven't been able to track him back to a specific computer, but I think he may be in the state of Florida."

"What was it he was looking for last time?"

"Information on the background of a retired army colonel, James Bruno. Also, he accessed his driver's license record in Florida."

"Can you set some sort of trap for him?"

"I already have; when I came in this morning I had an alert from the mainframe waiting on my work station."

"But you can't track him to a specific computer?"

"That's hard. The guy—or girl—is very smart. If he continued to use the same computer chain, that would make it a lot easier, but both times I discovered him he had created a new chain. It's like he's making big geographical leaps around the country every time he logs on."

"And to stop him we'd have to change all the log-on codes?"

"Right. And circulate the new codes to every authorized Agency employee around the world, in a highly secure manner."

"And that's a big job."

"It is, and every time we do something like that we run the risk of opening new security breaches, of having the codes fall into the hands of some hacker lurking out there."

"When was the last time the codes were changed?"

"Six years ago. We had teething problems, of course, but the mainframe has remained secure since we worked those out. If we issue new codes, we'll have to start all over again."

Shit, Lance thought. He stared at the desk in front of him.

"If I could make a suggestion?" the kid said.

"Go ahead."

"This guy has not shown any evil intent with these intrusions; he's just looking for information. It might make sense to let him continue and hope that he'll make a mistake that will make it easier to nail him. I've got the alert on the mainframe, and if he makes a more threatening move, then we can act on a code change."

Lance was pleased to have a way out of this mess. "All right, do that, but every time he logs on I want to know what he's looking at."

"I'll see that you do," the kid said. He gave a little wave and left, closing the door behind him.

Lance was still thinking, though. This intruder had made two visits to the mainframe, both looking for information about Holly, and he didn't like that. Of course, it could be somebody from Holly's past: an old lover, maybe, who had worked at the Agency and still harbored a crush on her. But he kept returning to another possibility: Teddy Fay.

Lance had really begun to believe the man was dead; certainly that was what he had repeatedly told the director, though she still seemed skeptical. To be frank with himself, he didn't care if Teddy was alive and well as long as he didn't call attention to himself and embarrass everybody, particularly himself but up to and including the director and her husband, President Will Lee.

Lance turned to his phone and pressed a speed-dial number; then he stared at the screen.

Holly was jarred awake by the ringing phone. She rolled over and looked at the bedside clock: seven fifteen. Then she realized the television screen at the foot of her bed had come alive, and Lance was staring at her—and at Josh, who had not yet woken up.

"Call me back on your secure line," Lance said, "as soon as you can be alone."

Josh woke up. "Huh?"

"It's nothing. Go back to sleep," Holly said. She grabbed the remote and switched off the TV.

"I heard a man's voice," Josh said.

"No, you didn't," Holly replied, placing a hand on his forehead and pushing down. "Go back to sleep."

She got out of bed, threw on a shirt and jeans and went downstairs to her Agency cubbyhole. She tapped in the code that opened the door, then went inside, closed the door behind her and logged on to her computer. A few keystrokes later, she had Lance on the screen.

"I'm here," she said.

"Sorry to wake you; something odd has come up."

"Go ahead."

"One of those geeks in computer services has come to me twice, now, with the news that someone outside the Agency has managed to log on to the mainframe, at least twice."

"Yes?"

"Yes. Of course, he may have logged on before, but he has been caught at it only twice."

"Who is it?"

"Unknown. He creates a sort of channel through several computers around the country, then logs on from one of them, so we haven't been able to pinpoint his location."

"What has he been doing on the mainframe?"

"Both times we've caught him he's been looking at information about you."

"Me?"

"Yes. Is there some old lover of yours out there who used to be Agency who might still be obsessed with you?"

"No. I don't know anybody who fits that description, especially the obsession part. What did he want to know about me, do you think?"

"The first time, he was looking up background information on one Colonel James Bruno."

"What kind of information?"

"The trial record of his court-martial and Bruno's Florida driver's license application."

"Bruno is a suspect in the series of rapes and murders we've been having here," Holly said. "The search could be related to that."

"The other time we caught him, he went into your personnel records."

"Holy shit," Holly said involuntarily.

"Exactly. Who would want to do that?"

"I can't imagine," Holly said.

"I can imagine somebody who might be just a tiny bit obsessed with you."

"Enlighten me, please."

"You attended the opera with him once, and you may have put a bullet in him at one point. Let's not mention any names."

Holly winced. "You say you haven't been able to pin down his location?"

"Not yet. He may be on the move, but the last time, our geek thought he might be somewhere in Florida."

"You think he might be looking for revenge?"

"Possibly, but he wouldn't need your personnel file for that; he'd just find you and kill you."

"Well, yes. Maybe he hasn't gotten over our last encounter."

"Perhaps not, but I don't have any sense that you're in any real danger. You might keep an eye out for him, though, or for someone who might be him."

"I take your point."

"Then go armed and be careful."

"I'll do that," Holly replied.

The screen went blank. Holly shut down the computer and left the little office. She walked into the kitchen to find Josh, naked, making coffee.

He jumped. "Where did you come from?"

"I was just on the phone."

"Where? I couldn't hear you."

"In a secret place," she said. "You look very nice."

"Oh, no, you don't," he said, backing away. "I've got to get to work."

"Oh, you have some time," she said, advancing on him.

38

Jimmy Weathers was sitting at his desk when Chief Bruno appeared in his cubicle door. "Good morning, Chief," he said.

"Somebody has vandalized my car," Bruno said.

"How's that, Chief?"

"Somebody cut one of my tires; I had to have it replaced yesterday."

"Why do you think it was a vandal?" Jimmy asked. "Couldn't you just have run over something?"

"It wasn't that kind of damage; it was a clean cut or, rather, two clean cuts. The tire would have blown as soon as I ran over a bump of some sort, like a pothole, and if I had been driving fast—say, in a pursuit—I could have been killed or seriously injured."

"But why would anybody cut your tire, Chief?"

"I don't know; I'm asking you for ideas."

"I'm afraid I don't have a clue," Jimmy replied.

"Are you sure?"

"I'm sure, Chief. I don't know anybody who would want to cause you harm."

"What about the Cade girl?" Bruno asked.

"Lauren? Why would she . . ."

"Oh, come on, Weathers. You know about the false charges she brought against me."

Jimmy colored slightly and decided not to deny it. "I just don't think Lauren is the type to do that," he said finally.

"She's a woman, isn't she? A woman with an imagined grievance?"

"I guess you could put a guard on your car," Jimmy said.

"We don't have enough manpower as it is," Bruno said.

"Well, we have a surveillance camera pointed at the back door. I guess you could aim it at the parking lot instead."

"Now that's a damn good idea, Jimmy," Bruno said. "Do it now." He walked away.

Jimmy sighed. Why hadn't he just kept his mouth shut? It was a fault of his that, around anyone of authority, he tended to talk too much. He got up from his desk, walked downstairs to the basement and found a ladder. He left the building through the outside basement door and set up the ladder on the back porch of the building; then he turned the camera so that it was pointing directly at Bruno's cruiser.

He was about to get down from the ladder when he saw a silver Toyota across the street pull out of a parking spot and drive away. The driver looked like that man he and Lauren had questioned— Smithson, his name was.

Jimmy climbed back down the ladder, stowed it in the basement and went upstairs again. He went to Bruno's office. "Chief, I turned the camera so that it points at your car."

"Let me see," Bruno said, turning to his computer. He tapped a few keys and a grid of images appeared on his screen, views of a dozen cameras set up inside and outside the building. "Yeah, there it is. What kind of tape loop do we have?"

"It's either six or eight hours, I think," Jimmy replied. "You'd have to call our tech guy for an accurate answer on that."

"Good work, Jimmy. Thanks." Bruno turned back to his desk.

Jimmy returned to his cubicle and sat, thinking about the tire and Bruno's reaction to it. His phone rang. "Detective Weathers," he said.

"Hi, it's Lauren."

"Hi, Lauren."

"Bruno had the tire changed before we could get to it and take a cast," she said.

"Yeah, he just told me. He noticed the cut and

was afraid he'd have a blowout at speed. Now he thinks vandals are persecuting him. He made me turn the back door surveillance camera toward his car, so he can watch it."

"Who does he think the vandals are?" she asked.

"You."

"Me? He thinks I cut his tire?"

"He mentioned it, but I'm not sure he really believes that. He's just getting paranoid."

"That's going to make it harder for us to nail him," Lauren said.

"Yeah, I guess it will make him more careful, but if he's the guy, he's already being real careful; we still don't have anything on him."

"No, we don't. But he's going to make a mistake eventually," Lauren said. "I just hope nobody else dies before he does."

"So do I," Jimmy replied. He took a deep breath. "Hey, uh, Lauren, would you like to . . . have dinner sometime?"

"Thanks, Jimmy," she said, "but I'm seeing somebody, and he's taking all my time."

"Oh, okay. Thanks anyway."

"Call me if you get any more ideas," Lauren said. "See you." She hung up. Oh, God, she thought, how's he going to take that?

39

Lauren was about to leave for the day when her phone rang. "Lauren Cade."

"Hi, it's Holly Barker."

"Hi, Holly."

"How'd your search for Bruno's tire go?"

"Not well," Lauren replied. She told Holly about the search at the tire recycling plant.

"That's a shame," Holly said. "Maybe if I'd gone with you we would have had a better chance to find the tire before it got sucked into that machine."

"Don't beat yourself up, Holly; it just didn't work out."

"Have you got anything else on Bruno?"

"Not a thing, nor on anyone else, either."

"Lauren, you remember the printout of those clippings and the juvenile record on Bruno I gave you?"

"Sure, I've still got them."

"Please shred them. They came from an Agency computer, and I don't want anyone else to see them. It's not like they're evidence; they're just background for you and Hurd."

"Sure, I'll do that right away."

"Something else, Lauren: has anyone else shown you anything that might have come from a CIA computer file?"

"No, in fact, no one has shown me anything from any computer file, except you."

"If anyone shows you anything that you think might come from an Agency file, will you call me immediately, please?"

"Sure. What's this about, Holly?"

"Someone is logging on to the Agency's computer system and extracting material on Bruno and me."

"Together or separately?"

"Both, and I've got to put a stop to that if I can figure out who's doing it."

"Doesn't the Agency have a lot of security stuff you'd have to go through to get into a computer?"

"Yes, a lot."

"Well, I don't think anyone I know would have that kind of expertise," Lauren said. "Certainly not anyone connected with the state police."

"That's what I thought; I'm just alerting you to the possibility."

"I'll keep an ear to the ground, sure."

"Thanks, Lauren."

"Say, you're seeing that doctor at the hospital, aren't you?"

"Yes, Josh Harmon."

"I've got a new boyfriend, too, and he's quite a cook. Why don't the four of us have dinner together sometime soon?"

"That sounds like fun, Lauren. Let me know where and when."

"I'll check with Jack and let you know."

"Bye-bye, then."

Lauren found Holly's computer files and shredded them, then straightened her desk, locked it and headed for Teddy's.

Teddy had a rib roast in the oven when Lauren arrived. He fixed them a drink, and they relaxed in the living room.

"Good day today?" he asked.

"No. We're back to square one after the episode with the tire."

"No suspects other than Bruno?"

"Not a one. I know he's doing this, but he's been very, very careful not to leave any usable evidence. I wish the man had a conscience; he'd blow his own brains out."

Teddy laughed. "I wouldn't count on that."

"Oh, Jack, I have this friend—well, acquaintance—named Holly Barker, who's in town for a while, and she's seeing a doctor in the emergency room at the hospital. Why don't we invite the two of them over for dinner one night soon?"

Teddy drew in a quick breath. "I'm not sure I want to share you with anybody just yet."

She dug him in the ribs. "Oh, come on. It'll do us both good to socialize a little."

"All right," Teddy said. "When do you want to do it?"

"How about this weekend? Saturday? I'll help in the kitchen."

"That's fine with me," Teddy said, his mind racing.

"Oh, good," she said, kissing him. "Holly's a great girl. I knew her in the army; then she was chief of police here, and now she does something with the CIA."

"What on earth is she doing here?"

"She's just taking her vacation; she has a house here, from when she was chief."

"And her boyfriend?"

"His name is Josh Harmon; he's a doctor and that's about all I know about him."

"Okay." Teddy took a deep breath. "There's something I want to talk to you about."

"Shoot."

"I think this relationship is going really well. How about you?"

"Really well," she said, kissing him.

"Something you said awhile back stuck in my mind: you said you hated the hot summers in Florida, that you'd like to live somewhere with a more even climate?"

"Did I?"

"Yes. Were you serious about that?"

"Well, it's not like I was contemplating moving."

"Let me tell you about two places I've thought about," Teddy said. "One is Santa Fe, New Mexico. Have you ever been there?"

"No, but I've heard good things about it."

"It has a warm summer but no humidity; it's seven thousand feet up in the mountains; the winter is cold but, again, dry, so it's not oppressive. It's the kind of weather where you can sit in a hot tub and let the snowflakes fall on your face."

"Sounds wonderful."

"The other place is San Diego, California, specifically La Jolla, a suburb, on the Pacific. The weather is delightful year-round: stays in the seventies, pretty much."

"Again, it sounds wonderful. Are you thinking about moving, Jack?"

"Yes," Teddy said, "but only if I can take you with me."

She laughed. "That's a pretty good offer. Are you serious or just kidding?"

"I'm not kidding, sweetheart."

"Wow. And how are we going to afford this? Can I get a police job out West?"

"Only if you want to. I'm very well off, so you don't have to work."

"That's very tempting," she said.

"There's no rush," Teddy said. "Think about it, and if it's what you want, well, when you get these murders cleared, we could just take off. I've got the airplane, remember?"

"I remember." She gave him a long kiss. "You're a very, very nice man, Jack."

"Thank you, ma'am," Teddy replied. He went back to the kitchen to take a look at his roast and start the vegetables. He had been contemplating telling her who he was but best not to lay too much on her all at once. Maybe best never to tell her who he once was before he was Jack Smithson.

40

Teddy woke up a little after two a.m. Lauren was breathing deeply beside him. She never woke up in the night. He rolled gently out of bed, got into the dark clothes he had left on a chair, took a small bag he had packed and left the house. He had parked farther away from the house than usual, so the sound of the cranking engine would not wake Lauren.

He drove at the speed limit, so as not to attract the attention of the local police, who were on the lookout for lone males driving late at night, and soon he was driving past the big church and into the quiet residential neighborhood where James Bruno lived. He drove slowly past the house, where he saw Bruno's cruiser parked in the driveway and no lights on in the house.

Teddy switched off his headlights and circled the block, looking for lights in the neighboring houses. He saw none. He parked behind Bruno's house, across the concrete drainage ditch and sat quietly in the car for a moment, looking for lights. None.

He popped the trunk and got out of the car. He retrieved the paper bag from the home store and the small bag he had packed, then crossed the drainage ditch, jumping across the narrow stream to keep his feet dry. He walked to the hedge at the rear of Bruno's property and passed through one of the gaps where a plant had been allowed to die.

He stopped just inside the hedge and opened the paper bag. He withdrew the painter's soft paper socks he had bought and put them on his feet, tucking his trousers into them, then he put on a paper hairnet and pulled on a pair of latex gloves. He took the .22-caliber semiautomatic pistol from the bag, racked the slide and secured the safety, then he tucked the weapon into his belt. He left his bag and the paper bag beside the hedge and walked slowly toward the house.

He looked through the back door into the kitchen and saw a night-light glowing, probably in the house's central hallway. He used a strip of flexible plastic to pop the cheap lock on the kitchen door, then, very slowly, he opened it and let himself into the house, leaving the door ajar.

As he expected, there was no security system in

the old ranch house, and he stood still in the kitchen for two minutes, listening for any sound. Finally, he walked into the hallway, found the night-light and unplugged it; then he stood still for another two minutes to allow his eyes to become accustomed to the darkness.

There was just enough light coming into the house from a streetlamp out front to allow him to move around with confidence, and he made his way to the rear, where he thought the master bedroom would be. He stopped again to listen and heard a gentle, regular snoring coming from the rear room. He walked to the door and stepped inside.

James Bruno lay on his back, soundly asleep, snoring. Teddy walked toward him and stopped, perhaps four feet away, to get a better look at him. Then he saw the gun.

It was a 9-mm Glock, and it lay on the bedside table in its holster. This was an unexpected benefit; he wouldn't need the .22. Teddy lifted the holster and gun slowly from the table, tucked the holster under his arm and, very slowly, pulled the Glock free. He replaced the holster on the bedside table next to a half-empty bottle of Famous Grouse Scotch whiskey and an empty glass.

Gently, he eased the pistol's slide back far enough to ascertain the presence of a cartridge in the chamber; then he eased it closed. He took a step closer to Bruno, and a board squeaked under his foot. Bruno stopped snoring and made a noise. Teddy waited patiently for him to fall fully asleep again.

Soon Bruno resumed snoring. Teddy held the pistol in his left, gloved hand and eased it slowly into position a fraction of an inch from Bruno's open mouth. He aimed carefully, not wishing to strike a tooth or a lip, then fired a single shot.

Bruno made a jerking movement and then relaxed. The shot had passed through his mouth, then severed the spine at the neck before passing into the pillow beneath his head.

Teddy held his position for just a moment, then he lifted Bruno's right hand, rubbed the pistol on his hand and forearm to deposit gunshot residue there, then dropped the weapon. It landed on Bruno's upper chest and slid off his body to the floor beside the bed.

Now Teddy switched on a small flashlight and had a look around the room, not seeing what he was looking for. He left the room and walked quickly down the hall, finding a small den with a desk. The center drawer yielded what Teddy was seeking: a medical insurance card that bore a sample of Bruno's signature and a stack of printed letterheads.

He took a sheet of stationery from the desk drawer, closed the drawer and then fed the paper

into a portable typewriter on the desktop. He held
the flashlight in his mouth, thought for a moment,
then typed:

> *To whom it may concern:*
>
> *I can't do this anymore. It is enough. The
> women were all innocent; that's what attracted
> me to them. I've punished enough, and now I
> will end this once and for all.*

Teddy typed the date at the bottom, then took the
paper from the typewriter and looked closely at the
signature on the card. He was a good forger, and
he didn't even need to practice. He signed the letter with a pen from the desk drawer and left it on
the desk.

He visited the bedroom once more to be sure
everything was in order; then he went back to the
kitchen and left the house, first locking and closing
the door.

At the hedge, he shucked off the paper socks,
hairnet and latex gloves; put them into the paper
bag; picked up his own small bag and returned to
the car. Halfway across town he came to a con-
struction Dumpster and deposited the paper bag
there.

He was at home and in bed with Lauren slightly
less than an hour after he left.

*   *   *

They both woke early, as usual. "Did you sleep well?" he asked.

"Like a baby," she said.

"So did I," he replied.

41

Detective Jimmy Weathers was at his desk early, as usual. He had been there only a moment when his phone rang.

"Detective Weathers."

"Jimmy, it's Lauren Cade."

"Good morning, Lauren."

"We have another one."

"Where?"

"On the Orchid Island golf course, north of Vero Beach, specifically, in a sand bunker beside the fourth fairway."

"I'm on my way," Jimmy said. He got his coat on and walked toward the back door, passing the desk of Chief Bruno's secretary. "When the chief comes in, will you tell him that we've had another woman murdered, and I'm at the crime scene? I'll call him when I'm done there and let him know the details."

"Oh, God, not another one," the woman replied. "I'll tell him. He has an interview here at nine with a candidate for the deputy chief's job."

Jimmy got into his car and drove out to the Orchid Island Club, a beautiful gated community out past the Disney Resort. He showed his badge at the gate and was waved through. He had played golf here once with Bruno, who was a nonresident member, and he remembered that he could drive nearly all the way to the fourth tee without getting on the grass. He parked near the tee and walked the rest of the way toward a group standing around a bunker on the left-hand side of the fairway.

"Good morning," he said as he walked up to Lauren.

"Not so good," she said, nodding toward the naked corpse, posed in a kneeling position in the sand.

Jimmy held his position, not wanting to interfere with the forensics people and the ME, who were already in the bunker. "Looks a lot like the last one, only without the car."

"Yeah, and we haven't found her car yet. They've mostly been left in or near their cars. I can't figure out how he got the body onto the golf course. He would have had to drive through the main gate, wouldn't he?"

"No, there's a second gate off Route Five Ten

that members can enter with a pass card." He paused for a moment. "Bruno is a member here."

"Ahh," she said.

There was a stand of tall evergreen trees behind the bunker, and a car could be seen passing behind them. "But that's not how he got the body here," Jimmy said, pointing. "There's a road behind the trees there that runs alongside the golf course of the Windsor development, which is right next door. There's a fence, but I guess he could get over that."

"That would account for some cuts and scrapes on the body," Lauren said.

"I guess it would," Jimmy replied.

The ME stood up from his work and came over to where they stood. "Death by strangulation, probably around midnight last night. Raped anally and vaginally, like the others. I'm supposing she was doped first, like the others."

Lauren nodded. "You find anything that might help us?" she asked one of the crime lab people.

"Not a thing," the man said. He pointed to a rake. "There's a rake in every bunker he could use to smooth over the whole area around the body and, of course, his tracks as he left."

"Shit," Lauren said.

Jimmy spent an hour with Lauren, walking the area around the bunker and checking along the fence behind the trees, but they found nothing else.

Jimmy was walking with Lauren back to where the cars were parked when his cell phone vibrated. "Hello?"

It was Bruno's secretary. "Jimmy, the chief hasn't shown up for his interview, and he's an hour late. That's unlike him, and he's not answering either his home phone or his cell phone, and he always has that cell phone with him. I'm worried that he might have had a heart attack or something. Would you swing by his house and see if he's there?"

"Sure, I will," Jimmy replied. "See you later, Lauren; I've got to check by Bruno's house and see if he's all right; he's late for a meeting, and he can't be found."

"Well, we can always hope, can't we? If you find him, question him about his whereabouts last night, and see if he has an alibi."

"Will do," Jimmy replied. He got into his car and headed for Bruno's neighborhood.

Bruno's car was in the driveway, so why wasn't he answering his phones? Jimmy got out of his car and rang the doorbell. He waited a moment, then tried the knob. The door was unlocked; he pushed it open and stuck his head inside. "Chief Bruno?" he called out. "It's Jimmy." He yelled again, but got no response, so he let himself into the house.

He walked down the central hall a few paces and

called out again; then he looked into the study and saw a note on the desk. He walked over and read it without touching it. "Uh-oh," he said aloud.

He left the room as he found it and walked down the hall to the rear bedroom. Bruno was lying peacefully in bed, and there was a Glock on the floor beside him. Jimmy walked over to Bruno and looked into his face. "My God," he said.

He turned and walked out of the house and to his car. Once there he got out his cell phone and called Lauren Cade.

"Sergeant Cade."

"This is Jimmy, Lauren. Bruno is dead in his house. Would you do me a favor and call the ME and the criminalist and bring them over here?" He gave her the address. "Maybe Hurd might like to be here, too."

"Will do, Jimmy, and I'm on my way."

Jimmy hung up and opened the trunk of his car. He lifted the lid over the spare tire and removed a paper bag, then closed the lid again. He took a roll of yellow crime-scene tape from the trunk and walked back to the house. He went inside and walked down the hall to Bruno's bedroom, then stood and looked around for a moment. He went to a closet and opened the sliding door. Bruno's uniforms and some civilian clothes hung neatly inside. On the top shelf was a shoe box.

Jimmy put on some latex gloves and took down

the shoe box, which was half full of some old photographs, some showing Bruno in army uniform. Jimmy opened the paper bag he had brought and shook the contents into the shoe box, then put the top on, replaced it on the shelf and put the wadded paper bag in his pocket.

He went back outside and taped the entrance to the house, then ran some more tape across the driveway between two trees. He went around to the rear of the house and taped the rear entrance as well, depositing the paper bag in his pocket in a garbage can by the door, under some beer cans. Then he walked carefully around the backyard, checking the ground.

He returned to the front yard in time to greet Lauren, who was followed shortly by the ME and the criminalist.

"Hurd's on his way," Lauren said.

Jimmy told them of his arrival at the house and the discovery of the body. "I didn't touch anything," he said, "so we've got a good crime scene here. Come inside, and I'll walk you through where I was."

He led them to the study and pointed out the note on the desk, next to the typewriter. "Read that," he said, then waited while they did. "The bedroom is down the hall to your left. I walked inside, looked at the body and walked around the bedroom. There's a Glock on the floor beside the bed and a shell casing on the floor between the bed and the chest of drawers. I'll wait here while you do your work."

Lauren looked into the room from the door but did not enter. "He ate his gun?"

"Looks that way," Jimmy said. "Come on, let's have a seat in the living room while they do their thing."

As they sat down, Hurd Wallace entered the house, and Lauren briefed him while Jimmy called police headquarters and told the secretary what had happened.

"I guess you're in charge, then, Jimmy," she said. "Chief Bruno never got around to hiring a deputy chief, and you're the senior officer. You better call the city council people and let them know what's happened."

"All right, I will."

Hurd spoke up. "We don't need a search warrant now, so let's go through this place thoroughly."

"What are we looking for, Hurd?" Jimmy asked.

"Any evidence that might connect Bruno to these murders. Jimmy, you take the kitchen; Lauren, you take the bedroom."

"I don't want to go in there, Hurd," Lauren said. "I'll take the study and the second guest room."

"All right," Hurd said, "I'll take Bruno's bedroom as soon as the body is out of there."

42

Jimmy went into the kitchen and carefully searched every cabinet, the pantry and the refrigerator; then he walked back into the hallway.

Lauren was coming out of the study. "Nothing I could find in there," she said, "except the suicide note."

They stood back and allowed the ME and a forensics guy to wheel the corpse past on a gurney.

"I'll be right back and give you my preliminary," the ME said.

Hurd, Lauren and Jimmy waited in the hallway. "What did you find?" Hurd asked.

"Nothing in the study, except the suicide note," Lauren said.

"The only thing of any significance in the kitchen was half a case of Famous Grouse Scotch and a refrigerator with at least a case of beer in it. Looks like Bruno was drinking a lot."

"There's half a bottle of Scotch and a glass on the bedside table," Hurd said.

The ME returned. "All right, death was by a single gunshot wound through the mouth, apparently self-inflicted; Forensics found the slug in the pillow, and he's taken charge of the gun, the shell casing and the slug. He'll run ballistics on all that today. I found some Ambien, a sleeping pill, in the bathroom medicine chest, one left from a prescription of twenty-five, and there's a booze bottle by the bed, so my guess is I'll find both of those things in the stomach contents."

"Can you do the Bruno autopsy first, before the woman victim?" Hurd asked.

"If you like."

"Call me when you're done," Hurd said.

"Call me, too," Jimmy added. The ME left.

"Okay, time for the bedroom," Hurd said. "Lauren, you can wait in the living room; Jimmy, with me." He led the way into the bedroom.

"I'll take the chest of drawers," Jimmy said.

"All right."

Jimmy began opening drawers and emptying the contents of each, one at a time, on top of the chest, returning them to the drawer after his search. He was on the bottom drawer when Hurd, who was searching the closet, spoke up.

"Jimmy, I've got something here," he said. "Lauren, come in here!" he yelled.

Lauren came to the door. "I don't want to come in there."

"Get your ass in here," Hurd said quietly. "I want you to witness this." He set an open shoe box on the bed. "I found this on the closet shelf."

Jimmy and Lauren came in close and watched.

"Give me an evidence bag," Hurd said. "No, two, and big ones."

Lauren opened her large purse and produced the plastic bags.

"We've got two, four, six pairs of women's panties," Hurd said, dropping them one at a time into an evidence bag. "We'll want DNA from those." He held up something the size of a staple gun with a small bottle attached to it. "And we've got a vaccination gun with a chemical attached." He dropped it into the second bag, then emptied the shoe box onto the bed. "Nothing else but some old photographs," Hurd said, poking through them. Finally, he returned them to the shoe box and replaced the cover.

"Ten to one, that's a Rohypnol solution in the plastic bottle attached to the gun," Lauren said.

"Right," Hurd said. "Jimmy, we're going to take charge of this evidence. We'll log in everything, then photograph it all, test the panties for DNA matches with the victims, check the serial number on the vaccination gun against hospital records, then, since you're the lead investigator, return it all to you to lock up in your evidence room."

"That's fine with me, Hurd," Jimmy said.

Hurd took a small evidence bag from his pocket. "I'll bag the suicide note. I think we're done here for the moment."

"Hurd," Jimmy said, "We should get out a press release at some point."

"Let's wait for the autopsy, the ballistics and the DNA tests to be completed," Hurd said. "I'll write something up and fax it to you for your approval before I release it."

"All right," Jimmy said.

"One more thing," Hurd said. "You've both seen everything I've seen. Did either of you find any indication that this might be a homicide, instead of a suicide?"

"No," Lauren said.

"Me, neither," Jimmy added. "It all seems straightforward."

"Okay," Hurd said, "the letter gives us his guilty conscience over the murders as a motive for suicide; he apparently took Ambien and booze, then shot himself with his service pistol. The women's underwear and the vaccination gun are corroborating evidence. Anything to add?"

"No," Lauren said.

"No," Jimmy said.

"God," Hurd said. "We might have just saved

that last woman's life, if we'd gotten to that tire recycling plant in time."

"We did everything we could, Hurd," Lauren said. "It was the delay in getting the search warrant that made us late, so the fault lies with the judge, if anybody, certainly not with us."

"I guess you're right," Hurd said. "Lauren, post some do-not-enter notices on the front and rear doors, and let's get out of here."

Jimmy drove back to police headquarters. The watch was changing, so most of the force roster was in the squad room.

"Let me have your attention," he shouted. Everybody got quiet. "The information I'm about to give you is not for public consumption until you read it in the papers or see it on TV. Everybody got that?"

There were murmurs of assent.

"A couple of hours ago I was at a crime scene out at Orchid Island, where another female victim was found, left in a sand trap. While I was there, Gladys called me and told me the chief was an hour late for a meeting and he wasn't answering his phones, and she asked me to go to his house and see if he was all right.

"I found the chief lying in bed, dead, with his Glock on the floor beside him. I summoned the ME and a rep from Forensics and Hurd Wallace and Lauren Cade, too. We found a suicide note, and Hurd found a box of stuff on a closet shelf that included half a dozen pairs of women's panties and a vaccination gun, like the one stolen from the hospital. It appears from the available evidence that the chief was the murderer of all these women who have been found dead lately."

Everybody started to talk at once.

"Quiet!" Jimmy said. "Like I said before, this is not for public consumption until it hits the papers. The chief never appointed a deputy chief, so for the moment, because I'm the senior officer here, I'm acting chief until the city council does something official. They've already been notified of what's happened.

"I don't want to answer any questions right now. You've been told everything I know, so let's get on with the watch change and start doing our jobs again. Thank you."

Jimmy walked back to Bruno's office. "Gladys," he called, "please come in here. I'm going to search the chief's office, and I want a witness."

Gladys came in and stood by the door. Jimmy searched the desk and the cupboards and didn't find anything relevant to the murders, except a nearly empty bottle of Famous Grouse Scotch in a bottom desk drawer.

"Thank you, Gladys. That's it," Jimmy said. "Please close the door behind you."

Gladys left, and Jimmy sat down behind Bruno's desk. He was the chief now, by God, and Bruno was dead, with all the murders hung around his neck. The suicide note was a fake, and he figured Lauren Cade or Holly Barker for having shot Bruno, but he wasn't about to pursue that. This was the best day of his life.

43

It was Holly's last day of training on the Malibu, and she was now certified to pilot her new airplane. She drove home, excited, ready to grill steaks with Josh, and as soon as she walked through the door she saw the light on the phone flashing. She pressed the voice-mail button on the phone and listened.

"Holly, it's Lauren. Please call me on my cell as soon as you get this message. Something good has happened."

Holly dialed the number.

"Holly?"

"Yep."

"I've got good news and good news."

"Tell me the good news first."

"Bruno is dead; he ate his gun."

Holly had to sit down. "I don't know what to say."

"Then let me tell you the good news: he left a suicide note confessing to the murders of the women."

Holly took a deep breath. "I'm just flabbergasted, Lauren."

"There's more: we searched his house and found six pairs of women's panties in a shoe box in a closet—they're being tested for DNA matches with the victims now—and a vaccination gun that matches the serial number of the one stolen from the hospital."

"I would call that a slam dunk," Holly said. "Who found the body?"

"Jimmy Weathers. I forgot to tell you the bad news." Lauren told her about the latest victim and about the phone call asking Jimmy to check on Bruno. "He found him dead in bed, with half a bottle of Scotch on the bedside table. The autopsy results have just come in: he had Ambien and six ounces of Scotch in his stomach, and the ballistics are good for his service pistol. All we need are the DNA results on the panties, and they're due any minute. Hang on a second." Lauren spoke with somebody else, then came back on the line. "The results are in: the DNA results match the victims. No semen present, though."

"Then Bruno is cooked as well as dead. Nice of him to save the state of Florida the trouble, wasn't it?"

"It sure was. I can't remember when I've been so happy. It's like the world has been lifted from my shoulders. Don't tell anybody I said this, but I've thought more than once about killing him myself, and if I'd had an opportunity, I don't know if I could have answered for myself."

"You deserve to be happy, Lauren. Congratulations on clearing the murders, and congratulate Hurd for me, too, will you?"

"I sure will. I've gotta run, now. Oh, can you and Josh join Jack and me for dinner at his house Saturday at seven thirty?"

"I think so. I'll ask Josh and confirm with you."

"Bye-bye."

Holly was salting the steaks and making a salad when Josh arrived. "Hey," she said, accepting a kiss. "Drink?"

"I'll make it; you're busy," he replied. "You seem a little dazed. Something wrong, or is it just the bourbon?"

"No, everything is good," she said. She gave him the details of Bruno's death and the clearing of the murders.

"That's fabulous news!" Josh said. "But you don't seem all that happy about it."

"It's just that it's all too good to be true," Holly said. "It's too neat a package."

"Bitch, bitch, bitch," Josh said.

"I know."

"Sometimes things just work out the way they should," he said. "I mean, Bruno was always the suspect, wasn't he?"

"Yes, but if he was the murderer, he was getting away with it, and I don't see him killing himself because of an attack of conscience. In my experience of him, he didn't have a conscience."

"You have a counterhypothesis?"

Holly picked up the phone and dialed Lauren again.

"Hi, Holly."

"A question, Lauren."

"Okay."

"What was the time of death on the last victim?"

"Midnight to four a.m."

"And what was the time of death on Bruno?"

"Two a.m. to six a.m."

"And what time did Jimmy get the call about Bruno not showing for work?"

"A little after ten a.m."

"And what time did you get to Bruno's house?"

"About ten thirty."

"So how long would Jimmy have been at Bruno's house when you got there?"

"Ten minutes, maybe."

"Okay, that's all I wanted to know."

"You were thinking Jimmy might have offed Bruno?"

"I just wanted to eliminate the possibility, and the time line does that. Oh, who found the panties and the vaccination gun?"

"Hurd. I didn't want to go into Bruno's bedroom, so he and Jimmy were searching it. Hurd called me in to witness the evidence find."

"That clears up my questions, then. Thanks, Lauren."

"Bye-bye, Holly. See you Saturday."

"Hang on a second, Lauren." Holly turned to Josh. "Lauren has invited us to dinner at her boyfriend's house on Saturday night. You available?"

"I'll have to switch a shift, but that shouldn't be a problem."

"Lauren, we're good for dinner. You said seven thirty?"

"Yep. I'll give you the address."

Holly wrote it down. "And Jack's last name?"

"Smithson."

"See you Saturday at seven thirty." Holly hung up.

"You look happier," Josh said.

"Lauren had the right answers to my questions."

"I heard the questions; what did the answers prove?"

"That Jimmy Weathers couldn't have killed

Bruno." She explained the time line and the details of Jimmy's finding Bruno's body.

"Jimmy's the cop I met at the hospital, right?"

"Right."

"And you thought Jimmy might have killed Bruno?"

"Not really. I was just covering all the bases, eliminating Jimmy as a suspect; it's how cops think."

"Interesting," Josh said. "Jimmy didn't have time to kill him and forge a suicide note."

"That's it."

"But . . ."

"But what?"

"He had time to hide the panties and the vaccination gun, didn't he?"

"You're thinking that Jimmy could have murdered the women?"

"Can you eliminate him as a suspect in the women's murders?"

"I see your point," Holly said, "but something else eliminates him as a suspect in those crimes."

"What?"

"Bruno's suicide note; he claimed credit for the women, and that excludes Jimmy and everybody else in town."

Josh nodded. "Got it."

"You're thinking like a cop, too," Holly said.

"Maybe cops and doctors aren't all that different," Josh said. "I was thinking that Jimmy had been at the hospital, and he could have stolen the vaccination gun."

"Good point."

"But you're right; Bruno's suicide note clears Jimmy."

"It's good enough for me," Holly said.

"You're sure he couldn't have murdered Bruno and written the note in ten minutes?"

"Listen, I know Jimmy well. He's a nice young man and a good cop, but I don't think he has the low cunning or the skills to commit murder and forgery on the fly."

"How about if he finds Bruno already dead, then forges the note and plants the evidence?"

"Just barely possible, but the investigation will include authenticating the suicide note."

"So you're happy, Holly?"

"I'm happy."

"In that case, so am I."

44

Holly was having breakfast the following morning when the phone rang. "Hello?"

"Holly, it's Jimmy."

"Good morning, Jimmy. I heard about the clearing of the Bruno murders; I want to congratulate you."

"Thanks, Holly. It's a big relief. I want to ask a favor of you."

"What do you need?"

"I need a letter of recommendation to the city council."

"Recommending who for what?"

"Me for chief of police."

"I see."

"Bruno never appointed a deputy chief, and I'm the senior officer, so I'm acting chief. I'd like to have the council make it permanent, and a letter from you would be a big help."

"All right, Jimmy, I'll be glad to do that."

"Can you fax it, then mail it?" He gave her the number.

"Sure, I'll have it out within the hour. Have you asked Hurd?"

"Yes, and he's agreed. You and Hurd are the best recommendations I could have."

"When's your interview?"

"This afternoon."

"Good luck, Jimmy." Holly hung up and put her dishes in the dishwasher; then she went into her secure office, fired up her computer and wrote the letter:

To the Orchid Beach City Council:

I wish to recommend James Weathers for the position of chief of police. Jimmy has been on the force for twelve years now, and I participated in his training as a detective. I always found him eager to learn, organized, efficient and meticulous in his work, and I am sure he would bring these traits to the position of chief. He has the respect of the entire force and mine, as well.

Holly signed it, faxed it and left the envelope in her mailbox for pickup. When she got back to the house, the phone was ringing.

"Hello?"

"Holly, it's Hurd."

"Good morning, Hurd, and congratulations on wrapping up the Bruno case."

"Thanks, but you know very well that we got lucky."

"Sometimes you need luck."

"I know. Has Jimmy Weathers spoken to you this morning?"

"Yes, and I wrote him a recommendation, faxed it and mailed it. He told me you had agreed to do so, too."

"I did, after he told me you had agreed."

Holly thought it best not to mention that Jimmy had told her Hurd had already agreed. "I think he'll do a good job."

"I guess he will. He never gave me any cause to doubt his ability."

"Well, I hope he gets it."

"Yes. Lauren told me you asked some time-line questions about Jimmy."

"I did."

"I just want you to know that I had the same questions, but they were answered to my satisfaction. Also, I had the benefit of seeing Jimmy work the scene, and I thought he did a good job there, too."

"I'm glad we're in agreement, Hurd, and I know you're glad to get this one off your desk. I'm sure the governor will be pleased, too."

"I expect so. Well, I'll get my letter for Jimmy off now. I hope to see you again before you go back to Virginia."

"You'll have to come by for a drink, Hurd."

"Thanks." He said good-bye and hung up.

Well, Holly thought, I underestimated Jimmy's capacity for low cunning; he was smart enough to tell both Hurd and me that the other had agreed to write a letter.

Clad in a freshly pressed suit, Jimmy Weathers presented himself in the offices of the city council. He stood and waited in the reception room, not wishing to spoil the crease in his trousers.

The phone on the reception desk buzzed, and the secretary answered it. "Yes, ma'am," she said, and hung up. "You can go in now, Jimmy," she said.

Jimmy walked into the council chamber and found all the chairs at the long table filled. He knew these people; some of them had known him since childhood.

"Please sit down, Detective Weathers," said Irma Taggert, the council chairperson.

Jimmy took the lone chair facing the curved table. "Good morning," he said to all of them.

"Good morning," Irma replied. She seemed less unpleasant than usual. "Detective, we each have a copy of your application and a package containing your performance reviews since you joined the force. We want to congratulate you on amassing a very good record over the past twelve years."

"Thank you, ma'am," Jimmy replied.

"You're . . ." she consulted his application, "thirty-six years old—is that right?"

"That's right."

"We've never had a chief that young," she said.

"I know," Jimmy said, "but I do have twelve years on the job, and I would like to point out that all my experience has been in Orchid Beach, which I think gives me an advantage over applicants from other jurisdictions."

"Good point," Taggert said. "And we do have favorable recommendations from two past chiefs, Holly Barker and Hurd Wallace."

"I appreciate those," Jimmy said, "and I'm confident that the late Chief Marley, who originally hired me, would have recommended me if he could have."

"Does anyone have any questions to ask the detective?" Taggert asked.

"Jimmy," one of the men said, "how do you feel about the current staffing of the force?"

"Well, we're short a deputy chief, and we should have one."

"Do you know why Chief Bruno didn't offer you the job?"

"He told me he was considering me and he

thought I was qualified, but I had the impression he might have preferred to bring in someone he had known in the army."

"If you're promoted, is there anyone currently on the force that you'd promote to deputy chief?"

"No, I don't think so. I'd hire from outside. However, I would promote someone from within to fill my detective's slot."

"I see. So all you'd need to hire would be a deputy chief?"

"For the moment," Jimmy said. "I'd also continue to work cases as a detective. I don't think there's enough administrative work to take up all my time."

"So we could decrease the departmental budget?"

"I'd rather you didn't," Jimmy replied. "I'd like to have the budget to hire another officer, should we need one."

Jimmy was asked a few more questions, then thanked and dismissed.

"We'll be in touch," Irma Taggert said.

Jimmy left the room, feeling that his interview had gone well.

45

On Saturday evening, Teddy was up to his ears in preparing dinner and, simultaneously, preparing himself for his third face-to-face meeting with Holly Barker. On the first occasion, he'd had a fine production of *La Bohème* to distract her from paying attention to him, and, moreover, he was heavily disguised. On the second occasion, on the island of St. Marks, he had gained twenty-five pounds and sported red hair and a thick mustache; now he had lost the twenty-five pounds and perhaps a bit more, which had the pleasing effect of making him look younger. His hair and wig were graying, but he was still passing for sixtyish. He was also more tanned, since he had been living on the beach for a while.

He seared a whole, well-seasoned tenderloin of beef in a large skillet while he spread a chicken liver and mushroom pâté over rolled-out puff pastry.

When the tenderloin was thoroughly browned, he placed the pastry in a roasting pan, set the tenderloin on it and wrapped the pastry around it, pinching it decoratively at the top to hold it together and for an attractive presentation. He then set the pan in the oven.

He heard the driveway alarm go off and a minute later the screen door slam.

"Honey, I'm home!" Lauren shouted over the jazz playing on the living room stereo. "I brought my best china."

She came into the kitchen and kissed him. "How's it going?"

"I'm halfway through," he said. "The roast is in the oven. That was the time-consuming part. Why don't you set the table?"

"Will do," she said. "My good crystal is in the car. I'll go get it."

Teddy put the vegetables on, then went into the bedroom and changed into a silk shirt and new trousers he had bought at the Ralph Lauren outlet store in Vero. He slipped on a new pair of alligator loafers that he had gotten on sale on the Internet, then checked himself in the mirror. He was definitely *not* the man he had been when Holly last saw him, and, besides, he had been employing a soft Southern accent since his arrival in Vero Beach.

Teddy walked back into the living room and

viewed the first place setting. "Great!" he said. "You brought linen napkins, too."

"Oh, yes. My mother would have turned over in her grave if I'd put out the good china and crystal and not put out the linens."

Teddy picked up a wine goblet. "Baccarat," he said. "My favorite."

"What do we have for wine?" Lauren asked.

"Two bottles of Far Niente chardonnay in the fridge and two of Far Niente cabernet for the main course on the sideboard, one breathing. They're delicious, and they have the advantage of the world's most beautiful labels." He set the open bottle on the table, between the silver candlesticks she had brought.

"There," she said. "Just perfect. Now I've got to go change." She ran into the bedroom with a garment bag.

Teddy went back to the kitchen, just in time to turn off the vegetables. As he did, he heard the driveway alarm chime, so he took off his apron and went to the door, running through his mind the differences between his Jack voice, which was mostly his own, and the last voice Holly had heard him speak.

He opened the door and went out onto the porch just as Holly and her friend were getting out of a Mercedes. "Good evening," he said, "I'm Jack Smithson."

"I'm Josh Harmon," the man said, extending a hand.

Holly came from around the car. "Hi, I'm Holly Barker," she said, offering her hand.

"And I'm Jack Smithson," Teddy replied, shaking it. "Come on in and let's get a drink. Lauren is still dressing, as you might imagine." He led them into the house. "What can I get you?" he asked.

"Knob Creek on the rocks," Holly said, "if you have it. Not everybody does."

"I have it," Teddy said, scooping up some ice and pouring the drink.

"Scotch for me," Josh said.

"I have Johnnie Walker Black or Laphroaig, a single malt."

"Oh, the Laphroaig, that's a real treat."

Teddy poured Josh's drink, and then one each for Lauren and himself. He carried her drink into the bedroom, zipped up her dress for her and handed her the drink. "They seem very nice," he said.

She took a quick sip of her Scotch. "Well, get back in there and charm the socks off them."

Teddy returned to the living room, seated them on the sofa and settled into a chair. "So, Josh, you're an ER doctor at the Indian River Hospital?"

"That I am."

"Sounds exciting."

"Sometimes exciting, sometimes a little too exciting," Josh replied.

"And, Holly, you're with the CIA?"

"That's right."

"In what capacity?"

"I've recently been appointed assistant deputy director of operations."

"Operations, is that the analysis part or the spy part?"

"It's the spy part," she said.

"Sounds very mysterious. I won't ask you a lot of questions about it, because I'm sure you won't answer them. I would like to know if you enjoy your work, though."

"More than anything I've ever done," Holly answered.

"What did you do before you went to work for the CIA?"

"I was the police chief in Orchid Beach, and before that I was a career army officer, serving in the military police."

"That's quite a background," Teddy said.

"What do you do?"

"I'm retired, now. I was a machinist and a mechanical engineer."

"Where did you go to college? MIT, perhaps?"

Teddy laughed. "Oh, no. I apprenticed as a machinist, and I'm completely self-taught as an engineer."

"Did you work for an engineering firm?"

"No, I was self-employed. I invented things."

"What sort of things?" she asked.

"Office equipment, small kitchen appliances and gadgets."

"Did you sell them on late-night TV?"

"No, but some of the kitchen stuff was sold that way. I usually sold the ideas to a company that would manufacture and distribute the product and pay me a royalty."

"Was that lucrative?"

"Surprisingly so," Teddy said. "My wife was astonished; she always expected me to remain as poor as I was when we married."

"Are you divorced?"

"No, widowed: four years ago, ovarian cancer."

"I'm sorry," Holly said.

"It's often misdiagnosed," Josh contributed.

"As it was in her case."

"Teddy . . ." Holly began.

"It's Jack." He didn't twitch.

"I have the feeling we've met someplace before."

"Not that I recall," Teddy replied. He smiled. "I think I would have remembered. Do I remind you of this Teddy? Who was he?"

"Just someone I knew a while back, and, yes, you remind me of him a little."

"Well, I hope your memories of him are pleasant ones."

"Not entirely."

"Uh-oh," Teddy said. "I'm going to get blamed for the old boyfriend. I can see it coming." He laughed.

Holly was about to reply when Lauren walked into the room, looking smashing in a tight dress. "Is everybody drunk yet?"

"No," Josh said, "but we're working on it."

"Dinner's in twenty minutes," Teddy said, looking at his watch, "so you've got time for a refill." He got up and freshened the drinks.

Twenty minutes later, Teddy was slicing *boeuf* Wellington and serving vegetables. Holly had nailed him, or had she? Maybe she had only caught a whiff of his identity and had already dismissed it. In any case, she hadn't taken a shot at him yet. He poured the wine and sat down to dinner.

46

They had finished dinner and were on brandy.

"Lauren," Holly said, "you're a lucky woman to have a man who cooks like that. It was the best dinner I've had in years. And beef Wellington! You don't see that anymore."

"Thank you," Teddy said. "I like the old dishes best, the ones before cholesterol was invented."

"My father died of things like beef Wellington and bacon cheeseburgers," Josh said. "But he loved every minute of it." He turned to Lauren. "By the way, I haven't congratulated you on capturing your serial killer."

"Well, thanks," Lauren replied, "but I'm afraid he captured himself before we could. Fact is, we were getting nowhere fast."

"I'm sure he would have tripped himself up soon," Teddy said. "These criminals always do, don't they?"

"Nearly always," Holly said. "It's tough when you have a police officer as a repeat criminal; he knows all the investigative techniques and how to avoid leaving trace evidence."

"Well, in any case, good riddance," Teddy said, raising his glass.

"Good riddance," they all said, and drank.

"I have some other news," Lauren said. "Jack and I are thinking of . . ."

Teddy held up a hand. "Stop," he said, laughing. "That's still a secret."

"Does it have to be?" she asked.

"For the time being."

"Oh, all right," she said.

"Then your answer is yes?" he asked.

"That's still a secret, too," Lauren said.

"Holly," Teddy said, changing the subject as fast as possible, since he didn't want her to know his plans, "you're on vacation?"

"Yes, but I'm having to start thinking about going back."

"Have you enjoyed yourself here?"

"Very much."

"Where are you staying?" he asked.

"Oh, I still have my house here, from the old days," she said.

"Are you considering selling?"

"No. I think I'll always want it to come back to," Holly said. "Why? Are you thinking of buying?"

"Well, I'm renting this guesthouse," Teddy said, "but it's getting small fast."

"Especially with me around," Lauren said.

"That is a factor," Teddy said, laughing.

"You wouldn't want to live in Holly's house," Josh said. "It's like an armored hothouse, with all the improvements her employer has made."

Teddy knew about the improvements made for higher-ups in the Agency, but he pretended not to. "Improvements? What kind?"

"I don't think we need go into that," Holly said.

"It's top secret, huh?" Teddy asked.

"No, just not talked about outside the Agency. You'll have to remember that, Josh."

Josh threw up his hands. "I'm sorry. I'm unaccustomed to keeping state secrets."

"Don't make too big a thing of it," she said.

"I can see why they would be protective of their people," Teddy said. "After all, there are terrorists out there who would love to lob a few sticks of dynamite into an American intelligence officer's bedroom."

"Now, that's a disturbing thought," Josh said.

Holly elbowed him in the ribs. "Unless you change the subject, you're not going to have to worry about the safety of my bedroom."

"How 'bout them Gators!" Josh said.

"That's too big a change of subject for me,"

Teddy said. "The only sport I follow is Tiger Woods, and he's out for the season."

Jimmy Weathers was getting ready for bed when his phone rang. "Hello?"

"Jimmy, it's Irma Taggert," said the chairwoman of the city council.

Jimmy's heart sank. She was going to tell him he didn't get the job. "Good evening, Irma."

"I'm sorry to call so late, but we just got out of a very long council meeting about a lot of subjects."

"That's all right, Irma."

"I just wanted to be the first to congratulate you; you're the new Orchid Beach chief of police."

Jimmy was stunned. "They voted?"

"We did, and we voted for you. It was . . . well, nearly unanimous."

"I don't want to know who voted against me," he said.

"Then I won't tell you," she said.

"Irma, I really appreciate your confidence, and I hope you'll pass that along to the others, first chance you get."

"I'll do that, and you'll get a confirmation in writing tomorrow morning. We'll have to negotiate a contract, of course, but I can tell you it will be very close to what Bruno got. You'd better hire a lawyer to represent you."

"I'll do that, Irma, and thank you again for letting me know so quickly. I'm not sure I'll get much sleep tonight, but I'm very, very happy about this."

"So am I, Jimmy. Good night."

Jimmy hung up the phone and got into bed. He stared at the ceiling, thinking about himself wearing the chief's badge and sitting in his office with his own secretary. And best of all, he had now made himself completely safe, since he could control any further investigation into the series of rapes and murders.

All he had to do now was learn to control his impulses.

Josh and Holly were driving home from Jack Smithson's house.

"I'm sorry I mentioned the fortifications at your house," he said. "Too much to drink, I guess."

"Oh, it's all right. Part of our training is never to discuss our work, so when somebody does, it sets off alarm bells."

"I won't do it again."

"Thanks."

"Say, what made you call Jack Smithson 'Teddy'?"

"That was kind of strange, wasn't it? I think that, almost unconsciously, he reminded me of someone else."

"Who's Teddy?"

"You remember a few years back when an ex-Agency employee went on a killing spree, knocking off various right-wing political figures?"

"Teddy Fay!"

"That's right."

"You thought Jack Smithson was Teddy Fay?"

"Not really. He just sort of fits the general description—that is, he looks like Larry David, on *Curb Your Enthusiasm*—but so do thousands of other men."

"So I don't have to worry about another serial killer living in the area?"

"No, you don't," Holly said. "If Jack were Teddy, he would *never* invite me to dinner."

Teddy and Lauren were getting into bed.

"Why do you think Holly called you 'Teddy' at dinner?"

"Beats me," Teddy said. "I guess I remind her of some other fatally attractive man—maybe an old boyfriend."

"And why did you stop me from talking about our move?"

"I just don't want a lot of people talking about that. Why, have you decided to come with me?"

She sighed. "Maybe."

"Keep thinking about it," Teddy said, "but not talking about it."

47

Holly's phone rang. She looked at the clock: seven thirty. She found the TV remote control and switched it off, then picked up the phone. "Hello?"

"It's Lance. Getting sensitive about being seen in bed with a man?"

"None of your business," she said.

"Well, I miss your sunny face."

"It's Sunday morning. What's up, Lance?"

"He's back."

"Who's back?"

"Whoever is using the Agency mainframe without authority."

"What's he looking for this time?"

"More on Colonel James Bruno."

"Well, there's good news on that front: Colonel James Bruno ate his gun the night before last and is no longer a problem to anybody."

"Did he, now?"

"He did."

"Anyone know why?"

"He left a note expressing remorse for raping and killing half a dozen women."

"You're sure it's suicide?"

"I'm not even sure he's dead, but I have the word of the Orchid Beach Police Department, which I used to lead, and a special investigative unit of the Florida State Police. Both agencies have investigated thoroughly and confirmed the details."

"Lots of tests?"

"Autopsy, DNA, ballistics—the works. Plus, they found panties in Bruno's house containing the DNA of each of the victims, along with the vaccination gun he used to subdue them."

"Sounds like there's no doubt."

"Not much."

"You have doubts?"

"Not exactly. It was all just a little too pat, but I can't find any holes in it."

"How do you feel about the passing of Colonel Bruno?"

"I regret only that it didn't occur much sooner."

"So he had a bad conscience?"

"He had enough in his life to have dropped dead of guilt, without benefit of the Glock. Only problem I can see is, he didn't have a conscience, so why off himself?"

"I have the impression you think he might have been a victim of homicide?"

"I think it's a possibility, but I don't have a suspect, and neither does anybody else."

"How about whoever's using our mainframe for research on Bruno?"

"Tell you what, Lance, you name a suspect, and I'll look into it."

"How about your father?" Lance offered.

Holly sat up in bed.

"You still there, Holly?"

"Yeah."

"You asked me to name a suspect, and I did, and I haven't heard a demurral from you."

Holly still didn't speak; she was thinking too hard.

"I mean, one wouldn't think Ham would possess the necessary codes to enter our mainframe, but he is close to someone who does. In fact, does he even possess the computer skills to get in, even with the codes?"

He certainly did, Holly thought. "Ham's not the guy."

"You didn't answer my question, Holly."

"Even with the skills, he wouldn't have the codes."

"If you say so. To tell you the truth, I couldn't

care less who terminated Colonel Bruno, even if it's only himself."

"I couldn't care less, either. Well, maybe a little, just out of curiosity."

"You and I both know that's not so, Holly. I mean, you may not care who killed Bruno, but you always care and care deeply about *getting it right*."

"Put Bruno out of your mind, Lance," Holly said. "And Ham, too."

"If you wish."

"I wish."

"There is just one small thing I think you would want to know."

"Are you sure about that?"

"Oh, yes," Lance said.

"And what would that be?"

"Our geek was finally able to establish the exact locale from which the intruder was operating."

"And where would that be?"

"Though not a street address."

"From where is the intruder operating, Lance?"

"From Vero Beach, Florida. Or its environs."

Silence.

"Orchid Beach would qualify as environs of Vero Beach, wouldn't it?"

"Good-bye, Lance." Holly hung up the phone and sat, staring, at the blank television screen.

Josh grunted and turned over. "Everything okay?"

"I don't know," Holly replied, getting out of bed and into her jeans.

"You going someplace?" he asked.

"To my father's house."

"I was sort of looking forward to a Sunday morning in bed."

She leaned over and kissed him. "You stay right there," she said, "and I'll be back. There's something I have to ask Ham."

"How about you ask him by phone."

"I want to look him in the eye," she said.

Ham was on the back porch, doing something to his fishing tackle while Ginny was busy in the kitchen.

"Hey, Ham," she said, pulling up a chair until she was knee to knee with him.

"Hey, Sugar."

"Ham, did you shoot Jim Bruno?"

Ham stopped fiddling with the tackle and looked straight at her. "Not yet," he said.

"I guess you haven't heard yet."

"I haven't read the paper this morning. Did somebody cheat me out of killing him?"

"Yeah. Maybe him."

"Figures," Ham said. "The man was a coward, through and through."

"Yes, he was."

"Details, please?"

Holly told him everything.

"How come you think he didn't do it to himself?"

"I don't know yet. It hasn't gelled."

"You think it's going to gel?"

"Eventually."

"Good luck. You want to stay for Sunday dinner? Ginny has a roast in the oven."

"Thanks, but I've got something cooking myself."

48

Holly got back to the house and found Josh, wearing only an apron, in the kitchen.

"Did you get your question asked?"

"Yes, thank you." She kissed him and pinched him on the ass.

"Gee, thanks. Get the answer you wanted?"

"Yep."

"Happy now?"

"Nope."

"Will eggs Benedict help?"

"Couldn't hurt."

"Then pull up a stool, have some orange juice and tell me your problem."

Holly sat down and sipped her juice. "I don't think Bruno was a suicide, but I'm not sure why I think that."

"Do I get to play policeman again?"

"Yes, please."

"Okay, who had a motive?"

"I did, and so did Lauren."

"Do you want to answer the next question, or do you want a lawyer?"

"Ask."

"Did you kill Bruno?"

"No," she said.

"That leaves Lauren. Anything else I can do to help?"

"Lauren didn't kill him; she's living with Jack, and she would have to have left in the middle of the night and come back without waking him. Anyway, she didn't do it. I know that."

"Can you prove she didn't do it?"

"If I had to. Just take my word for it."

"Okay, Lauren is eliminated as a suspect on your personal say-so. Who else we got?"

"Nobody," Holly said. "At least, nobody who makes any sense as a suspect."

"Who else had anything to do with declaring Bruno a suicide?"

"Hurd Wallace and Jimmy Weathers were investigators. The medical examiner and a forensics guy were there, too."

"Any of them got a motive?"

"Not that I know of."

"Any of them have anything to gain by Bruno's death?"

"No, I don't . . ." She stopped.

"Think of somebody?"

"Well," she said, "Jimmy got Bruno's job."

"I think this is where I'm supposed to say people have killed for less."

"Yeah."

"People have killed for less."

"Good point, but I don't make Jimmy for a murderer. Unless he had more motive than that."

"Did he hate Bruno's guts?"

"Any thinking person would."

"Okay, that's two motives."

"But the time line doesn't work. We talked about that before, right?"

"Right. Maybe he did it at a time that wasn't our time line."

"When?"

"When did the ME say that Bruno died?"

"Something like two to six a.m."

"How's that for a time line. Does that work for Jimmy?"

"If it did, that would have given him time to write the suicide note."

"Does Jimmy live with anybody?"

"I don't know."

"I guess you ought to find out whether he has an alibi, then, 'cause I'm starting to like him for the homicide. Isn't that what they say on the TV shows?"

"Yeah." Holly got her address book and dialed

up the home number for Jane Grey, who was the secretary at the station.

"Hello?"

"Hey, Jane, it's Holly. I'm sorry to disturb you on a Sunday morning."

"That's okay, Holly, but I've got to go to church in a minute."

"I just have a couple of questions. Do you know if Jimmy Weathers lives with anybody?"

"Yes, he lives with his mother."

"Does he have a girlfriend?"

"Not that I know of. He's always looking for dates, though. I don't think he gets many."

"Okay, thanks, Jane. You go on to church."

"Why do you want to know about Jimmy, Holly?"

"I can't say right now, but please don't tell him I asked."

"All right. Bye-bye." Jane hung up.

Josh turned on the Cuisinart and started adding butter to the egg yolks. "So?"

"Jimmy lives with his mother."

"Didn't you once say that one thing in the serial killer profile is that he would probably live with his mother?"

"Yes, I did. And something else: Jimmy doesn't have a girlfriend, and he told me he did. When we were down at the marina after Daisy and I found that body on the beach. Jimmy lied to me, and Jimmy has a boat."

"Maybe he just didn't want to admit he didn't have a girlfriend."

"No. I didn't ask him; he volunteered it. Said he and his girlfriend like to go out on his boat together."

"So now do we suspect Jimmy of more than killing Bruno?"

"In theory," Holly said. "I want to know if he has an alibi."

"How are you going to find out?"

Holly checked her address book again and dialed, this time on speakerphone, so Josh could hear. She motioned for him to turn off the Cuisinart.

"Hurd Wallace."

"Hurd, what are you doing at your desk on a Sunday morning?"

"Hey, Holly. You know how it is; I'm just going over all the reports on Bruno again."

"Anything in there cast any doubt on the suicide?"

"Not exactly."

"But you're beginning to doubt it, aren't you?"

"Yeah, but I'm not sure why."

"I'm thinking the same thing. Any anomalies in the reports?"

Josh spoke up. "Hurd, it's Josh Harmon. In the ME's report, what did the blood work say?"

There was a shuffling of papers on Hurd's desk. "Blood alcohol was point two four, three times the legal limit for driving. And he had taken at least two Ambien."

"There's your anomaly," Josh said.

"How's that?" Hurd asked.

"Nobody could stay awake long with that combination in his bloodstream."

"He could have shot himself before the Ambien took effect," Hurd said.

"My point is," Josh said, "anybody could have gone into Bruno's house and stomped around all he liked, and Bruno would never have woken up. It would have been easy to kill him."

"You still thinking suicide, Hurd?" Holly asked.

"It's still possible, but I'm leaning the other way."

"Did you do any work on Bruno's signature on the note?"

"No experts, but there was an insurance card in the desk drawer with his signature on it, and they looked like they matched."

"If you found that card, Hurd, maybe the killer did, too, and he used it to forge the signature."

"That works for me," Hurd replied, "but all we've got is the possibility of homicide. We don't have a suspect."

"Is there any other anomaly in the reports?"

"Well, there was a partial print on the vaccination gun that wasn't Bruno's. Forensics ran the print, but there wasn't enough for a match in the database."

"Then how do you know it wasn't Bruno's?"

"Because he had printed Bruno's corpse and couldn't match it to the right pinkie, which is the finger he said it was."

"So if we had another suspect, he could do a direct comparison and maybe get a match?" Holly asked.

"That's right."

"Hurd," Holly said, "pull Jimmy Weathers's prints off the computer and have the guy do a direct comparison."

"Wait a minute, Holly. Jimmy and I together examined the contents of the box that held the panties and the vaccination gun, and he was wearing latex gloves. And he never touched it. Lauren observed; she can confirm that."

"Maybe Jimmy touched the gun earlier," Holly said. "Without gloves."

"What are you saying, Holly?"

"Maybe he touched the v-gun when he was hiding it and the panties in the box in Bruno's closet."

Hurd was silent for a moment. "Good God," he said finally.

49

Holly hung up the phone, and Josh went back to running the Cuisinart. When he was done, he poured the sauce into a pan and began thickening it, stirring very slowly.

Holly just stood there and thought. "Josh," she said, "I think we're back to square one."

"And exactly where is square one?" he asked, taking the English muffins from the toaster oven, draping them with Canadian bacon and spooning a softly poached egg onto each.

"Square one is where we were with Bruno: we thought he did it, but we had no corroborating evidence."

"So," Josh said, pouring Hollandaise sauce over the muffins, "now we just substitute Jimmy's name for Bruno's?"

"That's about it."

"But you still haven't proved that Bruno did not

do the murders. Even if somebody came into the house and shot him while he was zonked out on Scotch and Ambien, then wrote a suicide note for him, Bruno could still be the killer."

"When you put it that way, yes," Holly said.

"Can you think of another way to put it?"

"No," Holly said, "I can't."

Josh set the two plates on the table with a pitcher of orange juice, then opened half a bottle of champagne and held the chair for her.

"Mmmm, mimosas," she said, as he poured champagne into her half-glass of juice.

"Or Buck's fizzes," Josh said, sitting down, "if you live in England."

"That's a nice name," Holly said, sipping her Buck's fizz.

"There's another point you have to consider," Josh said, cutting into his eggs Benedict.

"What's that?"

"Even if Bruno is innocent and Jimmy Weathers murdered him and wrote his suicide note and planted the evidence, it seems unlikely that Jimmy is going to get caught."

"Maybe the partial print on the v-gun will turn out to be Jimmy's?"

"You think the DA would be willing to hang his whole case on that and a bunch of circumstantial evidence? By the way, what is circumstantial evidence, anyway?"

"Circumstances that strongly suggest guilt," Holly said, "or words to that effect."

"So, if it *seems* like Jimmy did it, he's guilty?"

"It's not as simple as that," Holly said. "First, he would have to have no alibi for any of the killings."

"Which all took place late at night?"

"Yes."

"So, his alibi is that he was home with Mom, asleep."

"I guess that would be it."

"If Mom corroborates that, then what circumstances would apply?"

"Jimmy has a boat, so he could have dumped one of the corpses in the sea; Jimmy has an unmarked police car at his disposal and a policeman's uniform and badge, so he'd have no trouble posing as a cop; Jimmy is single and horny, and that's a kind of motive; Jimmy had opportunity to steal the v-gun from the hospital, but so far we have no way to put him in the room with it; Jimmy had the opportunity to plant the panties and v-gun in Bruno's bedroom, even if he didn't kill him."

"So Jimmy has motive, means and opportunity," Josh said. "Isn't that all you need?"

"In theory, but in practice we need corroborating evidence, and we don't have any: no witnesses, no trace evidence at the crime scenes."

"I suppose it would help if you could find a

couple of women in Jimmy's past whom he raped, or nearly raped, on a date?"

"Sure, but I'm beginning to wonder if Jimmy has ever had a date. And even if he has, what are we going to do, run an ad in the local paper? 'Have you ever been raped or nearly raped by this man'?"

"Here's a more pleasant thought," Josh said. "None of this is your responsibility; you're not a cop anymore. You're returning to your day job shortly."

"Yeah, that's just great," Holly said disconsolately. "It's Hurd and Lauren's baby."

Teddy and Lauren were having a good breakfast, too.

"Looks like you've wrapped up your big case," Teddy said, holding up the paper.

"How 'bout that!" Lauren said, giving him a big bacon-flavored kiss.

"How 'bout you and I pack up and head for Santa Fe?" Teddy said. "And if you don't like it there, we'll try La Jolla; and if you don't like it there, we'll find someplace you do like."

"That's a breathtaking idea," Lauren said.

"Have you been thinking about it?"

"Of course, I have."

"And what is your decision?"

Lauren got up and squeezed herself into his lap,

and she put her arms around his neck. "My decision is YES!!!"

Then her cell phone rang.

Lauren picked it up, and Teddy could hear only her side of the conversation.

"Hello? Hi, Hurd. Okay, I'm listening." Long pause. "Oh, shit. Yes, I see, square one. You want me to come in today? All right, I'll see you tomorrow morning, and we'll start over." She hung up.

"I didn't like the sound of that," Teddy said. "What does it all mean?"

Lauren enlightened him at some length.

"So Hurd thinks Jimmy Weathers killed Bruno and all the women?"

"He can't prove Jimmy did it," Lauren said, "and he can't prove he didn't, either."

"So you're back at square one?"

"That's about the size of it. And, Jack, I can't walk out on Hurd with the whole thing just hanging like this."

"I can see that," Teddy said. "Well, I'll just have to try to be patient."

"I would be very grateful if you could," Lauren said.

Teddy thought about it. "This is really interesting," he said. "You've had only two suspects, both cops—one is dead and the other is suspected of killing him, plus they're both suspects in the killing of all those women. You've got enough evidence to call Bruno the killer and wrap the whole thing up, but you can't, because now you think Jimmy is the killer. I don't think I've ever read a thriller with such a convoluted plot."

"Any suggestions?"

"Yes," Teddy said. "It's wrapped up in the papers, so leave it that way and wait for another murder."

"You think Jimmy would kill again, now that he's off scot-free?"

"If he's already killed half a dozen times, it's because he really, really likes doing it. I predict he'll kill again, but be even more careful."

50

Hurd Wallace was sitting at his desk on Monday morning when Lauren knocked at his door. "Come in," he said.

Lauren sat down but didn't speak.

"Good morning," Hurd said, to break the silence.

"This is bad," Lauren said. "The case, I mean."

"It's difficult, yes."

"It's impossible," Lauren said, "unless . . ."

"Unless what?"

"Unless he kills again. Or tries to."

"I don't know that I'm comfortable with the idea of sitting around, waiting for Jimmy to murder another woman," Hurd said.

"I'm not comfortable with it either," Lauren said. "Not for a minute."

"We're in a difficult position," Hurd said. "We've already announced to the press that Bruno committed suicide as well as all the murders, and everybody is just delighted with that."

"You mean the governor is delighted."

"I mean everybody: the press, the city council, the public and, yes, the governor."

"So we can't issue another press release saying that maybe it didn't happen that way, that maybe the Orchid Beach chief of police did it all."

Hurd managed a chuckle. "I don't think so."

"And we don't want to wait for Jimmy to kill again."

"No, we don't, but, short of checking his alibis for the killings and waiting for word on the partial print to come back and, in general, continuing to work the case, there's not much else we can do."

"I think we should do all of that, but I think we should work on the basis that we're stuck with Jimmy."

"Without another alternative, yes," Hurd said.

"There's another alternative," Lauren said.

Hurd shifted in his seat. "I'm all ears."

"Maybe if I interest Jimmy in me . . ." Lauren said.

Hurd sat as if frozen and said nothing, just stared at her.

"Jimmy is attracted to me," Lauren said. "He even asked me out a few days ago."

"And how did you handle that?"

"I told him I'm seeing somebody, which is true, and he backed off."

"Just tell me how you see this playing out, Lauren."

"Okay. I let Jimmy know that I'm newly available."

"That you've stopped seeing your friend?"

"No, I don't think that's the way. I think Jimmy should think that I'll see him even though I'm seeing somebody else."

"Then you're forbidden fruit?"

"Exactly. I think he might find that more exciting."

"I can't disagree with that," Hurd said, "but . . ."

"Yes, I know. There are a lot of *buts*."

"But how do we control this? We could have a squad of people following you and Jimmy around, waiting for him to try . . ."

"Yes, and that would be awkward. And we have to remember that Jimmy is not stupid; I'd have to be a pretty good actress to pull this off."

"And are you a pretty good actress?"

"Yes."

"That's not enough, Lauren. Jimmy is a big guy, over six feet, muscular. He looks like he spends a lot of time at the gym."

"Yes, he does."

"Why do you think you can handle him? Physically, I mean."

"I'm not at all sure I could; I have to keep it from coming to that."

"Let me tell you bluntly why I can't authorize this," Hurd said, "either officially or unofficially."

"Tell me," Lauren replied.

"In order to pull this off, you're going to have to make Jimmy believe that he's going to . . ."

"Yes."

"He has to believe that you want him to fuck you." Hurd blushed. "I said I'd be blunt."

"It's all right, Hurd; be blunt."

"If he thinks that's going to happen and you try and stop him, you could make him very angry."

"That's kind of the idea."

"You've seen his victims. He wasn't gentle with them before he killed them. There's no reason to believe he would be gentle with you."

"I suppose it would be up to me to control him," Lauren said.

"And you think that, if you led him along, you could stop him from fucking you without . . . consequences?"

"The consequences would have to be for him."

"Lauren, let me be even blunter. Are you willing to kill him?"

"As you say, he's a big guy. I would probably have to kill him to stop him."

Hurd blushed even more. "Are you willing to fuck him, just to break this case?"

"If I have to. I mean, if I kill him, there'd be no witnesses, and we'd need evidence that he raped me."

"You mean semen."

"Yes. Inside me."

"What would your boyfriend say about this?"

"I have no intention of mentioning it to him."

"And suppose you did fuck Jimmy. Is there any way to resolve the case without killing him?"

"I think that, if he were excited enough, he might well talk about what he'd done. Especially if he thought I knew and that I was excited about knowing."

"Lauren," Hurd said, "one more question, and I want a straight answer. After what you went through with Bruno, why would you want to do this?"

Lauren regarded him evenly. "I think I want to do it *because* of what I went through with Bruno."

Hurd swiveled his chair around and gazed at the wall for half a minute before turning back to her. "Here's my decision, Lauren," Hurd said. "I will not allow you to try this. In fact, I *order* you not to. Is that perfectly clear?"

"Perfectly," Lauren replied.

"I want to explain why I'm giving you this order."

"I understand. You don't have to explain."

"Yes, I do, and I have three very valid reasons. One: such an attempt would place you in mortal peril. Two: even if you survived, the chances of your getting a confession from him would be remote. Three: even if you survived and got a confession, it's likely that either a judge would refuse to allow your evidence on grounds of entrapment, or the defense would characterize it as entrapment and say that Jimmy confessed only because he wanted so badly to fuck you."

"I see your point," Lauren said.

"Will you follow my order?"

Lauren hesitated.

"Lauren, unless you tell me that you will follow my order—and *mean* it—I will fire you out of hand right this minute, and then you will have no legal standing to attempt what you propose."

Lauren regarded her shoes. "All right, Hurd, I accept your order. Really, I'll table this plan."

"It's not a plan," Hurd said. "It's a dangerous fantasy. This is not how we solve homicides."

"Then," Lauren said, "we're probably going to have to accept another murder. Maybe more than one."

"We can't control that," Hurd said.

"Maybe we can," Lauren replied.

"You have an alternate plan, then?"

"I do."

51

Holly walked into the Ocean Grill in Vero Beach, stood just inside the door and looked for Lauren Cade.

"I'm right behind you," Lauren said.

"Hi," Holly said. "Let's get a table."

When they were settled in and iced tea had been served, Holly looked closely at Lauren. "What is going on?" she asked. "You look funny. Is something wrong?"

"No. Well, not yet. I want to run something by you."

"Go ahead."

Lauren told her about the plan she had considered.

"Did you propose this to Hurd?" Holly asked.

"Yes."

"I was hoping you wouldn't say that."

"Hurd turned down the idea. In fact, he ordered me not to do it."

"Of course."

"In fact, he said he would fire me on the spot, unless I agreed not to."

"Good for Hurd. What you proposed is not good judgment."

"Holly, what would you do in the circumstances?"

Holly thought about that.

"That's what I thought," Lauren said.

"I was thinking, not deciding to do something stupid."

"So you're against it?"

"In every possible way," Holly said.

"I had another thought, which I proposed to Hurd."

"Let's hear that one."

"We bug Jimmy's cruiser with a microphone and GPS."

"This is sounding better already."

"We follow him at a distance of, say, a quarter of a mile, just out of sight."

"Good," Holly said. "And you rush in as soon as he makes a wrong move?"

"Right."

"I like it, but I'll tell you how I would like it even better."

"Please do," Lauren said.

"You install multiple audio *and* video cameras, along with the GPS. It's too easy for something to go wrong with the equipment; you've got to have backup. And you're going to need the video for the trial."

"You're right."

"The problem is, you may have to tail Jimmy for days or even weeks before he makes his move. I mean, right now he's home free, and he knows that if he commits another murder the whole Bruno-as-killer thing will be blown."

"I think he would change his MO, make it seem that there's a different murderer out there," Lauren said.

"You may be right," Holly agreed, "but you're still going to have to wait for the pressure to build inside Jimmy, and that could take a while."

"It won't take a while," Lauren said.

"How can you make it happen sooner?" Holly asked.

"By being the victim."

"Lauren, I thought we agreed that was a stupid idea."

"Listen to me, Holly. If I don't do this we have only one other alternative: we wait for Jimmy to grab another woman. We'd be using an innocent person as bait, and who knows what could happen?"

"You have a point," Holly said.

"But if his intended victim is me, we have two advantages: we choose the time, and we have him on video and audio. All I need to do is use a code word, and backup is all over us. They have the location, and they're close."

Holly shrugged. "Again, you have a point."

"Cops do this sort of thing all the time," Lauren pointed out. "It's just like an undercover drug bust, and the state police have the equipment to make it work. They have surveillance vans that can track his car in real time, pinpoint it, and they have real-time viewing of what's happening in the car. Hurd can make that happen."

"Lauren," Holly said, "do you know what transference is?"

"I think so," Lauren replied. "It's like when you transfer your feeling about someone, like your wicked stepfather, onto someone else, like your boyfriend."

"Right. And do you see any transference going on here?"

"Yeah, I'm transferring my feelings about Bruno to Jimmy. That's a perfectly valid conclusion, and I think I have perfectly valid reasons for doing it. I hate rapists."

Holly thought about that for a few seconds. "I think you should have a helicopter, too," she said. "There's going to be a very short time between when Jimmy makes his move and you're in real trouble. Remember, all the other victims, including me, were unconscious immediately."

"We've got the vaccination gun," Lauren said.

"You can buy those things at a medical supply store," Holly said, "or shoplift one."

"I think Jimmy would want me conscious," Lauren said. "I think he would want a real sexual experience, at least at first."

"The problem is, Lauren, if you give him a real sexual experience, a consensual one, you've got no case against him; it's just two people fucking."

"No, no. I make him think it's real; then I say no."

"In that case, you'd have to fight him off," Holly pointed out.

"Not for long; I'd yell the code word, and help would be there."

"He could kill you in seconds."

"I'd be armed."

"If you're unconscious, that won't help. And you can't just shoot him without provocation, Lauren; you'll be on camera the whole time."

"How I handle it will have to be left to me," Lauren said.

"There's something else," Holly said. "How are you going to get hold of Jimmy's car long enough to do all this installation work on it?"

"That's why I came to you," Lauren said. "You

know Jane Grey, the station secretary, well, don't you?"

"Sure, Jane was my secretary when I was chief."

"Will you call her? Hurd doesn't want to do it for some reason."

"And tell her what?"

"Tell her to tell Jimmy that his car is scheduled for service, and she'll give him another. Then we can take the car into a shop and get the work done. If she gets his keys the night before and returns it two mornings later, we'll have plenty of time."

"Sure, I'll do that. Do you know when you want the car?"

"I'll let you know when everything's set."

"Okay, I'll wait for your call. One other thing, though."

"What?"

"I don't think you should carry a weapon; he's liable to notice. I think it should be concealed in the car. In fact, I think there should be two weapons concealed, say, one under the dash and one under the seat, and you ought to be there when they're planted, so you'll know exactly where they are."

"Good idea," Lauren said. "Anything else?"

Holly thought about it. "No, but I'll probably think of something. I'll call you when I do. And, Lauren?"

"Yes?"

"I want to be in a chase car," Holly said. "Clear it with Hurd."

"I will."

"And, Lauren, does your boyfriend know about this?"

"No, Holly, and I'm not going to tell him until it's over."

52

Teddy Fay picked up the new stick-on aircraft registration numbers at the design shop and drove home. He was working through a checklist of things he had to do before he and Lauren departed Vero Beach for good.

This was a different kind of escape for Teddy. Ordinarily when abandoning a location, he also abandoned his identity, his appearance and everything else about himself—he burned all his bridges—but he had made a decision not to tell Lauren who he really was, and that entailed becoming Jack Smithson permanently.

Teddy had been working for much of the day on fleshing out the identity: creating a better credit report, adding information to his pre–Vero Beach existence in north Georgia, creating the kind of past a real person would own. He had even fabricated the record of a past speeding ticket from Dalton, Georgia, with the fine paid on time.

Back at the beach house he had one last task: change the aircraft registration number on his airplane. It wasn't hugely important, but it would make him a little more difficult to trace if anybody tried. He finished the job on the computer and logged out of first the FAA computer, then the Agency mainframe. The phone rang.

"Hello?"

"Hi, it's me," Lauren said.

"Hey, kiddo."

"Have you started cooking dinner yet?"

"Not yet, but soon."

"Why don't we go out tonight? You like barbecue?"

"Yeah, sure; every Georgia boy does."

"There's a great little joint on 1A that does wonderful things to a pig. Want to meet me there after work? Say, six?"

"Sure," he said, noting the address.

"See you then." She made a kissing noise and hung up.

Holly was sitting out behind the house in the late-afternoon sun, with her bikini top off and the bottom pulled down, filling in her tan and watching Daisy play in the dunes when her cell phone buzzed. "Hello?"

"It's me," Lance said. "Are you near your secure room?"

"Yes."

"Call me when you're locked in and logged on." He hung up.

Holly got to her feet, pulled up her bikini bottom, grabbed the bra top and called Daisy, who loped toward her. Inside the house, she put on a robe, just in case Lance wanted to talk face-to-face, and let herself into her little office. She logged on, then called Lance. "It's Holly."

"The geek has visited me again. Our intruder logged on twice today, most recently less than ten minutes ago. Because of a glitch, the geek could only track his last log-on, which was the FAA computer, and wasn't able to figure out where in the FAA databases, so he doesn't know what the intruder was doing there."

"If he's who you think he might be, he could be making a new pilot's license for himself or creating an aircraft registration."

"That's right; our man flies himself."

"Any news on his location?"

"He's narrowed the possibilities to about a three-mile stretch of Vero Beach, less than a mile wide. I'm sending a map."

Holly watched the screen as the image popped onto her computer screen. "It's the southern half of Vero's island," she said.

"Yes, and somewhere between the western shore of the Intracoastal Waterway and the Atlantic."

"Well, it's not exactly a street address, is it?" Holly asked.

"No, but we're getting closer."

"Are we really?" Holly asked. "We're talking about three square miles of densely populated Florida, with God knows how many houses and apartment buildings."

"I just thought you'd like to know," Lance said. "Good-bye." He hung up.

You just thought you'd like me to know, Holly thought. She had pretty much shaken off the desire to nail Teddy Fay, but Lance apparently hadn't. She had her suspicions about Jack Smithson, but she had already decided not to pursue them.

She logged off the computer and locked the door behind her. Maybe it was time, she thought, to have another look at Jack's house. She put on some jogging clothes and went outside. "Come on, Daisy," she called, "we're going for a run."

Teddy sat with Lauren at the barbecue shack, eating Brunswick stew, a conglomeration of chicken, corn, tomato and, if you were in the right part of Georgia, maybe some squirrel or possum. Delicious. "How's work," he asked. "Are you making ready to pull out?"

"I've got one more job to do," Lauren said. "Just a detail to wrap up."

"How long?"

"A week; two, tops."

"Have you told the boss?"

"No, I think I'm going to leave without giving notice."

Teddy thought about that. Such an action might excite too much interest in Lauren's departure. "Give him notice," he said. "Hurd's been good to you, and you owe him that."

Lauren sighed. "You're right. I'll tell him tomorrow."

Holly ran down the wet sand at a clip, a good three miles to where Jack's guesthouse sat, just above the beach, with Daisy happily running alongside her. She reached the house a little after six, and, after ascertaining that neither Jack's nor Lauren's car was parked outside, she picked the front door lock and stepped out of her running shoes. "Daisy, stay here," she said to the dog. Daisy sat down on the porch and watched as she went inside in her stocking feet.

Holly stood in the living room for a moment. Then she saw a flashing light on a black box on the desk in Jack's study. There was an alarm system, and now it began making a chiming noise. She walked to the desk, picked up the phone and listened. All she got was a dial tone, so she knew the alarm system wasn't calling a security service or Jack's cell phone.

She didn't know how much time she had, so she worked quickly. She went into Jack's bedroom and rifled all the drawers and the closet, careful to leave no trace of her unauthorized presence. Then she went back into the study and switched on Jack's computer. All she got was a window requiring a password, and she didn't have time to work on that, so she shut it down again. She found no papers of any interest in the desk, only a few utility bills, already paid. She got up and opened what appeared to be a closet door, and it was, but it contained something very interesting: a Fort Knox safe with a digital lock. The thing was five feet high, and she reckoned it weighed six or seven hundred pounds.

Now why would Jack Smithson need such a large safe? Did he have a camera collection or, more likely, a gun collection? Or maybe a lot of cash? She would like to know, but she would need specialized equipment to get the safe opened, and she would have to get that from her house in McLean, Virginia.

She let herself out of the house and locked the door behind her. The alarm would reset itself after a few minutes, and she doubted if it recorded to a computer log, so Jack wouldn't know she had been there.

She got her shoes on again, then took a couple of palm fronds from under a nearby tree and swept her path clean of hers and Daisy's footprints all the way to the high-water mark. Then she jogged back to her house, arriving sweaty and tired.

She still had her suspicions, but she couldn't back them up.

53

The following morning, Lauren knocked on Hurd's office door with some trepidation.

"Come in," he called out.

Lauren walked in and sat down. "Okay," she said, "I have a better plan."

Hurd sat back in his chair. "I'm all ears," he said.

Lauren explained her plan to conceal video and audio bugs in Jimmy Weathers's car, along with a GPS locator.

"I'll need a surveillance van, two chase cars and a helicopter," she said.

"Wait a minute," Hurd said. "We can't requisition all that equipment on the off chance that some night he might go after another woman. He might take weeks to do that."

"I still plan to be the woman," she said.

"Lauren, I've already ordered you not to do that."

"Listen to me, Hurd. We'll have the two chase cars just far enough away to be out of sight, and the helicopter maybe a mile away. All I'll have to do is speak a code word, and they'll be all over Jimmy."

"All right, suppose it takes them a minute or two to arrive. How are you going to handle Jimmy?"

"I'll have two weapons concealed in the car." Hurd started to speak again, but she interrupted. "And I have some fighting skills."

Hurd leaned forward and rested his elbows on his desk. "Lauren, I apologize for having to say this, but you weren't able to fight off Jim Bruno when he . . ."

"That's true," Lauren admitted, "but if I had had help to call for, the rape would never have happened. All I have to do is hold Jimmy off for a minute or two, and it will be that part of the video that will be valuable in court."

Hurd just looked at her and said nothing.

"Hurd, if this were a drug bust, you'd let me do it."

"If it were a drug bust, you wouldn't have to provoke a violent response to make an arrest."

"That's true, but you're underestimating me. I'm tougher and better trained than I was with Bruno; I could hurt Jimmy, if I had to, and I'll still have two weapons to fall back on: one under the dash and one under the seat."

"Something else," Hurd said. "Even if this

worked, we'd only have Jimmy on one count of attempted rape."

"I think I can get him to confess beforehand," Lauren said. "I think when he gets excited, he'll talk about it."

"But he'll know that if he did that, you could testify against him."

"Of course, that's the idea. Hurd, if Jimmy is the killer we think he is, he would plan not to leave me alive to testify."

"And you think that notion is the way to talk me into this?"

"You know it's true," she said.

"Everything will depend on the chase cars getting to you before he kills you."

"I know that," Lauren said. "Sometimes you have to take a chance to get a serial killer off the street."

"This is a big chance; it's your life."

"I know that, and I'm telling you I can handle him. The alternative is to let him go on killing until we can catch him at it. How many lives of innocent women might we have to sacrifice?"

Hurd slumped. "When do you want to do this?"

"As soon as we can get the equipment in place," Lauren said. "Holly is going to call Jane Grey and have her tell Jimmy his car has to be serviced or inspected, so we can get hold of it for a day. All we need is to set the day."

"Let me make a couple of calls," Hurd said.

*   *   *

Holly sat in her office and called Lance. His face came on the screen.

"Yes?"

"Lance, I've got one suspect for our man, but I have no evidence to back up my suspicions."

"I'm not intending to try him," Lance said.

"I went into his house this evening. I found nothing except a large safe with an electronic lock. If there's anything that will prove or even indicate who he is, it will be in that safe."

"You've been trained to open it," Lance said.

"If I do that, I'm going to need an electronic device that Tech Services can supply. They call it an electronic combination resolver."

"Anything else?"

"Yes, time to get into the house and do the work. I got lucky tonight; he wasn't there."

"You'll have the device tomorrow morning," Lance said.

"All right, but understand this, Lance: I'll do the black-bag job, but I'm not going to go further than that. If you want something more done, you're going to have to send someone else."

"You're such a sissy," Lance said, chuckling. "Just get into the safe. All I need is confirmation of his identity, and then you're out of it."

Holly sighed. "All right," she said. She ended the call.

54

Holly woke up to the sound of the doorbell, alone, since Josh had worked a night shift at the hospital. She got up, struggled into a robe and walked downstairs. Daisy was already sitting in front of the door, on guard.

"Stay, Daisy," she said. Through a glass pane beside the door, she could see a black car. She looked through the peephole and saw a man, his back turned to her, wearing a black Windbreaker and a black baseball cap. "Guard, Daisy," she said. Daisy stood up and gave a low growl.

Holly put the chain on the door and opened it a crack. "Yes?"

The man turned around. He was young—mid-twenties—and wearing dark glasses. "Ms. Barker?"

"Yes." Holly put her foot tight against the door, ready for his shoulder against it.

He held up a small package. "I have a delivery for you."

"From whom?"

"From your friend in Virginia."

Holly slumped. "God, I didn't know who you were."

"That's kind of the idea," he said. "Nobody is supposed to." He held out the package, and Holly took it.

"I'm supposed to tell you, you should take very good care of that and return it when you're finished; it's not supposed to get lost."

"I understand," Holly said. "Thank you."

He turned and walked back toward his car.

"It's okay, Daisy," Holly said, locking the door behind her. "He was a friend."

Daisy relaxed.

Holly got a kitchen knife, cut the packing tape and removed the item. It was smaller than the one she'd trained with at the Farm, about the same size as a personal digital assistant, with a small LCD screen on top and a keyboard at the bottom. It could have been mistaken for a calculator. A wire ran from its base, ending in two very small alligator clips.

The box also held a sheet of folded paper. She opened it to find six photographs. A title read: "Six most widely used electronic locks," and there were arrows drawn, showing where the wires should be connected. Also in the box was a small pair of wire stripper/cutters.

She put everything back in the box, closed it and locked it in her small office, then went back to the kitchen, put the coffeepot on and began making breakfast.

She had gotten lucky the day before; was she going to be lucky enough again to find Jack Smithson out of his house? She had a feeling this was going to take a stakeout, and she hated stakeouts.

She ate her breakfast while glancing through the paper, then showered and dressed, slipping on a pair of rubber-soled loafers. Then she took the box from her office, called Daisy, got into her car and drove to Vero Beach.

Teddy Fay packed and sealed the two cardboard boxes, put them into the trunk of his car and locked the front door to his house. He got into the car and drove out from the driveway, turning north on A-1A, headed for the airport.

Holly had been sitting in her car, a block to the south, for less than an hour when she saw Smithson's silver Toyota pull out of the driveway. She waited for a while, until he had driven away from her, then started her car and turned into his driveway. She had been here before, for dinner, and she remembered seeing the driveway sensor planted just inside the entrance. She checked again to be sure that it was still there. It would give her a warning if he returned.

She checked the second hand on her Rolex as she passed the entrance, then drove down the narrow road to the guesthouse at a normal pace. She drove past the little house, checking her watch; just over a minute. She drove behind the house and parked so that the car was headed toward the beach but concealed from the drive by the house.

She left the engine running, tucked the box under her arm, then went to the front door and picked the lock. Leaving her shoes on the porch, she went directly to the study and opened the closet door that concealed the big safe. Using the sharp end of the wire stripper/cutters, she popped off the cover of the electronic lock, exposing the battery and the electronics; then she opened the box, retrieved the combination resolver and unfolded the sheet of photographs.

She compared the photos to the lock on the safe and immediately saw the correct one. Then she took the wire strippers and cut through the insulation on the two wires indicated on the photograph. She pushed back the insulation an eighth of an inch and attached an alligator clip, then did the same on the other wire. That done, she switched on the resolver. A message appeared: "How many digits?"

She looked on top of the safe, saw a yellow pamphlet and picked it up. It was the instructions for changing the combination for the safe. Of course, one needed the original, five-digit combination to change it, but all she needed was the number of digits. She entered 5 into the resolver.

A stream of numbers began scrolling up the LCD display, and at the top, a clock, indicating the time required to try all possible six-digit combinations for the lock: an hour and six minutes, and counting. That was the maximum length of time; the resolver might hit the right combination at any moment.

She set the instrument on top of the safe and had another look around the study. She tried the computer again, hoping he had left it on, but as it booted up, it required a password again. She shut it off and began going through the desk drawers again, finding only a telephone book. She imagined that Smithson kept his personal phone book on the computer.

Teddy was admitted through the airport gate and drove out to his airplane. He stowed the two boxes in the luggage compartment, then, using a 12-volt hair dryer, stripped the old registration numbers from the aircraft and affixed the new ones. The task had taken less than half an hour. He got back into the car and headed home.

* * *

Holly was startled by a sudden, electronic beep. The driveway sensor! She went to grab the resolver and heard a noise from the safe, the bolts opening. The beep had signaled only that the resolver had found the combination. She checked the clock: it had stopped on 83220 after fifty-one minutes.

Holly detached the alligator clips from the lock and replaced the cover; then she packed the resolver, instructions and wire strippers back into the box. Finally, she turned the wheel that opened the safe; the final bolt retracted smoothly, and swung the door open. As she did, lights came on inside the safe. On the top shelf was a stack of money about two inches high. There was nothing else in the safe.

She picked up the stack of bills and riffled through it: hundreds, fifties, twenties and tens—several thousand dollars, she guessed. Then she noticed that behind the stack of bills was a single bullet: she picked it up and looked at it. A military-issue .223 cartridge. She replaced it on the shelf, put the stack of bills in front of it again, just as she had found it, then closed the door of the safe and turned the wheel to relock it.

She tucked her box under her arm again and closed the closet door, then left the house and locked the front door behind her. As she did, she heard an electronic chime from inside the house: the driveway sensor. She glanced at her watch.

She grabbed her shoes and ran down the porch toward her car. She vaulted over the railing, landing as far as she could from the porch, since there was no time to brush away her tracks.

She leapt into the idling car, slammed it into gear and eased her way through the sand. The four-wheel-drive Cayenne managed nicely, and when the sand firmed up a bit, she accelerated toward the ocean. As soon as she crossed the high-water mark and reached the damp, firm sand, she turned right and raced south along the beach. She looked over her shoulder, back toward the guesthouse, and found it obscured by trees on the property next door.

She checked her watch again: thirty-five seconds. He would not have seen her as he drove up to the house. She had been very lucky.

55

As soon as Holly got home, she taped up the resolver in its box, then let herself into her office, fired up her computer and called Lance.

"Yes?" he said, as his face appeared on the screen.

"It's Holly. I did the job on the safe, and it was empty, except for a stack of money—several thousand dollars—and a single .223 cartridge."

"Why would anyone own a large safe and have only that in it?"

"I don't know. Maybe he's clearing out."

"Has he given you any indication of that?"

"No."

"You say he owns an airplane?"

"Yes."

"Look him up in the federal aircraft registry, then check the airplane to see if it has the correct tail number. If he has changed it in the computer, it might not match the numbers on the airplane."

"Oh, all right, Lance. By the way, I'm supposed to report any large purchase to you, am I not?"

"Yes. What are you buying?"

"I've bought an airplane, and I'll be flying it back to Manassas."

"What sort of airplane?"

"A Piper Malibu Mirage."

"How much did you pay for it?"

She told him.

"Would an investigation of your financial condition reveal enough substantiated funds to cover that?"

"Yes."

"I'll note it in your personnel file. You may be sure that such a large purchase will raise a flag, and someone will get on the mainframe and check out your assets, perhaps want to question you."

"I expected that."

"Thank you for telling me."

"Anything else you want done on the subject of our friend?"

"I can't think of anything else, can you?"

"No."

"Then let's let it rest for the time being."

"I was hoping you'd say that," Holly said.

"You'll be back next week?"

"Yes. Thanks for the time off; I've enjoyed it."

"Oh," Lance said, "you probably know that your name was given as a reference by an employment applicant."

Holly was puzzled. "And who might that be?"

Lance picked up a sheet of paper and looked at it. "One Joshua Harmon, MD. He's applied to the medical division as a surgeon and emergency physician."

"Yes, I know him."

"Do you recommend him?"

"Yes, unreservedly."

"I'll note that on his application."

"Will he be hired?"

"With your recommendation, I should think so, unless his background check turns up something that contradicts your opinion. He's already passed the basic computer check; the interviews of his friends and past employers are being conducted now."

"When did he apply?" Holly asked.

"Ten days ago," Lance replied. "What is your connection with him?"

"Purely social."

"Is he the lump I saw in your bed once, when I phoned you?"

"Good-bye, Lance," Holly said, then hung up. Lance's face disappeared from the screen.

*　　*　　*

That night Holly and Josh went to dinner at the Yellow Dog Café, up near Melbourne. They got drinks and then ordered.

"How was your day?" Josh asked.

"Passable," she replied. "And yours?"

"Fairly dreary. Setting a femur broken in a skateboarding accident was the highlight of my day."

"That must mean that most of this part of the world is healthy, then."

"I suppose."

"Tell me, Josh, are you happy in your work?"

"I'm bored with it," Josh replied.

"Were you thinking of changing your employment?"

"Well, I've been here over four years, and a change would be . . ." He stopped talking and looked at her. "You know," he said.

"I'm CIA," Holly replied. "I know everything."

"I shouldn't have given you as a reference," he said.

"I'm glad you did."

"I was going to surprise you."

"You did."

"Pleasantly, I hope."

"I was surprised. You didn't tell me what you were doing."

"Then it wouldn't have been a surprise."

"I guess not."

"Look, I can always withdraw my application, if you don't want me around, but I have to say, I thought you'd be pleased."

"I am," she admitted. "My life at Langley has been all about work since I've been there. It'll be nice to change that a little."

"I'll do what I can to help," Josh said, squeezing her thigh.

"How did you even know there was a medical division at the Agency?" she asked.

"They tried to recruit me near the end of my surgical residency," he said.

"Why didn't you accept?"

"I wanted to make some money before I went into . . . public service."

"And why did you reapply now?"

"You have to ask?" Josh asked.

Holly smiled. "You're sweet."

"Do you think I'll be accepted?"

"If they don't find out that you've been a North Korean sleeper since grade school."

"Oh, God, I didn't think they would check on that!"

She laughed. "My recommendation won't hurt."

"You recommended me?"

"I did, just this afternoon."

"I guess that must mean you want me around."

She took his hand. "It does."

He smiled.

"Something you should know, though," Holly said.

"What's that?"

"You're going to have to work hard at the Agency; you may not have much time to see me."

"I'll figure something out," he said.

"And, if you don't, I will," she replied.

56

Hurd Wallace telephoned his nominal superior, Colonel Timothy Wyatt, who was head of the state police. Hurd effectively reported only to the governor, but he made a point of making equipment and personnel requests through Wyatt, as a courtesy and to maintain good relations for situations like the one he now faced.

"Good morning, Hurd," Wyatt said without warmth.

"Good morning, Colonel," Hurd replied.

"What can I do for you?"

"I want to request some equipment for a special operation," Hurd said.

"What is the nature of your operation?"

"To obtain evidence against and arrest a suspect in the rapes and murders of several women in the Vero Beach area."

"Was the most recent of them named Patricia Terwilliger?"

"Yes, Colonel."

"I was under the impression that the suicide and confession of one James Bruno cleared her case and the others."

"Did you have a particular interest in Ms. Terwilliger?"

"She was my wife's sister."

"Colonel, I apologize for not speaking to you directly about the case; I was unaware of the relationship."

"I would have thought that a crack investigator such as yourself would have known that, Captain."

"We made the family notification to her mother. One of my people visited her personally to break the news."

"My wife was grateful for that. You have not responded to my question: I thought Patricia's murder had been committed by James Bruno."

"There is some question as to whether he acted alone," Hurd half-lied.

"You think he may have had an accomplice?"

"It's a distinct possibility. It's also possible that the accomplice may have murdered Bruno and staged the suicide."

"Well, this case just gets more and more interesting," Wyatt said.

"I've made a practice of copying you on every report I've submitted, Colonel, and I will continue to do so."

"What equipment do you need to continue this investigation?"

"I need GPS, audio and video equipment to be concealed in the suspect's car by state technicians and a van equipped to conduct electronic surveillance on the car. I also need a helicopter, as a backup, to provide visual surveillance."

"Anything else?"

"I can provide the two chase cars I'll need, but should something arise on the technical front, I'd need in-depth advice and assistance from appropriate personnel."

"I see," Wyatt replied. "When and for how long?"

"From this Friday through the weekend plus a couple of more days. I'll need the helicopter only on the day of the operation."

"I assume you will have the proper warrant."

"I will deal with that locally," Hurd replied.

"Please hold," the colonel said.

Hurd sat, the receiver to his ear, for eight minutes by his watch. It seemed like half an hour. Then there was a click.

"I have my chief of technical services, Mike Green, on the line," Wyatt said. "I have authorized him to supply your needs, so I'll hang up and let you two work out the details. Good-bye and good luck, and I'd appreciate it if you would transmit to me any further details that emerge in the case we discussed." Wyatt hung up.

"Mike?"

"I'm here, Captain. What can I do for you."

Hurd told him.

Holly and Lauren Cade met for lunch at the Ocean Grill, as was becoming their habit.

"Hurd has requisitioned the equipment we need for the operation," Lauren said. "Now would be a good time for you to call Jane Grey and get her cooperation."

"When will you need Jimmy's car?" Holly asked.

"If she can get it Friday night and return it Monday morning, that would be ideal."

Holly produced her cell phone, looked up Jane's direct line and called.

"Orchid Beach Police Department, Jane Grey."

"Hi, Jane, it's Holly."

"How you doing, Holly?"

"Real well, but I need your help on something."

"Anything I can do, sure."

"First I have to tell you some things that have to remain with you and no one else."

"Gotcha."

"Jimmy Weathers has become a suspect in the rapes and murders."

"It wasn't Bruno?"

"Maybe. We're not sure, but in order to find out, we're going to have to place some equipment in Jimmy's car, and we'll need the weekend to do that."

"I see," Jane replied.

"Can you get him to use another car from Friday afternoon until Monday morning while his car is worked on?"

"I think I can manage that," Jane said.

"Thank you, Jane. Would you call me back when that's all set up?"

"I will. Anything else?"

"That's all."

"I'll call you later." Jane hung up.

"Jane is with us," Holly said to Lauren. "I had to tell her those things, but she's completely trustworthy."

"That's all right," Lauren said.

"Anything else new in the case?"

"Well, I've had all sorts of thoughts about it."

"What thoughts?"

"Whether Jimmy and Bruno were in it together, and if they were, did Jimmy kill Bruno."

Holly thought about that. "I'm inclined to think that Bruno would want to work alone, but I certainly can't discount your theory of their working together. I think it's entirely possible, maybe even likely, that Jimmy killed Bruno, simply because the combination of drugs and alcohol found in Bruno's system would have made it nearly impossible to wake him up. Anybody could have stuck a gun in his mouth and written a suicide note."

"That's what I think," Lauren said, "but I think Jimmy's only motive for doing that would be the involvement of both of them in the rapes and murders."

"Jimmy would have Bruno's job as a motive. Maybe when he went to wake Bruno, he couldn't rouse him and took the opportunity to remove Bruno as an obstacle to his career."

"That makes sense. Bruno was about to start interviewing for a deputy chief's slot, and Jimmy had no assurance that he'd get the job."

"When do you make the run at Jimmy?" Holly asked.

"Monday, if the work on the car goes okay," Lauren replied.

"Like I said, I want to be in a chase car."

"I wouldn't have it any other way," Lauren said.

57

Jimmy Weathers arrived at work the following morning and had no sooner settled at his desk than Jane Grey was standing in his doorway.

"Good morning, Jimmy," she said brightly.

"Good morning, Jane," he replied.

"I'm going to need your car at five o'clock on Friday for maintenance; it'll be back Monday morning."

"What kind of maintenance? It's pretty new." He was now driving Bruno's car, which had been purchased when the new chief had arrived.

"Our maintenance contract calls for periodic inspections, not always at the manufacturer's specified times," Jane replied smoothly. "Tell you what. I can let you have that Mustang convertible we confiscated in the drug bust a couple of weeks ago; it hasn't come up for auction yet."

Jimmy brightened. "Hey, good deal," he said.

She handed him the Mustang's key. "You can pick it up at the impound lot any time Friday before five. It's only a short walk to impound. Just leave your keys in the car."

"Will do," Jimmy said, and Jane went back to her office.

Jimmy was getting a little restless, and he thought maybe the Mustang might make it easy to pick up a girl over the weekend. It was too flashy to use for the big job—it might get noticed—but it was great for just getting laid in.

Lauren sat at the breakfast table and watched Jack wolf down his scrambled eggs and sausages. He ate a lot, she reflected, but never seemed to gain any weight.

"What have you been up to?" she asked.

"Well, I cleaned out the safe, packed up my stuff and loaded it into the airplane," he said. "Thought I'd get a head start on our move."

"Good idea," she said. "How much stuff can I take in the airplane?"

"Take a week's clothes, have the rest packed into boxes at a pack-and-ship place and tell them you'll call them with a new address soon. It's a good time to get rid of any clothes you don't really like, and the shopping's good in Santa Fe."

"In that case," she said, "I think I'll hold myself to two suitcases and give the rest to the Salvation Army store."

"That's the way to think," Teddy said. "I always travel light: if I buy a new jacket, I throw one away. How's your case coming?"

Lauren took his hand. "I think I'm going to be free to go early next week," she said.

"That's good news!"

"There's just one more arrest I want to be there for," she said, "and then I'm all yours."

"Want to tell me about it?"

"I'll tell you about it when it's over," she said.

Holly's phone rang late that afternoon. "Hello?"

"It's Lance."

"Hey. You want me to go to the secure phone?"

"No, it's not necessary. I just called to let you know that Joshua Harmon is being offered the position he applied for."

"Great! When?"

"Tomorrow morning," Lance said. "I thought you might like to tell him yourself."

"Thanks, I would. Tell me, Lance, how did this all move along so quickly?"

"Dr. Harmon has friends in high places," Lance replied. "Good-bye." He hung up.

Holly hung up, laughing.

*   *   *

She was getting dinner ready when Josh arrived, looking a little down. "Another bad day?"

"Another boring one," Josh said, pouring them both a drink and taking a stool.

"You're really getting tired of it here, aren't you?"

"That and I'm not very happy about your going back and leaving me behind."

"Are you sure you want to move to McLean?"

"I certainly want to move somewhere, and McLean is where you are, so that's good enough for me."

"So you would consider a job offer good news?"

"I don't want to think about it; then if I don't get it, I'll be less disappointed."

"I wouldn't want you to be disappointed," Holly said, kissing him on the forehead.

"Well, that's a nice thought," Josh replied. "That makes me feel better already." He raised his glass. "That and this Scotch whiskey."

"Congratulations," Holly said. "You got the job."

He looked at her closely. "Are you serious?"

"Perfectly."

"How could this happen so quickly?"

"You've got friends in high places," Holly said.

Josh came off the stool, grabbed her and kissed her. "That's the best news I've ever had," he said.

"And you're young yet," she laughed.

He began helping her in the kitchen.

"I was thinking," she said. "I've got to fly my new airplane back, so you could drive my Cayenne and rent one of those tow bars to pull your car behind."

"Good idea," he said. "And I can fill them both with my stuff."

"How much stuff do you have?" Holly asked.

"Well, not all that much, really. I always make it a policy when I move to throw away as much stuff as I can do without."

"That's a relief," Holly said. "I have only so much closet space."

"Huh?"

"In my house," she said. "You're not going to turn down a free sack, are you?"

He kissed her on the neck. "Certainly not."

"I'm glad to hear it," she said. "It's been nice having a roomie here, and I think it's a good idea to continue the practice."

"Why thank you, ma'am."

"You'll get a written offer from the Agency," she said, "and they'll ask you for a local address up there. Use mine."

"Shall I sign up as Mr. Holly Barker?"

"Not just yet, buster; I'm a cautious woman."

"I hadn't noticed."

"I'd rather have a long affair than a short marriage," she said.

"I guess that's one way to look at it," he replied, nodding.

"It's the only way to look at it," Holly said.

58

On Friday afternoon, Jimmy Weathers left his keys in his cruiser and walked the two blocks to the impound lot. The Mustang convertible, bright yellow and quite new, was sitting out, freshly washed, waiting for him. Jimmy signed the paperwork and got into the car, which smelled of new leather. The car had the hot V-8 engine, and when he turned the key it made a sweet noise. He tossed his service cap into the backseat and roared away, headed for the beach.

As soon as the Mustang passed the police station, a man wearing coveralls with the local dealer's GM name emblazoned on it got out of a van, got into Jimmy's cruiser and followed his partner, who was driving the van. They drove to a state police garage in Melbourne, parked in an available bay and went to work on the cruiser, starting by removing the steering wheel and the entire dashboard.

*   *   *

Hurd was at his desk when his phone rang. "Hurd Wallace."

"Captain Wallace, this is Mike Green. I just wanted you to know that your Orchid Beach police cruiser has arrived at our Melbourne facility, and work has already begun on it. I'm advised that they will be finished late Sunday afternoon, when it will be delivered back to the Orchid police station."

"Thank you, Mike," Hurd said, "but I and one of my people are going to want to check it out, especially for the placing of the weapons, before it's delivered. Will you call me on my cell when it's done, and we'll meet you somewhere between Melbourne and Orchid Beach." Hurd gave him the cell number.

"Will do, Captain," Green replied. "See you then."

Hurd called out to Lauren, who was walking past his office. "We've got Jimmy's car," he said, "and they're already at work on it."

"That's good news," Lauren said.

"Keep yourself available late Sunday afternoon; I want us to go over the car together and make sure you understand where everything is, especially the weapons."

"I'll be on my cell," Lauren said.

*   *   *

Jimmy sailed along Ocean Drive in Vero Beach with the top down and the wind in his short hair. He hadn't felt so good since he got the chief's job. He pulled into the parking area in front of the Ocean Grill and parked in a spot overlooking the beach. He took off his uniform shirt and tossed it into the backseat, then took a Polo from his briefcase and put that on. Finally, he locked his shirt, cap and weapons belt in the trunk and stood, looking out at the Atlantic Ocean. Half a dozen surfers were riding nice waves, and there were a few dozen people lying on the beach. He spotted a girl alone who was wearing a bikini, and as he watched, she untied the bra and lay on her stomach, letting the strings fall aside.

Jimmy put on his aviator shades, walked down the stairs to the beach and approached her. "Hey," he said, stopping next to her towel. "You need somebody to put some lotion on your back?"

She turned her head toward him but didn't sit up. "I'm okay," she said; then she turned her head away.

"Can I bring you a cold one?" he asked.

She turned her head back toward him. "No, thanks."

"You with somebody?"

"Uh, yeah. He's surfing." She waved a thumb at the surf.

"Which one?"

"Does it matter? Look, I'd like to be left alone."

"Nobody needs to be alone," Jimmy said, squatting beside her in the sand.

"I need to be alone," she said.

"Listen," he said softly. "I've got a new Mustang convertible right up there above us; why don't you let me show you some of the local sights? Ever seen the Jungle Trail?"

"No, and I don't care to," she replied, not looking at him.

"It's a beautiful drive, lots of wildflowers, even orchids, and wildlife, too—you see deer and raccoons, maybe even a Florida panther."

"The Florida panther is a myth," she said. "Now, will you please leave me alone?"

"The Florida panther is no myth," Jimmy said. "I've seen one twice."

She turned back and looked at him. "Look, do I have to call a cop?"

"No need for that," Jimmy said, pulling out his wallet. "I'm a cop." He flashed his badge. "In fact, I'm *the* cop; I'm the chief of police." He held the badge closer, so she could read it.

"In that case," she said, "you ought to know that harassment is against the law, and if I choose to push it, I could get you fired."

"Listen, lady, who are you going to complain to? I'm the boss."

She looked around at the other people. "You want me to make a scene? You want me to start screaming? Because I will. NOW GET OUT OF HERE!" she yelled.

"All right, all right," Jimmy said, standing up and backing away. Other sunbathers were looking at him oddly, now. He climbed the stairs and got back into the Mustang.

"Bitch!" he said aloud to himself, then started the car. He backed out of the parking place and yanked the stick into gear, leaving rubber and a roar behind him.

59

Teddy decided to make his special scrambled eggs on Monday morning. After putting the applewood-smoked bacon in the microwave and the plump Wolferman's English muffins in the toaster oven, he melted some butter in a small skillet, then added a little milk and a handful of shredded sharp cheddar cheese. While the cheese was melting he whipped up half a dozen eggs with a wire wisk, then poured them into the skillet, turned down the gas flame to low and slowly scrambled them with a spatula.

When the eggs were still soft but not runny, he spooned them onto the plates, added the bacon and muffins and poured two glasses of freshly squeezed orange juice. As if on cue, Lauren came out of the bedroom with a large handbag over her shoulder. She set the bag on the sideboard and sat down to breakfast.

"Oh, I love these eggs!" she said, tasting them. "I love it all!"

When they were finished, Teddy poured them coffee. "To your last day," he said, raising his mug.

"I'll drink to that," she said, raising her own.

"You look very happy about it," Teddy said, "but also a little nervous."

"I'm nervous about telling Hurd," she said.

"I thought you were going to tell him earlier."

"I sort of hinted at it, but I didn't resign. I wanted to know how tonight's operation would go before I did that."

"Is there any chance it won't go well enough to let us leave tomorrow morning?" Teddy asked.

"Maybe," she replied. "Excuse me. I've got to go to the bathroom." She got up and disappeared into the bedroom.

Teddy cleared the table, and when he came back he looked into her open handbag. Inside he could see a filmy pair of cotton pants and a tank top she liked to wear when they were going out and she was feeling sexy.

He went back to the kitchen and put the dishes into the dishwasher. As he returned to the living room she came out of the bedroom and retrieved her bag. "I'm off," she said, giving him a kiss. "I may be late tonight; don't wait dinner for me."

"Why late?" he asked.

"It's part of the operation," she replied, "and don't ask, because I can't tell you about it." She kissed him again and ran out the door.

Lauren's estimate of two suitcases did not come anywhere close to what she wanted to take with her, plus she had left two packed boxes she wanted sent ahead of them. Late in the day, Teddy put them into the trunk of the car and drove to the pack-and-ship place on A-1A.

As he walked in he was surprised to see Holly Barker there, sending boxes of her own. "Good afternoon," he said.

"Oh, hi, Jack," she replied, signing a check and handing it to the clerk. "I'm just sending some of my Florida stuff back to Virginia. What brings you here?"

"Just sending a few things to some friends," Teddy replied, setting the boxes so that she couldn't see the address of the Santa Fe hotel he was sending them to.

"Listen," Holly said, "I don't want you to worry about Lauren tonight. She's a capable person, and she's going to have a lot of backup. We all know how dangerous Jimmy is."

"I'm relieved to hear it," Teddy said, not feeling relieved at all. Lauren had not said the operation was dangerous. "Have a good trip home," he said.

Holly left and got into her Cayenne, which he had not noticed was parked outside, and drove away.

Teddy sent the boxes and drove home, wondering what the hell Lauren was getting herself into.

Lauren went into the conference room and met with the backup team. She had seen the car before, but the tech guys had photographs, and they wanted to explain everything again. Holly Barker came in and took a seat.

"All right, everybody," Mike Green said, "this is what we've got: two video cameras mounted in the air-conditioning vents on each side of the dashboard, here and here," he said. "There is a microphone with each one and another mike, on a separate circuit, in the center vent. We have three cameras mounted in the overhead light, one pointed forward, two covering the rear seat, each with a mike. There is another camera and mike in the rear seat light over the parcel shelf."

He held up a Zippo lighter. "Each of these would fit into the case of this lighter, and the lenses are pinpoint size. They are outstanding in low-light levels, and they can pick up audio as faint as a whisper."

"Where are the weapons located?" Holly asked.

"One here, under the dashboard," Green said,

"and one under the passenger seat, in spring clips."

"I've seen them and tried extracting them," Lauren said, "and it's a good setup. They're both loaded and cocked, safety on."

"What kind of weapons?" Holly asked.

"Two Colt Mustang .three-eighties," Lauren replied. "They're small, but they'll be good in close quarters."

"One thing, Lauren," Mike Green said. "If he wants to play the radio, turn it down low—off, if you can get away with it."

"How does all this stuff transmit?" Holly asked.

"Through the car's onboard antennas; we didn't have to add anything."

"He's got a police radio in his car, right?" Holly asked.

"Yes, but we're using frequencies reserved for the state police; he can't get them on his radio or even if he has a scanner."

Hurd spoke up. "Lauren has already had some contact with Jimmy," he said.

"Yes, I have," Lauren said, "and he's raring to go."

"What on earth did you tell him?" Holly asked.

"I stopped by the station and flounced around a little. Then I sat down in his office and told him that things with Jack and me were not going well, and why didn't we get together? He suggested dinner, but I said I couldn't make that, so why didn't we just hook up around nine and go someplace quiet?"

"I can see why he's raring to go," Holly said.

Teddy wandered around the house, worrying about Lauren; then he got into his car and drove to Lauren's office. It was after seven, and her car was still parked outside. He pulled into a little strip mall across the road and parked. Pretending to be browsing, he went from shop to shop, keeping an eye on her car, then had some dinner in a little café at a table by the window. Just after eight thirty Lauren, wearing her sexy outfit, came out of the building accompanied by Hurd Wallace, Holly Barker and four men.

Lauren got into her car, and the others got into two unmarked cars and a van belonging to a plumbing company, according to the sign on the outside. Teddy left money on the table, went to his car and followed the little procession. Near police headquarters, the two cars and the van stopped in different places, and Lauren drove into the police parking lot.

Teddy parked a half block away and waited.

60

Lauren took a deep breath to calm herself, then opened the back door of the police station and stepped into the hallway. Light from Jimmy's office spilled into the hallway.

She walked down the hall, turned and then leaned against the doorjamb, alluringly, she hoped. "Hi, there," she said.

Jimmy looked up and grinned. He had already changed out of his uniform and was wearing a short-sleeved shirt and khaki trousers. "Hi. You ready?"

"Whenever you are," she replied.

Jimmy locked his desk, got up and escorted her down the hall to the rear door and opened it for her. "Your car or mine?"

"Mine's a mess. Anyway, yours has more room, so let's take that." To her relief, Jimmy steered her toward his car, opened the door and let her inside.

She sat in the middle of the wide bench seat, so that when he got in they would be close together.

He entered the car and started it. She knew that the cameras would come on when the engine started and remain on for thirty minutes after the engine stopped.

"Where to?" he asked.

"I don't know," she said. "How about Jungle Trail? Nobody goes out there since the murders."

"Perfect," Jimmy said. He pulled out of the parking lot and drove away.

Teddy watched them get into the car, watched Lauren slide across the seat toward Jimmy, and he didn't like it. She was making herself bait. He looked around for the two police cars and the van, but they were nowhere in sight. He started his car and followed Jimmy at a distance.

Holly sat in the passenger seat while a state trooper, Charlie Towns, drove. She watched the blip on the GPS. "Got him on the screen," she said. "Let's go, but don't close on him. Stay out of sight."

They drove across the bridge, and Jimmy turned north, toward the southern terminus of Jungle Trail. As he did, he put a hand on her thinly clad thigh, and she put her hand on top of his. It was dark out; the moon had not yet risen.

*   *   *

Teddy alternated between watching Jimmy's tail-lights and looking for the police cars. Where the hell were they? How were they going to help Lauren if they couldn't see her?

Jimmy made a left turn off A-1A, and as he did, Lauren saw him take a long look in the rearview mirror. She knew that he wouldn't see anything and that they would be picked up by the GPS in all three pursuing vehicles, so she felt safe. Nervous but safe.

Teddy watched Jimmy make the left turn. He had an idea of where the lead car was going; he and Lauren had driven Jungle Trail once. He fell back a little, switched off his headlights and, without using his turn signal, followed the lead. He saw no other cars turn behind him. He watched as Jimmy turned right on the trail proper; then he slowed to let him gain more distance before he turned, too.

If it had been dark before, it was pitch-black now, with the canopy of trees shielding them from even the starlight. Lauren nearly panicked when, for a moment, she couldn't remember the code word. Then it came to her: *bastard*. Jimmy's hand slid higher up her leg to her crotch, but she didn't stop him.

They drove up the trail for another five minutes, then Jimmy stopped the car.

"Here okay?" he asked.

"Sure," she said.

Teddy saw Jimmy's brake lights come on, then go dark. They had stopped, and he had turned off his lights.

Hurd Wallace, riding in the surveillance van, watched the GPS screen. "He's stopped," Hurd said. He looked at the series of video screens. "She looks calm," he said. Then the screens went dark. "What happened?" Hurd asked.

"He's on Jungle Trail, so the tree canopy is blocking any light," Mike Green replied. "He's turned off his lights, so his dashboard lights have gone off, too, so we just can't see. But don't worry; we've still got audio."

"You didn't anticipate this?" Hurd asked.

"What, anticipate total darkness? Did you want me to install lights in his car?"

"You okay?" they heard Jimmy say.

"I'm just . . ." Lauren was saying, then stopped talking.

"What's going on?" Hurd asked.

Mike pointed at a dial on his control panel. "They're not transmitting audio," he said. "The system must have powered down when he switched off the engine."

"But it's supposed to continue running for thirty minutes," Hurd protested.

"What can I tell you?" Mike replied. "It didn't happen."

Hurd picked up his handheld radio. "Cars one and two: we've lost both video and audio, and oh, shit, the GPS isn't transmitting, either; it's blocked by the trees. They're somewhere on Jungle Trail. Close on them fast!"

Teddy saw the white sand of a road to his left and pulled a few yards into it. He got out of the car and peered into the darkness up the road but couldn't see a thing. He got back in, unlocked the glove compartment and took out a small but powerful Surefire flashlight and the 9-mm pistol he kept there.

"Step on it, Charlie," Holly said. "God, I hope we're not going to be too late!"

Jimmy reached down between his legs and released the seat adjuster, allowing the bench seat to move backward a good foot. Lauren suddenly realized that now she couldn't reach the gun under the dash, and she tried to calm herself. There was still the one under the front seat, though.

Jimmy put an arm around Lauren and moved his left hand to her crotch.

"Is this how you did it with the others, Jimmy?" Lauren asked. "Did they like it?"

"Sure," Jimmy said. "They loved it. They loved every minute of it." He stuck his hand inside the elastic band of her pants and reached downward.

Lauren still didn't stop him. "They were unconscious, though, weren't they?"

"A little," Jimmy said, "but they could still feel my dick inside them. I got the dosage just right."

"You bastard," Lauren said. She didn't know if what Jimmy had said was enough of a confession, but she was beginning to panic. "Not so hard," she said, pushing his hand away. "You bastard."

"Bitch!" Jimmy shouted. "You want it just like they got it, don't you?"

Lauren moved across the seat and was about to go for the gun underneath it, when Jimmy's fist smashed into the side of her face. In the darkness, she hadn't seen it coming. She fell onto the floor of the car, between the seat and the dash, but she couldn't seem to think clearly. She wanted something, but she couldn't think what. She fought to stay conscious.

Jimmy reached down, grabbed the waistband of her pants and hauled her back onto the seat facedown. There was a loud ripping sound as he tore her clothes from her body; then he got an arm under her and pulled her to her knees.

Her face pressed against the plastic seat, Lauren began to come to. Then she felt something cold and wet in her crotch. Jimmy had produced a lubricant from somewhere and was slathering it onto her vagina and anus. She reached under the seat and felt for the little Colt Mustang clipped there. She got a hand on it and pulled it free, but she was pinned facedown and couldn't turn over, and her elbow couldn't rotate enough to point the gun at him.

"Switch on the goddamned siren and the lights!" Hurd shouted at the driver. "I want him to hear and see us coming!"

"There's no siren on the van," the man called back.

Hurd pressed the switch on his radio. "Sirens and lights on!" he yelled into the instrument.

Lauren could hear Jimmy unzip his trousers and pull them down. She tried again to turn over, but he had her pinned with one hand. God, she thought, he's going to rape me, and there's nothing I can do about it. She had a flash of the scene with Bruno in his car years ago, and she felt the helplessness she had felt then.

Suddenly, the car was filled with an amazingly white, bright light. There was a loud noise, and then she was showered with glass, but Jimmy's hand was no longer on her back. She twisted around and, momentarily blinded by the light, pointed the Mustang in his direction. She fired three times and heard glass break again. Then Jimmy was on top of her.

Teddy heard the sirens and, looking back down Jungle Trail, saw flashing lights coming. He dove into the underbrush and began making his way back down the trail through the palmettos as fast as he could. He had gone perhaps fifty yards when the two police cars and the van blew noisily past him. As soon as they had passed, he moved back into the road and began running down the trail. A moment later, using the red setting on the flashlight, he found his car, got it started and was driving back up Jungle Trail. He avoided using the brakes and didn't switch the lights on until he thought he was near the turn back to A-1A. Above him, he saw the spotlight of a helicopter come on, but it was pointing behind him.

He slowed down when he reached A-1A, and drove toward home, keeping to the speed limit. A police car and an ambulance drove past him fast, in the opposite direction.

Lauren might be hurt, he thought, but she was in safe hands now.

61

Holly sat with Lauren in the back of the ambulance, mopping Jimmy's blood from her breasts with a wad of cotton soaked in alcohol. At first, she was hysterical, but soon she calmed down.

"I don't want to go to the hospital," she said.

"You need to be checked out, Lauren," Holly said.

"I'm not hurt, I'm not raped, and I want to go back to the office, where my clothes are." She was naked now, since Jimmy had ripped off her pants and panties, and the EMT had cut off her tank top.

"Are you sure, Lauren?"

"Damn it, I'm sure!"

Holly got on the radio. "Hurd, Lauren isn't hurt, and she insists on going back to the office for her clothes instead of to the hospital."

Lauren took the radio from Holly's hand.

"Hurd, I am perfectly all right; all I need is my clothes."

"Roger, Lauren," Hurd said. "We'll see you at the office for debriefing."

Lauren, dressed now, sat at the conference table, holding an ice pack to her face where Jimmy had slugged her, and gave a vivid account into a tape recorder of everything that had happened.

"You'll have to testify at the inquest," somebody said.

"There doesn't need to be an inquest," Lauren replied. "I shot a man who was attacking me. Didn't you hear everything?"

"We lost audio transmission," Mike Green said, "but I had a tape recorder planted in the dash that kept running."

"Is there any inconsistency in my story?" she asked.

"No," Hurd said; then he switched off the tape recorder. "This is off the record, everybody. Lauren, there are two things I don't understand."

"What?"

"One, the flash of white light."

"I think it must have been the muzzle flash in the darkness," she said.

"All right. I buy that," Hurd replied. "But there's one other thing: the driver's side window was smashed, but I understand that one of your shots must have gone through him and hit the window. What I don't understand is that the passenger's side window was smashed, too."

"Maybe one round went through the passenger window," Lauren said, "or richocheted."

"From what I could see, the window was broken from the outside; nearly all of the glass was in the car. It was all over you when we got there."

"Okay, Hurd, you've got me there; I have no explanation for that. All I've got is what I've told you. I think I was unconscious for a moment after Jimmy hit me, and I was semiconscious for another moment. Maybe something happened then that I don't understand."

"It's just a loose end," Hurd said, "and I don't like loose ends."

"Well, Hurd," Lauren said with some heat, "I was pretty busy in that car, and I'm sorry I didn't have time to tie up your loose end."

Hurd held up a hand. "It's all right, Lauren. I'm not going to make an issue of it. Anybody here have any problem with neglecting to notice the passenger window?"

Everybody shook their heads.

Holly thought she knew how the window was broken, but she kept her mouth shut.

*   *   *

An hour later, Holly drove Lauren back to her car at the police station parking lot. She was remembering how she had mentioned the operation to Jack Smithson at the pack-and-ship store.

"Lauren," she said, "did you tell Jack what you were going to be doing tonight?"

"God, no!" Lauren said. "He would have gone nuts! He wouldn't have let me do it."

"That's what I thought," Holly said. She dropped Lauren at her car but took another close look at her. "Are you sure you're all right to drive?"

"Holly, I'm just fine. Really I am. When you think about it, this operation turned out better than we could have hoped for. There'll be no trial for Jimmy, so the families won't be put through that, and so the whole thing is just over. I'm feeling really good about that."

"Okay, Lauren, just drive carefully on your way home."

"Don't worry about me."

But Holly followed Lauren at a distance, until she saw her turn into Jack's driveway.

Back home, Josh was waiting.

"When are we taking off north?" he asked.

"I'm going to stay one more day, just to be available to Hurd if he has any more questions for me. I also want to have dinner tomorrow night with Ham and Ginny; you can join us. I'll fly home the day after. I've been checking the weather every day, and Wednesday should be a perfect flying day."

"And when do you go back to work?" he asked.

"Monday morning, bright and early."

"I'll be at your house Thursday night, I think," Josh said.

"I'll just take a cab home from Manassas airport," Holly said. "I've already arranged for hangar space there."

"You want me to take Daisy with me in the car?" he asked.

"No, she's flown before with Ginny and me, and she's fine with it."

They fell asleep in each other's arms.

The following morning Holly called Hurd Wallace.

"Thanks for your help last night," he said. "I think it was a good idea having a woman with Lauren."

"She was perfectly fine after she calmed down," Holly said. "How is she this morning?"

"She didn't come in," Hurd said. "She left a letter in my in-box, and I found it this morning. She's resigned."

"I'm surprised," Holly said. "Did you see that coming?"

"No, but I think it had more to do with her new

boyfriend than it did with anything that happened last night," he said.

"Do you know what her plans are?" Holly asked.

"No, but she said she'd be in touch. We don't really need her to wrap up the case."

"Well, I'm off to Virginia tomorrow morning," Holly said. "It was good seeing you and even better working with you again, Hurd."

"Thank you, Holly. Same here. You keep in touch, hear?"

"Will do." Holly hung up. She was surprised at Lauren's resignation; it didn't seem like a spur-of-the-moment thing. She wanted to say good-bye, and she wanted one more conversation with Jack Smithson, too, so she got into her car with Daisy and drove over to his beach house.

When she pulled into the driveway, there were no cars parked at the house. She got out and went to the door. No one came when she knocked, but there was an unsealed envelope stuck in the door, addressed to a real estate company. Holly was too nosy not to look inside.

There were some keys, a check and a note from Jack saying that he was vacating the premises and paying the remainder of the short-term lease.

Holly used one of the keys to unlock the front door. She walked inside and looked around, but it had been cleaned out. The big safe was still in the closet, its door open and a note left on top of it, again addressed to the real estate company. She read it. "The safe is yours," it said. "The combination is TEDDY."

AUTHOR'S NOTE

I am happy to hear from readers, but you should know that if you write to me in care of my publisher, three to six months will pass before I receive your letter, and when it finally arrives it will be one among many, and I will not be able to reply.

However, if you have access to the Internet, you may visit my Web site at www.stuartwoods.com, where there is a button for sending me e-mail. So far, I have been able to reply to all my e-mail, and I will continue to try to do so.

If you send me an e-mail and do not receive a reply, it is probably because you are among an alarming number of people who have entered their e-mail address incorrectly in their mail software. I have many of my replies returned as undeliverable.

Remember: e-mail, reply; snail mail, no reply.

When you e-mail, please do not send attachments, as I *never* open these. They can take twenty minutes to download, and they often contain viruses.

Please do not place me on your mailing lists for funny stories, prayers, political causes, charitable fund-raising, petitions or sentimental claptrap. I get enough of that from people I already know. Generally speaking, when I get e-mail addressed to a large number of people, I immediately delete it without reading it.

Please do not send me your ideas for a book, as I have a policy of writing only what I myself invent. If you send me story ideas, I will immediately delete them without reading them. If you have a good idea for a book, write it yourself, but I will not be able to advise you on how to get it published. Buy a copy of *Writer's Market* at any bookstore; that will tell you how.

Anyone with a request concerning events or appearances may e-mail it to me or send it to: Publicity Department, Penguin Group (USA) Inc., 375 Hudson Street, New York, NY 10014.

Those ambitious folk who wish to buy film, dramatic or television rights to my books should contact Matthew Snyder, Creative Artists Agency, 9830 Wilshire Boulevard, Beverly Hills, CA 98212-1825.

Those who wish to make offers for rights of a literary nature should contact Anne Sibbald, Janklow & Nesbit, 445 Park Avenue, New York, NY

10022. (Note: This is not an invitation for you to send her your manuscript or to solicit her to be your agent.)

If you want to know if I will be signing books in your city, please visit my Web site, www.stuart woods.com, where the tour schedule will be published a month or so in advance. If you wish me to do a book signing in your locality, ask your favorite bookseller to contact his Penguin representative or the Penguin publicity department with the request.

If you find typographical or editorial errors in my book and feel an irresistible urge to tell someone, please write to Penguin's address above. Do not e-mail your discoveries to me, as I will already have learned about them from others.

A list of my published works appears in the front of this book and on my Web site. All the novels are still in print in paperback and can be found at or ordered from any bookstore. If you wish to obtain hardcover copies of earlier novels or of the two nonfiction books, a good used-book store or one of the online bookstores can help you find them. Otherwise, you will have to go to a great many garage sales.

Read on for a sneak peek at
New York Times bestselling author
Stuart Woods's novel

KISSER

Available now

E laine's, late.

Stone Barrington and his former NYPD partner, Dino Bacchetti, were dining in the company of herself, Elaine, who, as usual, was making her rounds. "So?" Elaine asked as she joined them.

"Not much," Dino replied.

Stone was deep into his *spaghetti alla carbonara*.

"Nice, isn't it?" she asked. Elaine had a good opinion of her food.

"Mmmmf," Stone replied, trying to handle what he had stuffed into his mouth and speak at the same time.

"Never mind," Elaine said. "Enjoy."

Stone swallowed hard and nodded. "Thank you. I am."

The waiter came with the wine and poured everybody a glass.

Stone began to take smaller bites so that he

could better participate in the conversation. As he took his first sip of wine, he froze.

Dino stared at him. "What's the matter? Am I gonna have to do the Heimlich?"

Stone set down the glass but said nothing. He was following the entrance of a very beautiful woman. She was probably five eight or nine, he thought, and closer to six feet in her heels. She was dressed in a classic Little Black Dress, which set off a strand of large pearls around her neck. Fake, probably, but who cared? She had shoulder-length honey blond hair and a lot of it, cascades of it, big eyes, and plump lips sporting bright red lipstick. Dino and Elaine followed Stone's gaze as the woman turned to her left and sat down at the bar.

"She can't be alone," Dino said.

"Who is she?" Stone asked Elaine.

"Never saw her in here," Elaine replied, "but you'd better hurry. She's not gonna be alone long."

Stone put down his glass, got up, and walked toward the bar, straightening his tie. Normally, the people at the tables didn't have much to do with the people at the bar; they were different crowds. But Stone knew when to make an exception.

"Good evening," he said to her, offering his hand. "My name is Stone Barrington."

She took the hand and offered a shy smile.

"Hello, I'm Carrie Cox," she said, with a soft and Southern accent.

Stone indicated his table. "My friends Dino and Elaine agree with me that you are too beautiful to be sitting alone at the bar. Will you join us?"

She looked surprised. "Thank you, yes," she said after a moment's thought.

Stone escorted her back to the table and sat her down. "Carrie Cox, this is Elaine Kaufman, your hostess, and Dino Bacchetti, one of New York's Finest."

"How do you do?" Carrie said. "Finest what?"

"It's a designation meant to describe any New York City police officer," Stone said, "without regard for individual quality."

"Stone should know," Dino said. "He used to be one of New York's worst."

Carrie laughed, a low, inviting sound.

"You must be from out of town," Dino said.

"Isn't everybody?" Elaine asked.

"I've only been in New York for three weeks," Carrie said.

"Where you from?" Elaine asked.

"I'm from a little town in Georgia called Delano, but I came here from Atlanta. I lived there for two years."

"And what brought you to our city?" Stone asked.

"I'm an actress, so after a couple of years of

training in Atlanta, it was either New York or L.A. Since it's spring, I thought I'd start in New York, and if I hadn't found work by winter, I'd move on to L.A."

Stone was fascinated by her mouth, which moved in an oddly attractive way when she talked.

"And have you found work yet?"

"Almost immediately," she said, "but not as an actress. I've been working as a lip model."

"I'm not surprised," Stone said.

"A *lip* model?" Dino asked.

"I've been modeling lipstick," she explained, "in the mornings. In the afternoons I've been making the rounds, looking for stage work."

"That's tough," Elaine said.

"Well, I've had one very attractive offer," Carrie said, "from a man called Del Wood."

Stone knew him a little, from a couple of dinner parties. Wood was a Broadway impresario who composed both music and lyrics and who owned his own theater. "The new Irving Berlin," Stone said, "as he's often called."

"Unfortunately," Carrie said, "the offer came with some very unattractive strings."

"Ah," Stone said. "Del Wood has that reputation. He is also known as Del Woodie."

Carrie laughed. "I can believe it. Do you know what he said to me?"

"I can't wait to find out," Dino said, leaning forward.

"He said—and please pardon the language; it's his, not mine—'I want to strip off that dress, lay you on your belly, and fuck you in the ass.'"

"Oh," Dino said.

Stone was speechless.

"I was thinking of suing him for sexual harassment," Carrie said.

"Well," Dino said, indicating Stone, "meet your new lawyer."

"Oh, are you a lawyer?" Carrie asked Stone.

"Yes, but I'm not sure you'd have much of a case."

"Why not?"

"Did he force himself on you?"

"No. I got out of there."

"Were there any witnesses?"

"No."

"Then I'm afraid it would be your word against his," Stone said.

"Well," Carrie said, "I did get him on tape."

SOPHISTICATED SUSPENSE
From the *New York Times* bestseller

STUART WOODS

Blood Orchid

Chief of Police Holly Barker returns along
with her father Ham and Daisy the
Doberman. This time, they get introduced
to the cutthroat world of Florida real
estate...and uncover a scam as dangerous
as it is lucrative.

ORCHID BLUES

From *New York Times* bestselling author

STUART WOODS

When Holly's wedding festivities are shattered by a brutal robbery, she vows to find the culprits. With nothing to go on but the inexplicable killing of an innocent bystander, Holly discovers evidence that leads her into the midst of a clan whose members are as mysterious as they are zealous. Holly's father, Ham, a retired army master sergeant, is her ticket into their strange world. What he finds there boggles the mind and sucks them all—Holly, Ham, and Daisy—into a whirlpool of crazed criminality from which even the FBI can't save them.